LUCID
awake in the world and the dream

GARDNER EEDEN

READ THIS BOOK AS FICTION, LIKE
EVERYTHING THAT HAS EVER BEEN
WRITTEN.

LUCID:

AWAKE IN THE WORLD AND THE DREAM

TABLE OF CONTENTS

4

LUCID is the next step in the evolution of human consciousness.

We've made rapid advances in understanding the human brain, but are still very much in the dark about understanding the human mind, much less the origin, power, and purpose of consciousness—and consciousness is all-encompassing, whether you are awake or asleep.

Even now, there are machines available and more to follow on the open market that will stimulate your consciousness within the dream and make you aware that you are within a dream, a phenomenon known as "lucid dreaming." This has the potential to change everything you think you know about consciousness, mental disorders, free will, morality, mortality, and even God.

Some of these machines show potential to spur a lucidity within your mind; some are junk. But what matters is that the evolution of this technology will only move forward and become more effective at stirring and provoking those regions of our brain that serve as a conduit between our mind and the universe.

Now that we can spur lucidity in the dream, we need a primer for what's possible as we shift our existence.

We are making possible a disembodied reality; but are we ready for it emotionally, psychologically, or spiritually? As your place in the world evolves, you could be learning how to navigate the next; you're living in it anyway, whether you know it or not.

WHAT IF GOD EXISTS
BUT IS COMPLETELY
UNAWARE HE'S GOD?

ARE YOU LUCID?

To be lucid is to have clarity, to be aware of one's self and surroundings. One can be lucid in the world, and one can be lucid in the dream.

We do not go to sleep to "dream," and we do not wake up "from" a dream. The dream is as constant a state as the world, and we inhabit various levels of consciousness between the two worlds.

The dream can sometimes move up a level from the "subconscious" into the immediate conscious forefront of your mind and perception. You'll call it confusion, delusion, déjà vu, elation, transcendence, or various psychoses, but we live in the dream as fluidly and temporally as we do the world. This ongoing flux of consciousness is the cause of many of our greatest problems and inspirations. The dream, and our level of awareness within it, as in the world, affects us constantly.

Biconsciousness is the state of being simultaneously aware in both the world and the dream. I am lucid to both worlds at once, as I suspect humans might have been a very long time ago—before our mythologies formed our fears and pushed dream awareness deep into the subconscious, before the evolution of our brains dictated what visions to trust and which to fear. For me, this ability was innate but needed to be honed, though I do believe others can learn to achieve levels of simultaneous lucidity. I certainly suspect there are other biconscious individuals in the world who simply haven't had the opportunity to recognize their condition, or they are diagnosed with mental or physical disorders that are masking their abilities.

Think of biconsciousness as a fluctuating, imperfect split-screen TV for your very existence, though one screen lays atop the other rather than side-by-side; one screen displays the world of weight, gravity, and consequence: the other screen has no laws and can be largely under your control. If you have lived with this and practiced varieties of control over longer periods of time, you can learn to slip into a tactile interaction with each environment—even at the same time. I have lived with this condition for most of my life. It's challenging and exhilarating—it enhances and supercharges the senses in both worlds and creates an intense paradox. Awake and experiencing the full clash of both worlds, one can truly grasp the concepts of heaven and hell.

The "dream" is a state of existence that runs parallel to the "world." Most people believe they go to sleep and have "dreams," intermittent visions in the night that come and go in tandem with sleep cycles. This isn't entirely accurate. People slip into the dream at different stages and most people only remember random scenarios and fragments. However, the dream is as fluid and constant a state as "reality," or what we think of as the "waking world." Some people can become "lucid" in the dream, as aware as they are in the world, and can achieve a certain level of control over events and denizens there. Some people can barely be called "lucid" or "aware" in the world, much less their dream.

There are times when one world actively engages the mind and senses; then something occurs in the other that demands attention. Sometimes long stretches go by when nothing of any interest happens in either world. And sometimes, we are deluged by events and overwhelmed by pressures in both worlds at once, and our limited perceptions are stretched to bursting. Unexplained emotional outbursts, mood swings, delusions, everything from mild fatigue to psychopathic delusion are the result of our constant interaction with both worlds simultaneously. When we become more aware of each world in every moment, we achieve a lucidity that strikes a balance in the world, and an amazing freedom in the dream. Consciousness is a constant, intertwining stream of frequencies, wavelengths and modalities that we are always tuning amidst so much static and white noise, and in which our experience alters the strength of our perception.

I am frequently asked, if we live in two worlds at once, which is true? Which is real? In the end, what difference does it make? The answer is both.

We do not know the reasons for our evolution into consciousness, nor can we technically map the neural pathways that send us back and forth, at least not yet. One thing is certain; our attention is up for grabs, and two worlds are simultaneously screaming for it.

ORIGIN

You must sometimes wonder where the "real" you originated, and where it resides. The world or the dream? Why do you so often feel like a lone traveler? Did you exist in the dream before you emerged in the world? You want to ask your parents if you were covertly raised through some secret government program that is being monitored by hidden cameras; or you'd like a doctor to sigh, take off his glasses and tell you how astonished he is that you've lived so many years with such a rare disease gone undetected, or your parents tell you on your eighteenth birthday that you were, in fact, discovered by them in a tiny steaming spaceship that crashed in the woods, and they heard your cry and raised you as their own. These explanations would give you some reason, some story for feeling like such an outsider through your life and could explain every hardship and challenge you've ever faced. Or you could find yourself in the dream and know that you have always been there, will always be there, and have never, ever been given a map. You are Alice trapped in Wonderland, Peter marooned in Neverland.

When I was very little, before language clouded my soul's ultimate freedom, I did not always know where the dream ended and the world began. In amniotic slumber, we are both awake and asleep, and that wonderment pervades the infant psychoses until communication, story and a sense of time put barricades around the phantom zone of consciousness.

I first became aware of the true difference between the dream and world at the age of 5, when I began remembering a series of images from the dream; semi-nightmarish phantasmic scenes of a ghost following me around. The landscape was my real suburban neighborhood infused with the flat but bright colors of a Saturday morning cartoon. The ghost would appear in my dream in different spirit-like cloudy, humanish forms; one night he would be visceral and terrifying, another he would seem melancholic, another he would blink cartoon eyes, but he kept following me in my dream, and eventually I realized that it was not normal for a ghost or spirit to be hanging out with me. This ghost did not appear to me in the world, and I felt certain in the world that I would not see him moving toward me across a street or field, as it did in the dream. Yet I would sometimes be aware that it was watching me from within, in the way that a figure in a TV set could peer through the screen and observe you in the world. This was how I began to make distinctions between two realities. This dream ran through me—and it was a place of very different possibilities.

Once aware on a nightly basis that I was slipping into the dream, and that my body was in a different realm though I knew my physical self was sleeping in bed, I became very curious as to how I could be in the dream and the world at the same time. I researched dreams—but in the age before the internet and with a limited small town library at my disposal, resources on dreams were pathetic. I was only able to find a few volumes of Sigmund Freud which had been thoroughly combed through by high school students for any sexual references (and littered with penciled-in phallic doodles smudgily erased by diligent librarians). One of the local bookstores had some dream "interpretation" books which, even so young, I realized were utterly ridiculous. Mentioning my nightly adventures to my father resulted in a lecture about all the dreams of the prophets in the bible; my mother simply attempted to change my diet (I was not allowed chocolate for months until I lied to her one day that I didn't have those strange dreams anymore).

The awareness of the dream and its concurrent existence with the world gave me a vast new playground to explore, and it began to happen more frequently that I could see the dream even as my eyes were awake and interacting with the world. It was disorienting, and I was frequently accused of being "spacy" and even diagnosed with some form of autism and attention deficit disorder. My parents rightfully fretted over my condition, but when the dream rose to the forefront of my conscious mind, I phased into it willfully, regardless of what my body in the world was doing. I had learned not to relate my experience to anyone—family, friend, teacher, or doctor. It would not be understood. I masked the condition well and bore the brunt of being labeled a "space case" through most of grade school, until I truly learned to figure out how to

WHAT CAN THE NOTION OF GOD
AND THE UNIVERSE MEAN TO
SOMEONE WHO DAILY PRACTICES
GODLIKE POWERS OVER THEIR OWN
INFINITE UNIVERSE?

manage the experience of two worlds. If I was engaged in something important in the world—a test, a lecture, walking across a street, staring at the back of Amy Sommers' hair—I could diminish the broadcast of the dream until I could idle my body and shift my conscious weight into the other world. It was like training for a highly demanding sport or art, trying to find the "zone" in which I could cross over, through the invisible wall, into hyper-focused concentration. I could often close my eyes and instantly be in the dream. If I allowed the dream to be predominant, I could still perceive any stimulus from the world and sometimes even carry on a conversation. I would continue to refine the techniques of consciousness in dual worlds as I matured.

Into puberty, my activities in the dream turned to exactly the sort of behavior puberty dictates in young men. I could be sitting behind Cindy W in biology class in the world, imagining all her body parts I would never see, while in the dream I was taking her clothes off and looking at the parts as I imagined them to be. As I matured and gained more "real-world" experience, my interactions in the dream became much more thorough (though, for a while, slightly less imaginative and fantastical).

In adolescent testosterone-fueled rages brought on by events in the world, I could easily phase into the dream and destroy entire buildings, fling annoying people off majestically high cliffs, and soar with a rocket's thrust into outer space to feel the cold embrace of the mind's cosmos. Finding little of value in authentic dream research, at least the variety to which I had access, I fell into reading science fiction and fantasy, which dealt with the possibilities of dreams in fantastic and imaginative ways that fueled my world. I devoured superhero comics and could, in the dream, conjure the same powers as those heroes and villains, unleashing them on my dream public. I was a terror in those years, but only to myself and the dream. In the world, I was a B-minus student who mowed lawns for spending money, tried to seduce girls with awkward humor, and was completely inept at sports.

Throughout high school, I was developing a bit of a crisis of consciousness and conscience alike because of my pillaging and wilding in the dream. The dream was surfacing more and more outside of sleep; by 14, I was not so much sleeping solidly as resting my eyes and meditating, and by 16, it had grown difficult to shut either world off for even temporary respite from any kind of activity. I could not yet bring myself to align and overlap the two. My reputation for being "spacy" followed me throughout high school. It also had many other students (and teachers) convinced I was a stoner constantly on drugs, and nothing was further from the truth; the dream kept me from even wanting to experiment with any form of drug or narcotic, even alcohol, because I did not want to destroy the purity of what I was experiencing. Other kids ranted about how great it was to get high. Their addled descriptions of drug-induced buzzes were lame. They had no idea.

One girl found me interesting, "deep, a little mysterious," and this led to my first sex in the world. She leaned to the gothic and intellectual and we shared a love of science fiction. She was a senior to my junior, and our sex life lasted about a year before she went off to college, but from our first encounter where I lasted about 20 seconds in her hand to our last, a marathon 6 hour sexcapade in her home (her parents were away for the weekend), I was coming close to aligning the worlds; the focused energy of sexuality was the key, but I would soon learn to apply that energy and approach to other areas.

I still could not speak to anyone about my condition. Mentioning even a "really funny dream" to someone seemed toxic; an instant glaze of disinterest clouded their mind and the subject was changed quickly. To most people, even my closest friends (all two of them), "dreams" were whatever culture told them. Like foreign affairs, it was easy not to think too deeply about them. My crises at this point stemmed from my worrying about my moral direction—if I were so powerful in the dream but normal in the world, what was God telling me, or had I already been possessed by the opposite of God? Philosophically and spiritually I was lost and no religion offered meaningful security. What can the notion of God and the Universe mean to someone who daily practices Godlike powers over their own infinite universe?

School became a frightful challenge; it was hard to focus on the work at hand when so many incredible experiences were available just on the other side of that sheer cosmic membrane. I muddled through and stayed out of trouble, avoiding further diagnoses of ADD and the prescriptions of Ritalin or Adderall, which I was certain would erode my lucidity or turn it into a sham. I knew teachers, students and even my own family felt certain something was off, but so long as I kept my grades passable and strived for some outward normalcy, I was left to my own devices. I had to contain myself from reaching out in the world the way I could in the dream. It was difficult—keeping a secret, like a mutant.

In the summer between my junior and senior years, I kept getting visited in the dream by a friendly couple who hinted that the solution to all my anxiety about the nature of which reality was "reality" was simple; just stay in the dream. I could vanquish them, laugh at them, abandon them and fly off to my usual adventures; but they kept reappearing at random and it worried me. I'd battled monsters, fucked movie stars, explored outer space and toppled entire cities; but the presence of these two, both seemingly in their upper 20s, unnerved me and I could not shed them—or their message of freedom. This couple, whose names I never asked, would appear bohemian in appearance in one encounter, and very professional in another, usually at odds with the energy or setting in which I was engulfed. I sometimes felt their presence before I saw them, or perhaps willed them into appearing. These encounters were like running into the neighbors down the street or three floors up. If, that is, you had a sneaking suspicion that those neighbors worked for the CIA.

Pressure and confusion mounted, a building isolation of feeling completely alone in the universe. I was all too aware that these were feelings that caused suicidal tendencies in some teens and homicidal tendencies in others. Such power in the dream imbalanced with such in-experience in the world, with a sad morass of spiritual uncertainty in the mix as well, kept putting a weight on me that became too hard to bear.

I once again told my parents I was having issues sleep-ing at night, and that I didn't want it to affect my college test scores—that shrewd tactic got them to agree to take me to a sleep clinic I had read about at a university in Chicago. I wanted my condition validated, scientifically, hoping for some explanation as to why my brain was in-tent on forcing me to live in two worlds rather than one. Maybe there would be a sympathetic, knowledgeable sci-entist I could spill my guts to, or maybe I'd learn there were others like me.

They took me to the clinic and I was attached to all the cool-looking but very annoying EEG wires and made to sleep overnight in a dark room for observation. It was all very clinical. They kept asking if I had sleepwalking or bedwetting tendencies.

I slept. I woke. It was like staying at Holiday Inn, only the housekeeping staff comes into the room to put pe-troleum jelly on your head and chest. Otherwise, it was disappointingly uninteresting.

Here's the report handed to my parents the following af-ternoon:

SUBJECT REPORTS INTENSE DREAM STATES DURING NAPS AS WELL AS REGULAR SLEEP. SUBJECT REPORTS ENTERING A DREAM STATE IMMEDIATELY UPON SLEEP ONSET REGARDLESS OF SLEEP AND R.E.M. STAGE MAT-URATION. SUBJECT REPORTS MAINTAINING DREAM STATE IN LINEAR CONSCIOUSNESS UNTIL INDUCING WAKEFULNESS ON PURPOSE. SUBJECT REPORTS VIVID MEMORY OF DREAM STATE AND DESCRIBES MINUTE DE-TAILS WITH EASE. SUBJECT EXHIBITS NO SIGN OF NEUROSES, SCHIZOPHRENIA OR INFLUENCE OF PARA-NORMAL AND/OR HYPNAGOGIC INFLUENCE. SUBJECT

HAS NO CRIMINAL BACKGROUND. SUBJECT IS NOT
ON PRESCRIPTION MEDICATION OF ANY KIND AND RE-
PORTS NO ALLERGIES. SUBJECT IS NOT A RECRE-
ATIONAL DRUG USER. SUBJECT IS NOT RELIGIOUSLY
ZEALOUS. SUBJECT UNDER OBSERVATION DISPLAYED
ABNORMALLY HIGH BRAIN ACTIVITY DURING REM AND
NON-REM CYCLES. SUGGEST COUNSELING AND THERAPY
UNTIL CESSATION OF ABNORMAL DREAM TENDENCIES.

These silly clinic people thought you only "dreamt"
during the REM cycle.

Revealing my truth and experience to the world elicited
an unfavorable "yawn," so there was no reason to keep
it a secret, I'd just come across slightly stranger than I
already did.

I decided to make it my life's work to understand what I
thought no one else could. My parent's budget and my
grades (i.e., my ability to fully concentrate in the world)
would not get me to the upper echelons and vanguard
of scientific dream research such as the labs at Stanford,
Berkeley or MIT. I had to settle. There were few paths
I could take to studying my condition through academic
means: psychology, neuroscience, and quantum physics seemed most applicable. Completely inept at science and math, I chose to major in psychology, and I was
doomed to endure yet more classes from professors who
felt that Freudian theory was the be-all and end-all of
dream research.

At university, they (jokingly) called me "REMbrandt" for
my ideas. Other monikers were Dr. Dreamenstein, Sigmund Fraud, "the lone wolf," and, justifiably from one
girl who was the recipient of my attempts at short-lived
machismo, "Dream On Boy." I'd had sex with her so
many times in the dream, my ego in the world got the
best of me; one of many experiments in maintaining a
biconscious relationship.

My grades were average, my theories "interesting," "far-
fetched," "not based in current scientific protocol," and

"delusional." I gained access to a sleep lab and convinced another student to hook me up. The brain activity on the EEG most certainly raised eyebrows; letters were written, a few researchers from the upper echelons of academia feigned interest in the possibility of this dual-conscious phenomena, but none could be bothered to contemplate the implications of my condition when they were all busy writing papers on their own outlandish dream and consciousness theories, extolling and repudiating Freud and Jung, sinking further into the quicksand of academia, or stepping out into the world of pop science or the New Age movement (where the real money was), blissfully holding dream and meditation workshops at seaside retreats.

My papers were well received but lacked scientific disciplines producing quantified evidence of my theories. I ended up taking philosophy courses that seemed more helpful in dealing with my more metaphysical conundrums. I barely graduated and did not have the credentials to open a practice; besides, I could not abide patients expecting me to tell them what their dreams "meant."

Never ask me what a dream "means."

For a while, I lived with a former classmate, Sheila, the only girl I've ever truly loved. She had been attracted to my theory, my energies, to me—she shared in my dream/world experiments, became my anchor on the world side and a willing avatar on the dream side, and treated me with an undeserved amount of patience. Living poorly in the big city took a toll on us, especially since she was earning her keep as a counselor in a well-established private school. I was job-jumping from bookstores to movie theatres to museums, trying to figure out how to make the compromises in the world and the dream that came with worldly responsibility. Doors opened for her in the world—the welcoming arms and material generosity of a wealthy administration, troubled and interesting youth to work with, and grateful, country-club parents who adored the perky young counselor their sons

YOU ARE ONLY READING THIS
IN ONE WORLD—I'VE BEEN
COMPOSING IT IN TWO.

and daughters were falling in love with, keeping their issues out of their perfect hair. The wines, the dinners, the sports cars of handsome young fathers all pulled her into her own waking dream, clearer and more immediate than looking at the closed eyes of her disheveled roommate lover, wondering where he was journeying, knowing that it was not to the kitchen to make her a romantic breakfast. She gave us a year but was emotionally gone long before that, and even the sisterly affections died off before the lease was up.

I took an even smaller, dingier studio apartment deeper in the bowels of the city, finagled a lowly job in the library system, and spewed words into a computer, blasting the dream for my losses and blasting myself for having no initiative to harness my powers like the fucking superhero I always knew I was.

With the pull of the internet, I could hide unbothered and glean information from the sleep labs around the world, remain anonymous and dispense advice to anyone expressing interest or ability akin to my experience. For a few years, I carried the moniker REMbrandt (it had grown on me, despite my being walking proof that dream activity was not dependent on the REM stage) and dispensed advice and ideas on discussion boards and in chat rooms. I figured I was safe; if anyone was interested in my theories, they would come forward; if not, I was perfectly happy working at the library by day, trawling the net at night, and chronicling something and, eventually, they came. People who were not quite biconscious—they were weirder, kinkier, more desperate— responded. Pathetic, brilliant and sometimes evil things were out there and I'd been giving them an excuse to reveal themselves. People whose conditions put them on the fringes of society recognized a kindred spirit, and I became good at weeding out the nonsense, the wannabes, and the false "searchers." I cautiously began to post my theories and some of my experiences, and they garnered the full gamut of reaction, some of which you will read in this book. "REMbrandt" became too precious a screen name, and too much like the new age gimmickry of scientists I abhorred. I adopted my current name, Gardner Eeden—

Gardner being my given middle name, and Eeden from Frederik van Eeden, the one psychologist from the classical era of the emergence of dream research as a scientific pursuit and who is credited with coining the term "lucid dreaming" (credit is also due to the Marquis d'Hervey de Saint Denys, who in the 1860s kept extensive dream journals and wrote the phrase "reves lucide.") Like the superheroes I admire, this alias is necessary to protect my identity from those who would seek to destroy me (and if you think "destroy" is being overdramatic, well, there will be stories about that). My cities, my university, my friends' names, are all either omitted completely or changed. Though if I name inhabitants of the dream, be assured they are honest names to the best of my recollection. But this is not a biography, so don't let those instances distract you.

This book is a handbook of lucidity, an introduction to the next phase of human evolution. It's not a how-to guide, because I can't teach you how to become lucid or even to expand your consciousness. I can try to inspire you to act. The day is rapidly approaching when technology enables us to stimulate lucidity within the dream. When that happens, what will you do with all the freedom, all the pleasure, all that power? The effects of being unprepared for this duality could kill you.

Some of this material has been posted in various forms online over the years. I admit fully to being a lazy writer. There is some science here, but I reside beyond science. I have no credentials in academia. The world of dream research and theory is rife with fraud, fantastical theories, and self-delusion, and there is no reason you should treat my musings any differently. It may prove disparate, or inconsistent, and for those of you who are scientifically engaged in the study of sleep, dreams and consciousness, it may fly in the face of all you believe you know. I mean no disrespect, so by all means, please carry on. Just bear this in mind: you are only reading this in one world—I've been composing it in two.

INITIATION

There is the dream, and the world, and they run concurrently, a constant flow of consciousness that we slip in and out of with various degrees of surrender and control.

Since the dawn of "self-realization," we have regarded the dream as separate and multiple "dreams," singular visions or events within our sleeping mind, the only access to them being our fragmented memory upon waking. My experience shows that it is not an altered state of consciousness, but the other side of the coin of consciousness. The coin gets flipped when our physical selves in the world are shut down; but it is ever present regardless of our sleep cycle. We can become as lucid to the dream as we are to the world. Inversely, we can be as detached and confused in the world as we ever are in the dream.

Science does not know why humans, or any animals, require sleep. We know that a sleeping state will often refresh our mind and rest our body; but, from an evolutionary standpoint, it leaves us completely vulnerable. What is so important about shutting down our active body that we take such a great risk each night to achieve? The engines roar in this world, but once the physical engines shut down and minimize, the propulsion shoots us into a full glide in the dream. It is theorized that we use approximately 5-10% of our brains (probably a myth), but our brains grew extraordinarily large for a reason; consciousness. We harbor the geography and stimulus of two worlds. For most people, sleep is the catalyst for opening an interactive gateway to the second world. But for some, those doors are always open.

I am a man who is conscious 24 hours a day. Slipping my primary focus between the dream and the world is an almost effortless, sometimes terrifyingly involuntary act (driving can be tricky). Over the years, I have had to learn to live within the world of laws, morality and gravity—and the world without them. These are not necessarily "parallel universes" and I don't see them as any mystical, metaphysical alternate realities. These are two fibers of the same conscious thread and they run concurrently. When I am in the world, I am aware of the dream, and

YOU WERE BORN IN THE
WORLD AND IN THE DREAM.

when in the dream, I am aware of the world. I can act, move and experience sensation in each world separately; but I can think in both simultaneously. It's a unified mind prone to scatter, shift and phase to and fro, like watching two television shows on the same screen.

I don't always think in terms of "waking up" and "going to sleep." Rather, I describe the transitions as "phasing." There is "hard phasing," which is when I make a more abrupt transition into the world or dream from the other; and "soft phasing" which is more of an attention shift from one to the other as I am engaged in each simultaneously.

First, throw out everything you think you know about dreams and dreaming. The dream is not a series of quizzical images that float through your head which you may or may not remember the next day. It is not the stored fantasies, wish fulfillments and rumblings of the "id" any more than daydreams or waking fantasies are such. There are no universal dream symbols any more than there are things people do universally, such as eat, sleep, run, walk, and lust. There is nothing in a dream any more sacred or symbolic or open to interpretation than anything that may occur to you on any given day. There are no messages or hidden meanings in your dreams that are the key to your mind's or soul's ultimate fulfillment. You can prescribe meaning to any sequence of events in the world or dream alike, all are open to your prejudices. If you only had brief, minor glimpses of your everyday life, they would suddenly take on great metaphysical weight and importance, whether it was a vision of you taking out the trash or making love with your partner. Take any random slices from your normal day; consider those the only things you can remember of the day. Try to make sense of them. They become more exotic—more filled with spiritual meaning and potential, because they are taken out of the flow of the day.

The dream is not present only during sleep or unconsciousness; it is a constant state, a flip-side conscious current in which we may swim, skim, dive, or avoid by staying on shore for fear of sharks.

The fact is, you do not know exactly what the dream is, but you exist within it as surely as you exist within this world. Lust, glee, humor, panic, confusion and certainty, interaction and connection are as essential in one as the other.

You were born in the world and in the dream. You were very likely conscious in the dream before you emerged in the world. Just as you were an infant and child in the world, trying to make sense of sounds and shapes and natural laws, so in the dream you were trying to learn as well (and still are). In the world, you had parents or guardians and teachers to shape your experience and guide you; in the dream, you had no guidance, just an endless playground of limitless possibility in which your imagination could run wild. Your world experience— terrors and elations and all—crept into the dream, and the dream qualities—wonder and the sense of ultimate ego—crept into the world. Instruction and limitation in the world increased through schooling; but in the dream, you still wandered and played and tried to make sense of the difference between the two states. If one never recognizes the dream as a habitable realm, it will always be a curious source of confusion, punctuated by occasional fears and absurdities. If one learns to be as aware in the dream as one is in life, then the power of harnessing one's duality is within reach.

The first time you have a sustained lucid dreaming experience, where you are perfectly conscious in your dreaming self and have some control of your dream environment, you will never see reality in the same way again. You have achieved a unique and immeasurable power. This power has come from within you—and though it can be affected by external stimuli, it is originated and maintained through your inner thought processes; the same thought processes you employ in the world.

Your most powerfully lucid moments in either world are not always extraordinary events. We are not always most lucid at the birth of our child or during significant rites of passage and crises; we can be too overwhelmed by our senses to be in control of them, as disoriented as in any "nightmare." More often, a mundane or tedious moment crosses into a perfect lucidity. Ultra-conscious moments come to us unexpectedly; we don't always get to choose them. Our consciousness has an elasticity, there are layers of awareness, and we modulate between moments of static and clarity. This happens in the dream as it happens in the world. The more aware and lucid we seem to the moment, the more layers of unconscious activity ignite and fire upon our reason and intellect with deep and endless stores of ammunition from our collective unconscious.

As we cannot hear the high and low tones of the sound spectrum, or feel the tremors in such low or high vibrations, so we cannot grasp the high and low levels of consciousness. They exist, they affect us, and we exist in them.

DEFINING THE DREAM

There is no more misunderstood word in the English language than dream. It is right up there with the words "God" and "love" in that it has such a powerful range of meaning and interpretation, yet defines nothing concrete.

You are "living the dream," "dreaming of that special someone," "following your dream." Dream is inspiration and aspiration, but it's "just a dream." In our society, dream is the opposite of "real." We are raised to think that we have "a dream," or "series of dreams" in the night, as if the inner TV gets turned on when the lights go out and our brain flips channels for a while. We are passive observers, or in the case of nightmares, we are victims. A bad dream gets its own name ("nightmare"), but a good dream is just "a good dream." Countless prophets, delusional or not, as well as artists, poets, scientists and preachers, have proclaimed that God speaks to them through their dreams, or that they receive divine revelation or mystical inspiration from their dreams. Even practical solutions to vexing problems are presented via the dream. We write stories of older, wiser, more primal cultures who have powers of communicating within their dreams and interpreting the dreams for the benefit of the world. A spiritual, even physiological connection to the dream is not solely an aboriginal conceit. It does not belong to the realm of ancient wisdom, and no sages or mystics hold the keys to understanding or experiencing the dream any more than I do. Some of them have just devoted decades to honing their body's and mind's functioning, and that gets you a little farther along. My hats are certainly off to the good monks of ancient Asian cultures, but I am well beyond them—and I can do it while drinking Jack Daniels and listening to loud music. Tea and silent meditation are good too.

Language slights us when it comes to describing the dream. Any standard dictionary lists multiple definitions for "dream" in English alone. Don't bother looking them up, you've heard them countless times and your "subconscious" is already running through them as you read this. Melt them all into a couple of definitions and you'd come up with "fantasy" or "aspiration." They deny anything tangible, concrete, or realistic about where you spend half of your existence.

My experience is that the dream is just life. It is consciousness writ large, the mirror twin of the world we have created, every bit as fleeting and visceral. Its objects and occurrences are not symbols or revelations any more than any object or activity in the world. It is a world I inhabit, as boring or exciting as I make it.

Regardless of how lucid one can be in the world or the dream, surprises do happen. There are degrees of lucidity, and "lucid" does not always mean one has full control; we surrender to the flow and tides of life, as we do in the dream. There are moments of control and moments of complete abandon in each realm. The "sub" in "subconscious" is accurate. It's our attention just beneath the surface.

There is an awesome power in aligning one's conscious duality. We are born with an amazing ability to connect with our creative origins. You can experience Eden and exile from Eden converging. You can merge with the other you in the mirror and explore that world beyond the reflection.

If you want to get profound about biconsciousness, consider how you can live within a complete paradox. It is the snake eating its own tail, the Escher steps, the vase faces, the Judas kiss. Jekyll and Hyde, where both the beast and the rational man exist at the same time, drawing the same breath.

You can kiss someone in the world while hitting them in the dream. You can reverse this scenario and take it to any extreme you like. You can begin to discover what your many self-conflicts are and put them at ease. Biconsciousness can ease fears and provide an amazing release from the tensions of the world, though it also introduces a host of challenges.

To define the dream is to define a combination of thought, instinct, urge and transcendence, a combination no linguist in any language has the proper terminology for. Any definition of lucidity can refer to either world.

ACHIEVING LUCIDITY

I cannot teach you how to achieve lucidity. I could create lots of suggestive exercises involving meditation, auto-suggestion, mind control and other techniques used by psychologists who think they're able to tap into something in the psyche, but it would be misleading and deceitful. Lucidity does not come because you want it, or because you've earned it. It does not necessarily emerge when all the conditions are magically right. Lucidity doesn't care if you are closed to it, fighting it, or full of desire for it. It may not be a natural function like orgasm, or an involuntary function like yawning. I can tell you that the more awareness you build of details in your sphere of consciousness, the more lucidity might be triggered. Carlos Castaneda's old exercise of concentrating on looking closely at your hands while awake and reminding yourself you are lucid is not a bad approach (the theory is that when you see your hands in your dream, you will remember the exercise and become lucid).

Becoming lucid is not unlike shifting your focus--as much your mental focus as any physical, ocular clarity. Think of those "Magic Eye" optical puzzles where you stare at a page filled with abstract color blots and waves (technically "Salitsky Dots") in sequential patterns, until you can shift into a "deep-vision" focus that reveals the hidden three- dimensional image within the pattern. Phasing into lucidity is a little like that; suddenly forms are clearer, deeper, the senses resonate more powerfully, and you feel as if you've gone behind the curtain or that some mental fog has cleared, enabling you to see the world in its true form.

There are many "guidebooks," articles and theories on how to try to achieve lucidity within the dream; there are even machines designed to use light and/or electrical stimulation to trigger a dream response. I can't argue their effectiveness or failure rates, and if you try these and they work for you, great. My primary advice when navigating the world of dream experience is that, once you're asked to accept any symbolism or sign up for subscriptions, bug out. It will be a very long time before we develop magic dream Viagra.

I can say from experience that you can build stamina in maintaining lucidity by exercising your lucidity in the world. Most people go through their day, every action voluntary and involuntary, without achieving a true lucidity or awareness of the moment and what they are capable of within the moment. Pause several times a day and look around at your environment; do you remember how you got there and where you will go? What other possible paths might you follow? Be aware of sounds and strangers; who is watching you, and who is oblivious to you? If you had unlimited powers, what actions might you take, if any, in that moment, in that place, at that time? There are no formulas for achieving a lucid state; if it's a natural function of our evolution, then we have been given few clues as to its place in our origin or future. I may posit that sleep is necessary not only for physical rest but to better isolate our dreaming, that we might recognize the dream as a concurrent but separate space in which we exist, and to practice and prepare for an eventual existence (or a return to that existence) in that realm.

The question is never "what does a dream mean?" Do not wonder why you woke up from a nightmare, or why you couldn't complete some act of pleasure. Why do we withhold pleasure in the world for fear of moral sin, yet the dream conjures far more taboo scenarios for us to experience? The question you must always ask is "what would I do if I were lucid?" Then, if you are truly lucid, do it.

It's Wonderland and Neverland, it's Alice being able to say "fuck you" to the Red Queen, throw the Dodo clear out of sight and stare down the Mad Hatter until he's quivering in the cream. Peter could put away his knife, turn Hook into the crocodile, and have a three-way with Wendy and Tiger Lily. Or the Lost Boys. Or Alice.

EXERCISES IN LUCIDITY

Dream researchers and avid lucid dreamers encourage a variety of techniques to help you achieve lucidity, and they usually fall into the variety of keeping a dream journal, looking at your hands to check your current state of "reality," and imagining what you'd do if you were in the dream. These are fine exercises but don't go very far in helping you to define the essence of the dream state as it interacts with the world; practicing lucidity in the world is crucial to achieving it in the dream.

Much preparation for a lucid mind begins in the world. Carve out some time, every day, several times a day, to shut out distractions and center yourself. This is, essentially, meditation, but there is no ritual, no mantra, no rule. You don't have to sit in a lotus position, palms up, or lay quietly in a dark room. Just start with your eyes closed in order to find your inner voice; say to yourself "I'm here, I'm in control of myself and my thoughts." Then open your eyes to your environment, but do not leave your voice; narrate to yourself what you are seeing. Do this at home, at work, on the bus, at the mall, during sex. Learn to dictate your own consciousness; if you let the day control your focus, you are ignoring so much lucid possibility.

Here are some exercises you can try to help achieve, or at least better understand, biconsciousness and the challenge of maintaining lucidity. It's not likely you'll be able to complete all these suggestions; do what you can. Lucidity loves an exploratory mind.

1) Try to have sex in the same room where your mother stands, as she's yelling that it's time for dinner. This is an exercise in acute concentration and mental focus.

2) Sit in front of two monitors or two television screens, placed side by side within your visual field, displaying unrelated programs but with occasionally similar places or faces appearing in each. Concentrate on each individually, then, as a whole, start to watch both; see what information you can retain. Draw connections between the two, but do not try to justify what you see, or create a story or narrative. Rather, pick out details and try to remember them later.

3) Through the day, as you look at an image (moving or still), picture yourself entering the image; what would you do there? Any image works--an advertisement on a bus, a horror movie, a work of art, web porn. Assure yourself that this image is a part of your current reality.

4) Go through a single day (even a single hour) excising all forms of story.

5) With a willing partner, have a sexual experience in an unusual location. I would advocate keeping it legal, but push the boundary. Anywhere with world denizens going about their business is ideal. Resist the urge to feel you should not be there. The challenge is that you are in a new and unfamiliar environment, yet needing to complete a task that requires physiological concentration.

6) Put yourself in a completely alien environment. For example, if you're a farmer, go into the inner city and sit in the lobby of a bustling office building. If you're a straight, middle-aged woman, go to a gay bar. Putting yourself in an unfamiliar space heightens your senses and awareness.

7) Hire a group of actors to appear as your mother, father, sister, boyfriend, girlfriend. You need to exercise a complete paradigm shift of roles and familiarity.

8) Get your face out of tablets, screens, smartphones and books. You do not spend time in the dream looking at devices like this. Touch surfaces, catalog textures, visually confirm the origins of sounds.

9) Be aware of environmental situations or factors that spike your senses; for example, storms fill me with lust. Driving at night looking at distant lights in the windows makes me more curious. Be aware of your emotions but do not let them create a narrative.

10) Sit in a public space and observe people. Focus on your trigger prejudices (for example, I can't stand smoking or precious hairdos). Affirm that here in the world, these people are no insult to you; they deserve your empathy and respect. Consider how you might address them in the dream. Imagining it in the world can instigate it in the dream. Do the same for those who might trigger your lust or your revulsion.

11) Make eye contact with anyone in your path. If speaking with someone, keep eye contact constant; not intense or challenging, just connecting. Eye contact holds you to the moment, to the now—it's a powerful, visceral connection.

12) Have sex with your partner, maintaining eye contact. You will be aware of your body movements and theirs, the environment and any sounds or smells, but you will block out those distractions by pinning yourself, your entire conscious being, to your partner. Do not break eye contact, even during orgasm.

13) Remember something that happened today, quickly. Was it the most important thing that happened to you all day, or a mindless triviality? Was the thing you remembered out of place, surreal or unexpected? Your memory of the dream is no different than your memory of the world. The act of memory recall is the same.

14) This is going to sound obvious, but open your eyes. When you're doing something pleasurable or experiencing something frightening, open your eyes and own the experience. When you close your eyes, you've already surrendered to another dimensional layer. Keeping your eyes open gives you an immediate feedback loop of information you can use to develop some level of control.

15) Sit with two or three friends. Focus your eyes on one, speak to them and then speak to one of the other friends without losing eye contact with the one friend. Take it seriously. Speak about something serious with the one you are locking eyes with, and something frivolous with another friend. Alternate friends and topics. Do not break eye contact.

TRUE LUCIDITY IS THE DIFFERENCE
BETWEEN USING ELECTRICITY AND
BEING ELECTRICITY.

PERCEPTION VS. REALITY

In the world, perception can be keen observation or mis-guided illusion; world–based reality is also tricky because our perceptions skew our ability to accept a true and concrete reality. We may say that a sensation—feeling distinct pain or pleasure—defines reality, but any lucid dreamer can tell you that sensation is every bit as real, even heightened, in the dream.

In the dream, perception and reality are one and the same; but the difference between being and being lucid is like the difference between a static shock and light-ning. True lucidity is the difference between using elec-tricity and *being* electricity.

In the world, I might perceive that the city skyline in the distance appears much closer; when in fact, it's 44 miles away. In the dream, if you perceive something to be close, with a simple thought you can make it appear right in front of you. In the world, visual perception is frequently a matter of spatial measurement; psycholog-ical or emotional perception is a matter of experiential understanding, and can be very wrong without the facts. The dream does not need to make these distinctions. Physical and emotional properties can be combined and adjusted at your direction.

DO NOT LET YOUR EMOTIONS CREATE A NARRATIVE.

FALLACIES

"Not ideas about the thing, but the thing itself"
—Wallace Stevens

Remembering

Many people will say that they do not remember their "dreams." It has been said by some psychologists that we were designed to forget our dreams so that we are not forced to make the distinction between "dream" and "reality". This could especially benefit those less able to distinguish between the states, such as small children or people suffering from some form of dementia. There may be a sort of 'dream amnesia' built into us so that we do not confuse the states, or allow our emotions to be too affected in one by something that happened in the other. The brain essentially immobilizes the muscles responsible for "fight or flight" response so that we do not physically act out our dreams (a condition known as "atonia"). This does not always work for everyone.

Black and White

Never has any interaction within the dream been black-and-white; the world has never been black-and-white. I thought people believed their dreams were black and white because of television. Did people call their dreams "black and white" before movies and television? Before photographs? I've never had anything less than a full-color, sensory dream. The claims say more about the power of the medium of moving pictures to make us believe we are in a dream world; the first people to witness moving images must have felt some connection to the screen and their own dream process. It was another way of putting pictures in the mind. Stories that provoke emotion create their own worlds. If someone's dream is in black and white, it is their own effect; the dream is not trying to be artsy.

Point of View

Most people are passive in the dream (as many are in the world). Even when they are the subject of the dream, their actions are passive. This is usually reflected in their daily life as well. They will deal with what comes to them rather than seeking out and creating their own agenda. Aggressors tend to be aggressors in either world; our world nature is echoed in the dream, though in the dream we are free to depart from our nature. More often, however, it is our true nature that finds us.

Lucidity requires a first person point of view.

Symbolism

Everything can be interpreted as a symbol, whether we're in the world or in the dream.

An important concept to grasp is that it is not how symbolic events in the dream can reveal themselves to be; it is how aware you are in the moment you are there. Are you aware enough to realize you're dreaming? When you encounter something that you've been told is symbolic of another thing, and you become lucid, you can simply change the object or make it disappear altogether—thus rendering any symbolism completely pointless.

DON'T EVER ASK ME
WHAT A DREAM MEANS.

Our dreams do not send us messages, omens or revelatory images for our edification. They do, however, portray our minds and thoughts on countless deeper and higher levels than our conscious selves can process. Any psychiatrist can take a dream event or sequence of events and find patterns and symbols that seem to completely address some issue or problem you may have in the world, just as any astrologer or palm reader can find messages in the positions of the stars or tea leaves to find the same. When you achieve lucidity in the dream—and in the world—you are able to actively seek out answers to issues you may be having. In the world, you will look up answers on the internet. In the dream, you *are* the internet. And, like the internet, those answers can be wrong, because their source is fallible. There is no ultimate truth; there is a series of choices you can make to build your character. You make better choices when you're completely aware of all the options at your disposal. In the world, those options are governed by physical and moral laws. In the dream, it is about experience, will power, and imagination.

MEMORY AND MEANING

In the dream as in the world, we have a merged set of memories, a composite of experiences. We are in a place unfamiliar to us (here) but do not question it (there) because it flows within the realm of the dream experience. We see someone—a relative or friend or celebrity—who doesn't look like that person (here) but we feel the association (there) intrinsically. We may catch ourselves between the streams of logic—here stream and there stream—and ask, but for a second—is that right? It doesn't look right, but it feels familiar. This familiar feeling is a thread that weaves throughout both worlds. The dream "avatar" of a person in the world says nothing about them, not even your own internal feelings regarding them. It feels like the person we remember from the world, but it is not them, and they are not a representation of themselves. They are a representation of yourself.

When we slip into the dream, we are sliding into thoughts and actions already in progress. The dream presents our moods, fears and pleasures slowed down to the point where we can literally step into them. They seem embarrassing, nonsensical, mundane or frightening because they are themselves the preposterous journey, broken down, bit by visual bit, of a notion, a thought. We want to believe they are themselves the final message, there for us to read and interpret. When we reach a conclusion, or define something in a single second as if by "intuition," that is because we draw from a deep well of visual, sensory and logical experience, and our brains are vast microprocessors. I suggest the dream can give us the frame-by-frame account of a thought, no matter how rambling; if we could slow it all down and watch it frame by frame, we would see the DNA strands or ones and zeros code of ideas weaving into a mental fabric projected for us not just to see, but to experience.

REVEALING HIDDEN TRUTHS

Your dream can be goofy and embarrassing, break sexual taboos or leave you breathless, and you're still trying to put it into the context of your waking world; what does it mean to me here. It's tiring and futile to do this. Take your dream on its own, for what it is making you experience in the moment. Much sensory information crosses back and forth from one world to the other; the worlds clearly affect each other, whether or not they share a common code or cosmological structure. Random shards of experience will cross over and litter in the other realm in mimetic play. In either realm, this can cause unexplained sudden onsets of depression, euphoria, wonderment, or desire. I say again, do not let your emotions create a narrative.

Do you ever have a "mind fart?" Do you lose track of something, forget why you walked into a room, experience déjà vu or suddenly sink into a depression? Occurrences in the dream may be dictating your world demeanor. You may not be instantly plugged into your unconscious mind, but it is that side of you that is poking out. It will often conflict with your desires and attentions in the world. If you only knew what the distraction was about, if you could only slip into the dream and address it, see it, fuck it or strangle it, you'd be amazed at the clarity that ensues. No matter what you achieve in the dream, it's probably not filled with messages of hidden universal truths. There are plenty of universal themes among people, especially those in a shared culture; they don't just pop up in the dream, they're everywhere.

DEATH

Most people, when in a situation in the dream in which they are about to be killed, get a split-second instant of realizing they are in a dream, and fear prods them to wake up. They do not convert that realization to lucidity. If you are lucid in a dream, you are not going to die. There has never been a recorded incident (outside of bad horror movies) of someone dying within a dream, as the result of some dream activity.

However, we can't simply ask those people who died while sleeping if they realized their moment of death from within the dream. If you die while fully awake, do you immediately slip into the dream to reside? Thousands of recorded "near-death" experiences could lead us to believe that you do.

When it comes to death, everything is pure speculation.

INTERPRETATION

Don't ever ask me what a dream means. The inane question "what does this dream mean" underscores that you are trying to find a story, a narrative to the dream, one that confirms your suspicions or gives you new revelations. Stop asking what a dream means. What does digesting mean? It's something you do, voluntarily or involuntarily, and you are sometimes more aware of it than other times. A pole is a pole; a hat is a hat. Sex organs are sex organs. In the lucid world and dream, we truly don't care much about fucking our mothers and killing our fathers; those notions in and of themselves are the real mythology and if they symbolize anything, it's that the people espousing symbolic theories need desperately to continue believing in stories. The wind does not have mystical meaning. It can feel good caressing your skin or it can rip you apart. It blows hot or cold depending on the molecules and energy through which it passes.

What has been your dream experience? Have you paid attention to your dream throughout your life, or has it been a casual afterthought? Have you bought into others' interpretations of dreams and the notion that there is somehow a universal key to understanding all our dreams? This is exactly like subscribing to a religion, with all its dogmas and mythologies. You are letting someone else interpret God for you, ignoring the profoundly original relationship to the universe which only you can have.

This is not to say that we can't take deeply meaningful lessons from the dream; we can learn from any activity in either state. We can also waste an incredible amount of time in either state. Even more so in the dream, since time is less fluid there. It is not easy, but I can sometimes be perfectly aware of minutes passing in the world, even as seeming hours unfold in the dream. This time distortion is one of the most jarring effects of biconsciousness, and it took me years to navigate it comfortably. It can still disorient me in so many ways. If I am stuck in the world in some dreary meeting, I am aware of time shuffling in the dream and at times it is as if I'm fast-forwarding in that world to make up for the lethargy in this.

Do not subscribe to the notion of universal symbols of objects or experiences in the dream. There is only the now, the current experience, and your level of awareness of it. When you can learn to control an object or an experience, it loses all power over you and its meaning to you will change. You may objectify it, study it or discard it, but it will not own you with the want of mystery.

MAINTAINING THE LUCID STATE

"I am one hundred billion cells in search of a leader."
– John Lilly

We have billions of microscopic life forms inhabiting our bodies, inside and out. Would it not stand to reason that we have countless waves of quantum energy surging through our conscious stream––the same particles and waves that flow through our bodies? If bacteria form colonies upon and within us, what invisible energies give us our being, and then further give us our ability to control that being, however briefly?

What is extremely difficult in maintaining a lucid state in both the dream and world simultaneously is achieving meaningful control over each state. You can rarely be at the same level of lucidity in each state. To say something is "dreamlike," "Kafkaesque," or "surreal" does not assume you are in the dream. Our experience alters the strength of our perception.

When in school, it seemed the harder I had to concentrate on something like a test or taking notes, the harder it was for me to keep dream events from commanding my attention there. I remember a particularly difficult

WE SEEK TO TUNE THE
WORLD OUT EVEN AS THE
DREAM WANTS TO RUSH IN.

geometry test during which, in the dream, a group of supernaturally powered strangers with malicious intent were attempting to kill me by hypnotizing me and dropping me off a tall building. Fully lucid there, I could banish them, tickle them, fuck them or otherwise make them disappear, but this gang was relentless and continued to challenge my attention in the world. The geometry test was a must-pass for me, I was in danger of failing my worst subject. This was a clash of attentions. It is hard to concentrate on being dropped from a ludicrously high skyscraper while erasing and reworking difficult mathematical proofs. In the end, I mustered my attentions in the dream to fly, fueled by anger, and smashed three assailants into the ether with spectacular purple explosions, and stopped briefly to bask in my dream awesomeness. I failed the geometry test. It's extremely difficult to concentrate on the laws of mathematics and physics when you are simultaneously engaged in breaking all those laws. Honestly, the dream was more fun.

Could I have wished the dream actions away, knowing I had to concentrate on that test in the world? With enough focus, yes. Was I irresponsibly choosing the distraction over the responsibility of the test? Ummm...yes. I have shuttered dream events so that I could maintain a more lucid attention in the world, but not always when it mattered most. I am certain I would find a complete focus in the world if I were saving someone's life or under extreme mental and physical duress.

To some, maintaining biconsciousness might be a matter of driving manual and automatic at the same time. Knowing when to shift into a new gear versus when to coast and when to idle. Then also knowing when to take a corner safely, and when to speed uncontrollably into a massive cement wall. Engaging passive judgment and active judgment simultaneously can be disconcerting. Just know that, regardless of where you might exercise your primary conscious actions, the other state becomes the subconscious; still flowing, still absorbing stimuli; still affecting the whole.

We all retreat and emerge from short periods of madness,

channels of thought in which we become trapped and are helpless to change, victimized by the realms within us that know more about us than we do, that reach back to long before we were born and want nothing more than to propel us with great force into the future, and it can't see whether or not there's a massive stone wall in the way or clear, blue sky. We stand peacefully gazing at the tides hour after hour, and when our guard loosens, the undertow of our psyche pulls us down. What defense do we have when we are matched by a greater, more powerful us? Ignorance, perhaps; blind acceptance. Or maybe a constant, subsurface anger that keeps the knowing world at a safe distance. Or we can visit these worlds within ourselves, shout at our demons and embrace our saints, or shout at our saints and embrace our demons. Or make our demons and saints alternately shout at and embrace each other as we stand by, bemused and in control. Yes, we're capable. I go there frequently.

I am filled with a menacing power. Some specter of control, or illusion that I have any control at all, shadows me in both worlds. We cannot, in the world or the dream, always choose our moments of clarity, of lucidity, of control. When we become truly lucid to a moment, the surge of power can be overwhelming. It can be surprising how little control we wield. The human response system and eons of instinct are powerful catalysts for jarring you into action in either state. "Fight or flight" still rules our physiology until some rational or creative thought can intercede. To concentrate more fully in one state is to lose some degree of power and control in the other, a mental see-saw of thought and action.

We seek awareness; and then we seek an escape from awareness. We seek to tune the world out even as the dream wants to rush in.

DEFINING "LUCID"

People often confuse lucid dreaming with having complete control over one's dream. There are degrees of lucidity in the dream just as there are in the world. An awareness of being in the dream does not mean one is able to control the dream; it's just the first phase. Lucidity is more like when you bring your mental wanderings, daydreams and reveries into alignment with your current reality.

"Lucid" does not necessarily mean "in control." Rather, it can be an awareness level that allows you to exercise your conscious reach and imaginative power. Just as in the world, at any time during the dream, you can lose control or fail to realize something. In a way, being lucid is the opposite of "nightmare," wherein you are terrified not just by the circumstance or monster that threatens you, but by the lack of control. When fully lucid, you can achieve near total control.

"Lucid" as a word generally means clear, transparent, or easily understandable. The origin is from the Latin, "lucidus," meaning light. The term "lucid dream" is credited to the Dutch writer and psychiatrist Frederik van Eeden (yes, from whom I took my pseudonymous name); van Eeden was a contemporary of William James and Freud. He is not the first to have written about becoming aware within the dream, but he supposedly coined the phrase.

To be "lucid" in the world or the dream is the same condition. You are clear about your state, you know where you are, who you are, and have a grasp of your surroundings; you are sensate and can move around in your environment with some degree of confidence. But being "lucid" does not mean one has "control." This is an important distinction. In a universe born of chaos, the notion of having absolute control over anything is an utter fallacy, an illusion.

For example: in the dream, I often seek the solace of a

location I return to frequently, an expanse of shallow, azure sea that stretches as far as the eye can see; its surface ripples with gentle movement but no waves, there is sunlight dappling the surface, and I can see the two feet or so to the soft, white sandy bottom. I can drop into this vast ocean and roll in the warm water with no fear of sharks, stingrays, rogue waves, or murky water. It is perfect and pristine. Yet, as I allow the indulgence of enjoying the sensations I've created, surprises do pop up. Little creatures will emerge from the sand and nip at me, storm clouds will threaten; once the sand gave way, sinking into a vast abyss that nearly pulled me under. The point is that, no matter how controlled an environment you create, you are always aware of the possibility of other objects or events superseding your desires; you have seen them in the world, in movies, on TV, read about them, and therefore, they exist and can occur. And they will. When they arise, you can choose to dispatch them however you please, but you cannot always keep the unexpected from happening. I am always surprised at what I encounter in my tropical lagoon, and the surprise is sometimes the greater pleasure.

Being lucid in the dream negates every theory of the dream as simply the mind's way of purging or sorting memory. It nearly obliterates Freudian theories of the dream as wish fulfillment (ironically, since when lucid you can do whatever you want); and it completely destroys the clichéd theories of dream symbolism.

To be "lucid" is to accept your awareness. When I was younger and first struggling to define my condition, I wrote ridiculous amounts of poetry and grandiose essays about being biconscious; thankfully I destroyed most of these pieces, then self-published the remains in a collection titled "The World Inside the World Outside." One piece in particular sticks with me; I've never been able to shake its depiction of what may describe perfect lucidity:

IT IS NOT ENOUGH TO BE HERE.
YOU MUST BE AWARE YOU ARE HERE.
IT'S NOT ENOUGH TO BE AWARE YOU ARE HERE.
YOU MUST WANT TO BE HERE,
AND YOU MUST BE AWARE THAT YOU WANT TO BE
HERE.
AND YOU MUST WANT TO BE AWARE THAT YOU
WANT TO BE HERE.
YOU MUST WANT TO BE AWARE THAT YOU ARE
HERE.
THOUGH YOU COULD BE IN ANOTHER PLACE.
YOU MUST CHOOSE TO BE HERE, AND BE AWARE
THAT YOU CHOOSE TO BE HERE.
YOU MUST CHOOSE TO BE.
YOU MUST WANT TO CHOOSE TO BE.

YOU *THINK*, THEREFORE, YOU *THINK* YOU ARE.

GEOGRAPHY

You might be tempted to think that all the landscapes and constructions within your dream are nothing more than psychic movie sets. They are never the same, always evolving to dress the scenarios being played out in your head. You would be mostly right. In the world, you never remember a place you've seen, no matter how often, with perfect clarity; memory is shifty and mutable.

Stronger lucidity can create more durable environments to explore, even to revisit frequently. We all visit places in our dream which "seem" like places in our world—I am partial to the urban environments where malls, museums and apartments all morph into labyrinthine constructions—and they do fade out as we surge to other places. I used to sketch out my favorite rooms, buildings, stores and spaces from the dream (using the dreamscape as my sketchpad—what good is a pencil and paper there?), and began a long-term project of mapping out the landscapes, cities, island oases and seas through which I traveled. It is impossible to measure distance in a world where distance is of no consequence, so the notion of travel becomes a psychological barrier, not a physical one.

Where does the dreamscape exist in relation to our geographical landscape? It isn't "above" or "below;" you could make an argument for a vague "within." Is it more like the internet's cloud, shared and spread out through some quantum code?

Space does not have a fixed geometry or position in the dream. You can feel you are "here" but you are also simultaneously "there," accessible by the tiniest shift of will, without the illusion of movement.

There are juxtapositions in the landscapes of the world, just as in the dream; images of utter mundanity punctuated by cities and parks filled with lush greenery, glistening metal high rises, surreal amusement parks or star-bright city centers such as in Tokyo, New York City's Times Square, or downtown Las Vegas. All of life is on a train looking out the window, and we preserve not only the landscape views that make an excitable impression on us but all the flat vistas in between. Who can look at the buildings of Frank Gehry or I.M. Pei and not think they would belong in the dream as easily as the world? I travel to New York City, to New Orleans, to Walt Disney World or to Toronto, and I'm one foot in the dream environment. When I travel in the dream, it's through generic mashups of multiple cityscapes and rural vistas, or in more energetic moments, I will sail through a cosmos comprised of countless breathtaking images courtesy of the Hubble telescope.

In the dream or the world, landscape is not truth, it is experience. Whether there are objects before me, or the illusion of objects, I perceive them, and only so much of them that I can see with my own eyes. Cheetahs and snails define "distance" very differently. Things are constantly changing, always in flux, yet we sense a stability and fixed position because, to us, these changes are happening at a glacial pace.

I would occasionally control my environment with some whimsical rearrangement—an upside-down mountain here, a lake in the middle of the air there. These exercises were fun distractions but would often grow tiresome; I am always excited by the landscapes of the world, and being able to explore combinations of those landscapes has always been more than enough to keep my nomadic wanderings fulfilled. It's like looking at art; as much as I love the fantastical illustrations of Roger Dean's alien landscapes from classic 70s rock bands, or Scott Mutter's surreal morphed photographs, or even the ponderous and illusory mechanics of M.C. Escher's sketches, I feel greater connections to stunning photographs of real places, whether on Earth or in another galaxy.

I could create more fantastical geography by visiting environments with which I was less familiar; star-strewn galaxies and nebulae layered with huge galactic formations—continents of dust clouds, vast floating, glowing

IN THE DREAM OR THE
WORLD, LANDSCAPE IS
NOT TRUTH, IT IS EXPERIENCE.

orbs and other ephemera which I had only seen in stunning astronomy pictures. Flying freely, I punch through these swirls and explosions and let them flow around and through me, often surrendering a lucid control just to see what the cosmos might surprise me with. It's in these spaces where I am most humbled, even as I recognize the cliché of being "one with the universe." It is a fearsome and anxious feeling to be suddenly enveloped by complete darkness, as all lights from all millennia fade away, recognizing that this, too, is a place.

In the dream, we all experience a metamorphous sense of place; a wide-open expanse suddenly shifts into a suffocating closet, a wall gives way to an auditorium, a dressing cabinet opens to a mythical world. We can change the scenery to the extent we have some lucid control, but our sense and perceptions of "place" and our role in a "place" are usually far more powerful than our psyche can master. In the world, place always has context, but our purpose in that space is not always clear. Does "place" define us? Or do we define it?

SPACE AND TIME

When you learn to move through the dream in ways impossible in the world, to become the nomadic dreamer even as your body is performing its necessary life-sustaining tasks in the world's stasis, you learn how to "force" time, or "force" space/movement. I do not have to physically fly or walk to a location I see in the distance; I can, essentially, "teleport" to that space. I do not have to physically open a door; I can phase to the inside of a location. This radically changes one's perspective in reviewing a certain cityscape or landscape and, when learning one's way around, offers a lot of wonderful and sometimes unpleasant surprises.

When I was a little boy, I remember going to the beach and just sitting for long stretches (probably just moments, but to a child, time is closer to the dream than the world) to feel the surf reach up to my toes, recede, and reach up again, like a massive liquid blanket being pulled and pushed. Even then I sensed the connection to the tide, a droning rhythm I could not quite fully hear. I was very satisfied to later learn how that rhythm of the ocean was tied to the spinning of the earth and the pull of the moon. In the dream, I would often (still do, in fact) sit at a precipice or an ocean and see if I could sense a tide, a rhythm or a pull. It is a world without gravity and beyond Newtonian physics, but it is not a world without natural rhythm. Things move of their own accord; a wind will pick up, a sound will emanate from the distance, some lonely peal of a creature or the thud and clank of metal will erupt. Though I understand these are echoes of sounds I know and have heard before, their place in the dream is not just filling blank space. It is me, constantly building an environment in which all my senses are exercised.

Time, in the dream or the world, is relative. An old cliché, but true. In the world, we "lose track of time," time speeds up when we're "having fun," we wonder "where did the time go"? In the dream, perceived time can shift wildly, and our physical measurements of time are generally meaningless. I cannot look to the sun for accurate time, and objects like clocks and watches will only keep time so long as I'm concentrating on their functionality. In the dream, if I want it to be time for something, I do not have to wait, I make it happen. Yet, in my unique biconscious life, I can say that I feel the presence of a kind of time within the dream; whether I am being the dream nomad and moving through multiple locations, daylight and night-dark environments, or whether I'm choosing to be sedentary and enjoying an environment unfold around me. There is a ticking, a hum, or some low-frequency sizzling current, a rhythm that is sometimes a 4/4 beat, sometimes punctuated with polyrhythmic signatures, and at other times free jazz. I cannot say that I believe time is a constant, but it is present when we ponder it, in either realm.

TO A CHILD, TIME IS CLOSER
TO THE DREAM
THAN THE WORLD.

Humans did not invent the notion of time, nor the basic means to measure the time. The natural rhythms of the universe do that for us; our orbit around the sun, the moon's orbit around the earth, the tides pounding the land. In the dream, you don't want to exert mental energy on consciously trying to keep track of time—it would be, for lack of a better phrase, a complete waste of time. Some physicists have theorized that time may not flow in a linear pattern but might, in fact, flow in many different directions at once. If we are conscious in the world, and conscious in the dream, and we see the evidence of that in the dream, does that confirm those theories?

We did not invent time, but humans have certainly tried to define it, control it, and manipulate it by creating stories around it.

We remember an experience even as it is happening to us; the experience and the remembering are the same. Things are realized through attention and materialized by concentration. If all the energy that will ever be contained in the universe was truly born with the Big Bang and all matter, motion and life are simply the conduits for transferring that energy, then how can we count the dream out of that eternal pulse? We are raised to imagine a linear timeline from our inception and even beyond, but we can manage our perceptions of time and distance differently. If the world is a clock, then the dream is a clock shop, with all devices set to different times from different time zones, some not ticking at all and others ticking mad as the Mad Hatter's watch. But a perfect lucidity, a complete control of your surroundings, cannot stop time.

Increased exposure to lucidity, over time, in an environment I'm able to manipulate, produces some profound effects in both the world and the dream. Humanity begins to dissipate...there is a tide to conscious control, an ebb and flow of possibility. Again, you go from using electricity to being electricity.

POINT OF VIEW

"Here We find that We have created Them who are Us."
– John Lilly

Though the dream, like the world, is typically experienced through our own subjective point of view, the dream can sometimes shift our viewing axis to make us feel as if we are watching ourselves or a projection of ourselves. This shifting of subjective to objective perception is jarring when one is non-lucid in the dream, and when lucidly engaged, the point of view does not shift so radically, if at all, depending on one's level of control. But if we're watching ourselves, then who have we become? Ourselves, we must assume. We harbor multiple layers, multiple perceptions of ourselves and the self is not contained within one physical form, either in the world or the dream. Fragments and shards can explore their own tangents and create their own pathways to travel. On every level our eyes, our projected eyes, and our projected senses are watching, gathering, and transferring concrete visions, abstract ideas, and paradoxical hallucinations. They move freely between the strata of our consciousness and often give us the sense of otherness, even as we may seek union.

We are, essentially, ghosts in our own dreams...drifting, like specters, usually not in control, a bit confused within a familiar but slightly altered environment, often disembodied until we encounter our body. Perhaps the denizens who populate our dreams are also ghosts, passing through the quantum-thin membranes of their own dreams into ours, phasing returning, in two places at once.

In the dream, we do sometimes slip into the point of view of a relative, stranger or fictional character, if not their being. It's usually too jarring to our sense of self and we do not get a good long look at ourselves from this "person's" point of view. We cannot seem to leave the stream or thread of our self and fully become another. I have

THE WORLD IS INFUSED WITH
WORDS TO THE POINT WHERE
WORDS BECOME THE WORLD.

tried this in lucidity many times and though I can get into the body of another, see through those eyes and feel what that body feels, I cannot split my point of view to be the one watching and the one being watched. Perhaps it's too much, as I'm already watching the world and the dream unfold at the same time, seemingly through two sets of eyes.

There are few profound insights to be gained in attempting this kind of role playing in the dream, since you are always a manifestation of your own being. It's fun to inhabit the form of the opposite sex, another race, a favorite hero, a historical figure, a complete stranger, or a wolf. To take the play fully into the pleasure zones you like, you must achieve a higher level of lucid control, and if you are at a higher level of lucidity, you are fully aware of your duality. Without lucidity, we can jump through other points of view in the dream and have some powerful experiences, but they are experiences of the self and become quickly lost or muddled as we find it too challenging to stray too far from our own shell for long.

KEEPING A DREAM JOURNAL

"When the going gets weird, the weird turn pro."
– Hunter S. Thompson

When I first started making sense of my rather aggressive dream voyaging, I read everything I could get my hands on, and even some of the best authors on dream theory always stressed the importance of keeping a journal. For a while I found this very useful, but within a few short years, my dream recall was as comprehensive as my waking day, and to reverentially write down every detail of the dream became unrealistic.

I encourage journal exercises for those just starting to explore the dream, because I've always found writing to be an excellent way of underscoring a fact, idea, or memory; it's a psychological commitment to capturing and exploring something, and one of the few ways of recording an event and keeping its memory from being lost or too terribly altered. But I recommend using the journal to record everything that screams to be captured, whether in the world or the dream. Do not differentiate between world or dream in the journal. After months, especially after years, you will be surprised at how normal the dream sounds and fantastical life events can be. You will get the bigger picture of how they are blended together, and maybe discover events that trigger certain behaviors, repulsions, desires, and prolonged states of anxiety or malaise.

The journal was an excellent exercise in the beginning, it gave me some discipline in my attention to the dream and gave me a long-term method of "playback." I highly recommend it as a means of capturing the only element of the dream you can carry into the world—your memory. If I could not lucidly carry the memory of the dream back into the world, I'm certain I would go mad.

Of course, when trying to describe events or emotions from the dream experience, words will often fail you. You must make up your own words, even if they seem nonsensical. For example, the unexpected disagreement between the "remembering" emotion in the world and the "doing" emotion in the dream is (to me) a "dismash." This word sounds stupid to you because you have no emotional resonance with it. Make up your own words and start using them; it's an excellent exercise for claiming an original form of power over your environment and breaking down established symbols of language and communication.

The world is infused with words to the point where words become the world. The naming, the myth behind all objects, the time it takes to form the words to make a language we understand—whether vocally or in our mind's silent pronunciation—turn words into tour guides through the meaning, feeling, even sensations of our lives. Yet words and their meaning are easily shattered by raw emotion.

In the dream, I can go for long periods with no intrusion from words; when things don't make sense, when there is no name or term for a fantastical experience or object, there is only intuition, reaction, acceptance or fear. There is interaction and a tactile and intuitive sense; we react more truly in the dream than in the world, for there are no filters of words distancing us from experience.

I do not identify labels or logos, morality, myth, or name people or objects. If I come across a dismash, a person who feels like my mother, but looks like a stranger, I accept it wholly on the basis of the feeling. I will not reject that she is my mother because I have not identified her by name and image or called her by name. Primal man felt thirst and he went to water, took it into his body, and was satisfied, no words. His language was all senses, outer and inner. When hit in the nose with the powerful pheromones of a potential mate, he used his strength to fulfill his biological imperative. This mindset is very much alive in the dream, and today it battles with our television and symbols and words—or the power they hold over us.

Words will fail you when it comes to the complexity of emotions and abilities within the dream. Do not employ them to strangle your experience. Keep a journal as a memory tool to navigate the world and dream together, but when biconsciousness kicks in, learn to let the words and the names go. Transitions are smoother.

I have spoken with blind and deaf persons who often live guided by these emotional instincts; when you cannot see something to visually label it, or hear something to verbally label it, you must create your own association born from your inner, sensual interaction with it. Doing this helps to create a powerful world of deeply linked associations that can free you from the strictures of other people's labels.

ARE YOU BICONSCIOUS?

I have yet to encounter someone whose experience is like mine. I've met those who are avid lucid dreamers, with terrific insights into their dream experience versus their world experience. I've come across many who have pretended to live with my condition, but it is very easy to catch untruths.

There may well be other biconscious persons in the world, and from throughout history. I'd like to think there have been mad artists—perhaps a Lewis Carroll, Edgar Allan Poe or Franz Kafka, a Bosch, a Coleridge, DaVinci—that worked and lived with this condition but could not truly comprehend it. It would most certainly have been diagnosed as madness or witchcraft up until the advent of Freud and Jung, so even creative geniuses probably knew best to channel all that extra conscious effort into their worldly work, grateful for the inspiration in the dream.

I do not mind the solitude of my condition; lucidity in the dream is a singularity, not a shared state. Though I do believe there are others who have not necessarily connected with one another, or perhaps the drugs they've been given have dulled their powers. I remain hopeful that I could someday encounter others who would completely understand this experience.

Despite my concern regarding the use of words and labels, the contact I have with others in the world needs a language that conveys my experience. I do hear from others who claim some similar abilities, if not full time; I hope there are more of us out there. For my sake, sure, but for the sake of the continuance of mankind. We could never be a movement, or a religion, or even an association, we are just humans who share the world/dream symbiosis. There could at least be a name for this ability to slip from the world to the dream. There are plenty of scientific sounding terms to adapt, with Greek and Latin "ixes" to mingle with modern tech jargon. Here is a list of suggestions from readers; have fun with it, make up your own term, and never take it too seriously:

Oneironaut
Dualist
Lucidist
Waker
Reve-lutionaries (from a French fan, "reve" is "dream")
REMmies
"Bi-C"

I can't foresee a great many people coming together with such similar experience that can be shared communally. The experience of the dream is the most subjective of our lives; it's the proverbial "blind men and the elephant." There will be no club, no church, no newsletter or convention that can contain the vast and profound experience inherent in the biconscious individual. Like secret agents given separate undercover assignments, we may nod in acknowledgement of each other but continue to move through our separate, covert missions.

I would like to think that a biconscious mind is particularly well-suited for long-term space travel, for invalids, for solitary confinement, those whose minds need to live in some form of release. It would not be a particularly safe condition for those who work in demanding or dangerous environments; it would be difficult to be biconscious while working in high-rise construction, or traffic control, or surgery.

A communal dream is, ultimately, most cultures' definition of "heaven." The ability to be with and interact with your loved ones who you've lost, or who you left behind; to be as one with those who share your faith. For some, it's the land of rewards and justice for a lifetime in which you've made better moral choices than not. But multiple personalities thrown together in any context will produce conflict (amazing family vacations, fun nights out with close friends and a weekend getaway with a lover can all devolve into a morass of resentment and regret). You

YOU CAN ONLY BE "AT ONE
WITH THE UNIVERSE" IF YOU
ARE A UNIVERSE OF ONE.

can only be "at one with the universe" if you are a universe of one.

"ALTERED STATES," DRUGS
AND THE "DEEP SELF"

"I do not take drugs. I am drugs."—Salvador Dali

I have never in my life taken recreational, "mind-expanding" drugs, even for "research."

When I was a teenager, enduring the thorny social acupuncture known as peer pressure, I wanted to be different. Being different meant not doing drugs. I found it pathetic that so many people were trying to proclaim their individuality by conforming to a mass notion of symbolic rebellion. Puking and losing control of one's faculties is not rebellion. Smoking is not an act of independence, it's an act of willful ignorance. They are symptoms of banal conformity that masquerade as individual expression and self-destructiveness.

I have never needed drugs as a stimulus or hallucinogen because I am usually "tripping" between two conscious states and neither have been "altered" by any substance. I have a literal high when I'm flying at full speed over quiet landscapes. I have an unparalleled buzz when I'm crashing through walls and throwing people around. And the rush of taking any sexual experience I want to when I'm prowling in the dream cannot be duplicated by any chemical or natural substance, controlled or not.

There are already too many chemical combinations in your brain, firing, oozing and snapping in a primordial biometric soup, sparking countless physiological reactions and making new connections. I need to know that what I do, the actions I take, the visions I move through, the worlds I inhabit, are of my own wellspring, not compromised or altered by drugs. None of which is to say that I find drugs wrong, or even useless. I'm bored when

I'm around people whose sole momentary purpose is to take drugs or drink to try to achieve some kind of buzz or high, or worse; to be a part of collective denial. I have at times seen the culture of drugs in a very condescending light. I think I have something better. It's not something everyone can achieve, and I don't condemn those who want substances to help in their consciousness explorations. I believe that if they could have my experience, they would gladly give up drug use as willingly as a child gives up a toy for the real thing. Lucidity should be the new drug. Achieve lucidity in two worlds and you are as high as you can get.

There are great thinkers who have pushed the boundaries of traditional dream and altered-state research through pharmaceutical means. John Lilly, Charles Tart, Timothy Leary, Carlos Castaneda, and others have certainly contributed to an "unshackling" of academic dream theory and have helped millions perceive the notion of consciousness in a different light.

I don't mean to belittle the valuable work of any of these men, all of whom I learned a great deal from and regard very highly. They've taken scientific research into the workings of the brain and the mechanics of consciousness to new levels with their experimentation with mind-altering substances (mainly ketamine, LSD and certain mushrooms).

In my view, psychotropic drugs run counter to the mind's pure ability to generate and power the dream. You already have all the utilities you need to inhabit and explore your dream world. Don't dilute your own possibilities. Drugs are a side-track to the main event. I saw lots of friends start drug courses with good scientific intentions, and others turn to drugs for misguided social intentions, and none ended up any closer to parallel consciousness, or with any greater understanding of some noble truth. When you take drugs to achieve a heightened experience, you become dependent on those drugs. You will not have them at your disposal when we make that transition to the dream.

ISOLATION THERAPY: PRACTICE
GOING IT ALONE

I did develop a tangent of Lilly's research on isolation. His work with isolation tanks was brilliant and few people picked it up after him. "Isolation Therapy," for lack of a catchier phrase, is simply one's need to shut everything out in order to concentrate on an inner self.

Here are some ways to achieve that, depending on your means and access to the right environment:

1. The isolation tank; these are not easy to find commercially, but Lilly's book *The Deep Self* is an excellent study of tank experimentation and includes instructions on how to build your own working tank at home. The tank is the best method for immersion into total isolation, primarily through the construct of floatation via the Epsom salts in the body-temp water. Leave out the ketamine and LSD.

2. A cave, if you are lucky enough to have access to one; go ahead and warm up the old jokes about hermits in caves and troglodytes. Throw in the morass of Plato's Cave symbolism. However, a few hundred feet into a decent cave passage can take you into a world with a total, natural vacuum of light and distracting sound. Look for wild caves in your area. Dress warmly enough (living caves tend to maintain year-round temps of between 55 – 58 degrees), bring a sleeping bag or mat, the minimum amount of food you need to live on for the length of time you want to be isolated (I prefer 24 hours at a stretch). And heed the basic rules of spelunking: carry 3 sources of light, don't destroy nature's furniture, and always tell someone exactly where you are going and when you plan to be back. Of course, spelunking's primary rule, never cave alone, must be absolutely disregarded.

3. A soundproofed room; first and foremost rule is to turn off all electronic devices, at least 24 hours before you move into isolation therapy. The residual mind junk

and energy needs to be dumped: stretches, breathing exercises, or meditation might help. Visualize the "recycle bin" of your mind's computer and dump everything that isn't life-sustaining.

4. Guided Imagery is probably useless for most people, because of the intrusion of another's voice. I have heard from some who record their own voice and play it back, guiding themselves into a meditative state from which to slip into the dream. For me, the inner voice is enough.

5. Do the exact opposite of all this quiet meditation stuff; turn your stereo up loud, put in the music that transcends your thoughts; spin, reel, rave your way to a heightened state. Amidst all the cacophony a kind of awareness will emerge, like punching your focus through to a different dimension. It might be skirting the stratosphere like a test pilot, then falling into a blackout zone before regaining control, but it's a worthy trip.

WHEN OUR BODIES FAIL US,
WE MOVE INTO OUR MINDS.
WHEN OUR MINDS FAIL US, WE
MOVE INTO THE DREAM.

THE JOURNEY

The realities of the world affected me as visions, and as visions only, while the wild ideas of the land of dreams became, in turn, not the material of my every-day existence, but in very deed that existence utterly and solely in itself.

Edgar Allan Poe, "*Berenice*"

When our bodies fail us, we move into our minds. When our minds fail us, we move into the dream.

Most people get interested in the concept of the dream, read about the amazing things others have done, and pursue the dream experience as some quest to find the fount of knowledge, the source of God, or "oneness" with the universe. That's ascribing values to an experience that is so beyond their comprehension they commit the same mistakes as those who start religions, even with the very best of intentions; they create stories and give mythic powers to the dream that are undue and meaningless.

Most people who write explanations of "dreams" write as tourists in a country they visit but don't live in, and they don't know the local language.

You must be willing to make the journey, in and of itself. Actions, experiences and interactions within will usually confound you, offer frustration, reveal inconsistencies and surprise reactions from yourself and your dream inhabitants. Just as in the world. There is no end to this journey, no final chapter, no summation, no revelation. Do not see this as a path to mystical revelation or self-enlightenment. It's a journey to the mailbox.

Just the journey.

I cannot suggest or guarantee that, even if you read this book or any other respectable dream research work, you would have any type of lucid dream or become more self-aware of your own conscious duality. You may claim that you don't even remember the "dreams" you had last night. Many people say this. Some also claim that they rarely or never dream. They are numbingly, ignorantly wrong.

When you have begun to achieve a dual lucidity (or even lucidity within the dream on a regular basis), questions arise. You will be confounded by the expectations you place upon yourself in the world, and it will hold you back. How do you progress within the dream when surrounded by the ethos of the world? What distinctions must be drawn?

The question is not "is this possible?"
The question is *"in what state is this possible?"*

MORALITY

"The unconsciousness of man is the consciousness of God, the end of the world."
--Henry David Thoreau

Saints throughout history have been terrified that God would punish them for their actions in the dream.

The most pious, God-fearing, good-hearted people on this earth commit acts of depravity. People of so many different faiths believe in a version of God and a version of the Devil, the balance of good and evil, yet ignore that duality within their own spirit. Many may be blissfully unaware of the activities they engage in that are counter to their world ethos, seeing within the dream only brief and sometimes terrifying glimpses of their naturally indulgent selves. When they waken, terror and doubt fade, shame and confusion linger but evaporate quickly enough; all we need do is mumble the comfort-invoking lie that "it was only a dream."

We spend so much of our world existence suppressing our urges, denying our desires, and shutting the door on our senses. We likely evolved to a higher consciousness because of our senses and their adaptability to our environment. Our senses in the world are tactile, physical, biological, and chemical; they do translate to the dream, they do evolve there, and they do transcend. We have not begun to explore the true range of human sensuality.

We cannot know what we are capable of until we are free to do everything that we are capable of. There are very good reasons why we can't explore all sensual facets of our capability in the world; but there is no reason we can't explore the range of our humanity—from base animal instincts to cosmic spiritual exploration—within the dream. When you are lucid to the terror or elation of the moment, whether from the world or the dream, you can fundamentally change the perception of your reality.

I've had the argument that, if it's a given that conscious ness is a constant force, weaving between the dream and the world, then shouldn't morality and conscience also be a constant? If that suits you, fine; but morality and conscience are constructs we need to survive as a species in the world; they define our social contracts, our civility, and our responsibilities to each other. In the dream, we are on our own.

There is a gravity to emotion and reality in the world, just as the laws of physics constrain us here, the ethos of humans that live in tribes and societies has its own structures and rules. In the dream, however, where the laws of physics do not rule, neither do the laws of morality, emotion, or ethics.

Many accuse me of engaging in immoral acts, depending on their religious beliefs. The truth is that, when lucid in either the dream or the world, I earn the power of choice. When it comes to behavior toward people or animals, I rarely choose to do in the dream what I would not do in the world. I have no interest in murdering my own dream population even though they are seemingly self-regenerating, though of course I will take pleasure from them whenever I want. In the dream, a girl won't look terrified at my approach, her expression is more likely to be as maddeningly indifferent as it would be at any bar. I do not force my own visions and creations into servitude. They (as avatars of my own thought processes) have something to teach me about separation, resistance, and control. And self-preservation.

The world, consisting of individuals with pleasures and fears, rights and opinions, relies on a moral code to ensure our mutual survival. Society requires this. In the dream, you are Creator, or perhaps more accurately, "acting creator." Our relationship to the universe in the world is governed by physical and societal laws—gravity and the Ten Commandments, for example. In the dream, we learn to shuffle our priorities, break free from the shackles of the world's laws, and embrace and explore a completely original relationship to the Universe. We are both creator and destroyer in the dream, and the worker ant within the world, but I never imagine for a moment in the dream that I am God. Having god-like powers does not make you the creator of all.

We have all had fantasies of what we would do given true, unchallenged power. That notion is with us from the time we understand morality and responsibility to the moment we die. It's with us because it is a power available to us. Tyrannical despots show what unchecked power is capable of unleashing in the world; but in the dream, you are not at war, you are not paranoid of losing power, and there are no traitors to stage a coup and assassinate you. Acts of violence or vengeance do not protect you, but nor do acts of magnanimity and generosity help your integrity or social standing. The New Testament's Book of Luke quotes Jesus as saying "The kingdom of God is within you." Any concept of Heaven and Hell are indeed within the dream, but they are not final resting places; you can come and go as you please.

MORALITY EVOLVED

LUCID is being aware, at any given time of day or night, of what you would do if you had nothing holding you back. In the world, you make moral choices that are bound by the laws of gravity and your own moral compass. In the dream, you are free to make any choice. Being biconscious means you can obey the laws in one world while simultaneously ignoring them in the other.

When I am fully lucid in the dream, I set out to do the things I feel like doing in the moment. Sometimes I study the details of the world around me, sometimes I wander. I'll fly or phase from place to place and see what connections I can make with the denizens of my landscapes and dreamscapes. Who will regard me with suspicion, who will ignore me? I am aware that these "who" are "me." The skill is in knowing this and forgetting it at the same time.
In the world, we believe in a moral purpose because our lives together depend on it. Still, millions ignore univer-

sal moral codes for their own fulfillment.

I identify with tourists, with their desperate struggle to be lucid as they move through a foreign place. They're seeking an experience in an alien world; they don't know what, or they think they know what they are looking for; but what most delights them is the occasional surprise. Even when fully lucid and engaged in the dream, surprises occur—the appearance of an object or change of circumstance so completely unexpected that you wonder if there isn't, in fact, a divine conductor directing the action.

One of the most difficult things to learn in dual lucidity is to let go of a sense of guilt and responsibility within the dream. These emotions serve their purpose in the world and lead us to moral action. In the dream, they are weights that must be overcome for the spirit to explore new realms. Before that spirit can be free, however, it must loosen itself from the bonds of flesh and bone, shake the cage of carbon, hydrogen and oxygen, and soar.

In the world, I have a random fear of heights; it's terrifying when it kicks in because it does not announce itself. One moment I can be on the 52nd floor of a building, looking out over the city through a large window, the next, I'm practically crawling toward the innermost part of that floor, desperate to get to the elevator. I'll be driving down the highway, approaching a bridge, and a third of the way across, I will look out at the water below; my skin will go clammy and I'll start to panic. I have to shout down my fear just to stay on the road and get across without causing a traffic jam. High, exposed roller coasters, glass elevators, driving on a mountain pass with open lookouts, these are actions that will set off my physiological panic. In the dream, I can fly unaided to the highest peaks, tallest buildings, even into the stratosphere, with nothing but elation and confidence.

I came to realize I wasn't afraid of the height itself in these situations. I could hike up a mountain and stand on the edge of a precipice, look straight down, and be fine.   My problem was in being in a high place in a man-made construction, one that was mechanical and could fail; even if the odds and statistics were greatly against it and all my intellect and rationale knew better. I could walk up a mountain side, but I could not climb up a sheer cliff face with ropes and pitons. I did not trust the mechanical conveyance; there were always too many possibilities beyond my control. A car, an elevator, a rope, stairs, a bridge, an airplane; these are all made of the same stuff as me. In the world, they are necessary and sometimes beyond our own individual control, due to the actions of others; in the dream, they are completely unnecessary. Just like morality.

I am frequently drawn to the story of Dr. Jekyll and Mr. Hyde; Stevenson was on to something there, and I wonder if he wasn't experiencing biconsciousness—he did claim profound inspiration from dreams (as did Samuel Taylor Coleridge and many other great writers and poets), though propriety of the day would probably demonize any claim to be able to exist in two worlds at once. I'd like to think that's why he fictionalized his experience into such a brilliant chronicle of the multifaceted mind and its ability to do in one world what would be considered horrible, brutal and criminal in the other. The character of Jekyll/Hyde might have been based on the real person Deacon Brodie, but I sense Stevenson found the true inspiration from within.

It's not that one is Jekyll in the world and becomes Hyde in the dream; it's that we are both in both worlds, each with its own set of rewards and limitations.

MORAL INSTINCT

For many, their sense of spirituality is in complete unison with their moral sensibility, and I respect that. It's true of me as well, and guides the choices I make in the world. Some have argued that to give in to base, hedonistic pleasures and experimental "depravity" in any dimension of consciousness invites moral failure and breakdown along whatever spiritual path our creator may have intended.

In my experience, when I see forces in the dream trying to do harm to others from the dream, my instinct is to jump in, save the "victims" and punish the "evildoers." Being the dream, I can conjure any means at my disposal, though typically my own Superman-like abilities take care of just about any such instance. It is the same instinct which I have in the world, but my physical limitations keep me from acting on. You can say that, if I had those powers in the world, I'd be using them to save people from others, but in the dream, I'm saving them from myself. That would be essentially true. However, it doesn't change the initial moral instinct that has come from my upbringing and experience. I will never deny the moral experience or my allegiance to it. I act in the dream with the full and lucid knowledge that those acts are of me, by me, for me or against me.

MORALITY SHARED

There must be a very good reason why there is a threshold between the dream and the world at all; to carry anything physical between the two realms would be impractical at least. We are, however, fully able to carry thoughts, ideas, concepts and memory from one to the other. We can carry perception and feeling between them—I can leave on a stereo playing music and hear it completely within the dream. The portal of the mind is a transducer for everything intangible, and each world constantly soaks up the other. But if we could carry physical objects or persons from the dream into the world, imagine the chaos; it would likely be the end of humanity. A moral code is all that protects us in the world. It's a veneer of protection that, alas, breaks down all the time.

If you take control over another person's body or cause harm to another person in your dream, is that a crime against that person? Is that a person in your dream as we define it in the world? Does your perceiving it as a person in the dream make it subject to any moral laws or conduct of behavior? Does any action in the dream that would be considered reprehensible in the world have mental or emotional consequences in either world?

Where Freud was brilliant was in recognizing that we had a dark side and that we masked our dark sides with symbols to make it palatable for the moral structure of society. He made an entirely new and acceptable method that could be spoken of in scientific and academic circles instead of the dark closets of churches, a language in which to discuss dreams, even the phallic in everything we see. The repressed desire here, the anal fixation there. Underneath every image a fetish, behind every action an obsession; every object catalogued as representing a dark aspect of the id, a repressed wish fulfillment granted. He was terribly wrong about the symbols—but he opened the doors for serious consideration of the terrain.

For me, the dream is a constant reminder that the greater universe does not employ any code of morality; a society needs a moral code to ensure respect and survival, but an individual in a world of his own making has no need for it. Hence the moral code of so many religious stories regarding moral action in the world would lead to fantastic rewards of pleasure, safety, and happiness in the "afterlife," (a.k.a. the dream). Whether it's a harp and wings and conversing with Jesus or enjoying a frolic with seventeen young virgins, it's the withholding of pleasure in the physical world, the control over instinct

WE FORGOT THAT WE
HAVE ALWAYS HAD
ACCESS TO EDEN.

that supposedly leads to the final reward. Which pretty much gives the final reward—hedonistic and spiritual freedom of body, mind and soul—all the power over the human condition. It is what we strive for, it is (as written in religious texts) the will of God that it be our reward. Indeed, it is the very place (the Garden of Eden) from which we emerged, when consciousness, self-awareness and awareness of others began to clash and shape our thinking from the dream to the world. The "fall" was our "exile" from the dream to the slums and offices of the world.

Somewhere in our subjugation of ourselves, we forgot that we have always had access to Eden. It is a matter of our humanity that we are given frequent glimpses of our versions of heaven and hell, each night (or, in my case, all the time). Perhaps it is our failsafe. Of course, our moral compass as humans is only as true as our state of mind allows.   People go insane (more accurately, we do not go insane; behavior wants to break through the dream and into the world, and we succumb because we have not achieved lucidity in either) and commit horrible acts upon themselves and others. People develop mental disorders both mild and severe and all these layers of our mental state in the world are mirrored in the dream. We become depressed and cannot understand why. Years of therapy, mind-dampening drugs and empty distractions cannot change us. They artificially block us from the dream, prevent lucidity, and make our mental state worse. The biconscious understand how thin the barrier is between "waking" and "dreaming" and it gives us hope, fortification, and unlimited personal power.

I was curious if a cultural and social meme, confining physiological conditions or other states that held sway over the consciousness of large swatches of like-minded people also infiltrated their dreams in the same way, directing and influencing their dream activities, or if they were free of the world's mindset. Fascinating studies have been done of the dreams of pregnant women, the dreams of young children, even the dreams of Germans

MAYBE THE DREAM IS
THE PROCREATION OF
THE SOUL.

during World War II (as in Charlotte Beradt's fascinating study, *"The Third Reich of Dreams"*. I have heard from amateurs who have attempted to conduct dream studies of their own for like-minded groups of friends; the problem is verifiable reliability, because when people suspect they are being researched along with other people, they tend to skew their accounts to "fit in" with the group so as not to be seen aberrant in any suspicious way. People also typically sugar-coat events of their dreams to align more with the moral code of the world; they do not want to be judged in either world.

There are so many groupings of people, though, that would bear fascinating studies of the dream, the mind, and where we might consciously evolve. I was especially interested in researching the dreams of those who cared little for the constructs of the world's morality; had they never made the connection with lucidity in the dream? What is the true reason that certain serial killers justify their actions? Do so many sociopaths claim they are heeding the "voice of god," not knowing that it is their own dream voice urging them on?

My conversations with some of these subjects were chilling. Talking about the actual crimes they committed in the world is one horrible thing; exploring the realm in which originated their justification for these acts is far darker. It is the subject of a very different project which I will complete when I can stop shuddering.

SEXUAL AWAKENING

We are introduced to sexuality—our fantasies, our curiosities, the preparedness of our bodies—through the dream. I find this ironic that it emerges from the dream, in which sex is an act of pure pleasure, versus a biologically driven mandate necessary in the world. Yet this is one area in which I might agree with Freud, regarding the dream's importance as an abattoir of repressed or taboo desires. The dream tries to introduce sexuality to us through the filter of our inexperience, resulting in (for me, anyway) some wildly imaginative speculation on what close-up female anatomy looked like, felt like, and tasted like. Not to mention how my newly functioning body was supposed to react.

For many, the most powerful and resonant dreams are the wet dreams that punctuate the onset of puberty but can be scattered throughout childhood and into adulthood. Boys and girls both have wet dreams, sexual dreams, explorations and experiments with their bodies. It is one of the few times in our life when we must notice the dream, because the dream actions have literally spilled into the world (the "wet dream" typically refers to young men ejaculating in the world from an experience had in the dream; but young women orgasm as well, they just don't usually need to change the sheets afterward). We have evidence of the power and effect of the dream. When enough real-world experience passes, when we have such specific references and sensations to draw from, then most people shut it down, or let real world experience suffice.

The ability to achieve some level of control over your mind and body during a sexual experience can be difficult. The notion of morality acts as gravity to hamper the rush of pleasure through the body. It's hard enough working through the attempts at mutual pleasure with someone, much less the dream body wanting in on the action. Believe me, when something as powerful as sexual pleasure fills the mind and body in the world, the dream self takes notice and participates, or wants to. It took years for me to be able to stand back within the dream while I was sexually engaged in the world, and by then I was used to the layers of possibilities that bi-world sex offered, and refraining within the dream seemed pointless.

Knowing exactly what it feels like for my cock to be gripped by a warm vagina in the world never meant that I did not still have flights of fancy at the same experience within the dream; a girl's vagina in the dream could still phase into a piece of exotic fruit, or she could shrink during the act until I was fucking a limp doll. Inversely, there were times during sex that in the dream I was conjuring the truly amazing experience (with or without the same girl in both places), even as the girl in the world was lifeless, passive or clinical. For a long time, just as I sought the permission of a girl in the world, I felt I needed to give myself permission to cut loose in the dream. Sex in and of itself is not a matter of morality; the treatment of another human being is the matter of morality. I could let go of that necessity in the dream. But treating your dream partner as a living breathing person who seeks mutual pleasure can have its rewards too.

Given that sex and pleasure derive from a biological necessity in the world, why then do they still hold so much power in the dream? Is it such a powerful force in the world that we are driven to mimic the act, the hunt, the control, or the submission, within the dream? Transcending the imperatives of the body is not as easy as it seems. Allow me to offer a rare attempt at spiritual supposition here; I can believe that the sexual drive carries so powerfully into the dream because, even stripped of biological necessity, it is still some means of lifeforce, of connection and unity. Curiosity alone may not be powerful enough to propel us onward into the dream journey; the life-force born of sexual union, whether it results in offspring or not, is still a procreative act. Students of biological evolution may argue there are more efficient ways of procreating, but the sex act as we know it has been the driving force of humanity since our creation, and will continue to be. Sex is not just a procreative mechanism—it's vital for biological survival, species regeneration and evolution. Yet, its more important function, cosmically, is the transference and exchange of energy. This could explain why it's as vital in the dream as in the world. Maybe the dream is the procreation of the soul.

There is a phenomenon known as "sexsomnia." It's essentially involuntary sexual acts carried out or attempted while one is sleeping. It might sometimes be referred to more loosely as "sleepfucking." This is rare but not

THE CONTEMPLATION
OF DREAMS IS NOT A
FRIENDLY PLACE FOR
THE SELF-RIGHTEOUS.

unheard of, and there are instances where it has led to accusations of rape and sexual abuse. It's essentially a glitch in atonia, the libido punching through the dream and the chemical stoppers that inhibit normal physical reaction during our various stages of sleep. Like sleep-walking, it's an exposure of the thin veil between the world and the dream and the average person's inability to maintain lucidity in either. If you are not capable of achieving some form of lucidity, in either or both, then you may well be putting yourself at the mercy of your physiological tides. This is not a very good thing in ei-ther world.

There are times I have caught myself in the world mim-icking motions within the dream, and I've had a few em-barrassingly close calls. Dropping my guard when I'm in a crowded space with lots of people, for instance, might someday result in my reaching out to touch some stranger intimately. When I am adept at melding the two worlds, I must be even more aware of my actions in the world. As it does in the dream, anything could happen.

TABOOS

We have all done things in the dream we could not tell our mothers, fathers, spouses, children, and best friends. We are too scared or ashamed to share our dream expe-rience with even our most trusted pastors, psychiatrists and counselors bound by oath to confidence. Every one of us has done things in the dream that are unspeak-able under the moral terms and obligations of our cul-ture. We've killed, raped, maimed, desecrated, fouled our bodies and others, not recognized our mothers and forsaken our children. I knew a 36-year-old woman who was extremely distraught over the fact that she'd never dreamt about any of her three children, and she was wracked with guilt over her subconscious omission of the central responsibility and joy of her life; it was making her question whether she was a good mother (in the world, she was in fact a great mother). She wanted to believe it was possible to seek out her children in the dream, which I could not help her do. She could not achieve a lucid state in the dream.

The world's major religions have conflicted counsel regarding one's actions in the dream; staunch orthodox zealots usually claim that if you are committing acts in the dream that are considered sins in the world, you're sinning, especially if you are in a lucid or semi-lucid state; others give a hall pass to subconscious ramblings, but only by dismissing the entire experience and validity of the dream. A particularly rabid and zealous Christian fundamentalist echoed many sentiments of like-minded persons of many religions by claiming that dreams were the "playground of Satan," created to tempt us. Unless they showed God or any prophet in a worshipful light, in which case they were truly prayers visited upon us by angels to confirm God's majesty. The same is true of a trip to the grocery when they either have or don't have my favorite nacho dip.

On occasion, I will have one of these zealots show up at a workshop—even going so far as to pay the full fee and sit through hours of discussion on topics that must make them squirm terribly. At some opportune moment of their own choosing, they shout out curses and accusations against me and my writings. I have a measured and temperate approach to these intrusions and have even conjured my assailants within the dream to release them into the air or throw them across the room, even if, in the world, I am speaking with deliberate consideration and patience. It always ends with my pausing, hearing them out until they sputter and quiver, and inviting them to continue with the group. Spent of their bile, sometimes embarrassed, all but one slunk off with outward posturing of victory on their faces. The contemplation of dreams is not a friendly place for the self-righteous.

In the dream, we commit what are considered terrible acts; we have gained no reward for these acts other than the fleeting second's satisfaction and pleasure. The unstudied question is, how often in unstable minds have these pursuits become pathological, to the point at which intent moves from the dream to the world, where a lustful action turns into a crime? I can't begin to express the immeasurable pleasure of reaching out and touching whatever you desire, whenever you desire it. A stranger's body, a cloud, someone else's food, a beautiful but poisonous animal, whatever. In the world, we must hold back; we're always censoring ourselves, checking our impulses, stifling our thoughts. Freud was correct that the dream is a repository for much of this withheld energy.

The notes of psychopath and sociopath interviews are riddled with mentions of dreams and compulsions born from the subconscious, often blamed on a separate entity—God, a demon, the devil or other controlling influence. Of course, this is just a manifestation of themselves, and an excuse to carry actions into the world. It is possible that if an awareness of dream lucidity were introduced into culture and the family framework early on, sociopathic tendencies that might become abnormal or criminal in the world could be recognized much earlier in life, as easily as recognizing that a child prone to abusing and torturing animals is on a likely path to doing the same to people. Yet we choose to belittle the dream, to dismiss it and ignore it, and without the benefit of lucidity and control, both worlds begin to break down and allow the worst to spill between the cracks.

RAVAGING

What is common to all men (and probably a healthy number of women)? Why do we look at strangers in airports, shopping malls and office buildings, and within a fraction of a second imagine a complete sexual conquest? If you were biconscious and capable of acting on those urges immediately, without consequence, wouldn't you?

Sex is about pleasure; ravaging is about power. Men of

today know that men in less civilized generations held much more power over women and may have had their way with them with little consequence other than disease. It is written that some kings and emperors had a virgin every night. There were no laws protecting women in many societies. In today's society, most of us would want nothing other than sexual respect and equality, but knowing the unchecked power enjoyed by the males before us can give the modern male ego a twinge of jealousy. The dream enables us to act out that male power fantasy. For women, the fantasy might be a rush to freedom from a male-dominated society, a wholeness with an environment uncompromised by the male ego. Being the more subjugated sex through much of history, women in fact report more euphoric connections to their dream worlds than do men, probably for the same reason they are more intrinsically connected to their emotional states than are men.

Acts of sex and violence in the dream are not acts of rape and murder, and it's vital to understand the difference. Within the dream, everything is yourself, your own construct, your own attention, and your own curiosity. The moral order and sense of responsibility that is crucial in the world is of little consequence in the dream because you are the god of your realm; not the creator of all life (another important distinction), but one with the power to change your scenario. When you ravage a denizen of the dream, you are essentially masturbating in a highly evolved holographic world. Exploration of anything or anyone is not an act of violation in the dream.

What are (rightly) considered depravities in the world are merely exercises in the dream. You are exercising your mind, stretching yourself to the limits of human possibility. Once experienced in the land of so much greater possibility, they lose their naughty luster. Believe me, the taboo things we obsess over in the world become very boring and unnecessary after exercised a few times in the dream. People often ask me if I'm able to "conjure" any attractive celebrity in the dream. Because this is a boring question, I will sometimes look them straight in the eye and tell them that I'm conjuring them within

THE DENIZENS OF THE
DREAM ARE REBELLIOUS
AND COMPLICIT.

the dream, right at that moment. This can be unnerving to a person. My conjuring them for a moment of dream pleasure is suddenly personal to them, even though they feel nothing physically. Whether I ravage them or a celebrity, it's no more thrilling than if I choose a random dream denizen.

MULTISEXUALITY

I have had many arguments with my gay and lesbian friends and acquaintances about the nature of a person's unbridled sexual potential; more specifically the notion that with all taboos and moral conflicts lifted, a person's sexuality would naturally become more universal and everyone would be truly bisexual.

I tried this in many experiments. Even in a world in which I was perfectly comfortable with any sexual experience, a world free of religious taboo and with no fear of disease, I felt no desire in my attempts to have a sexual experience with another man. I was always drawn to females. I tried engaging in sex acts with males, but even in the dream I couldn't generate the visceral desire necessary to complete any act. It simply gave me no pleasure.

My friends and debate partners reacted in disbelief, thinking my lack of desire was clouded by my conditioning in the world, or that I'm hindered by a lack of emotional investment. I can't change their thinking. I can't say that many people wouldn't become multi-sexual in the dream if they could live like me. In the dream, there is no biological imperative for attraction to a female, yet I remain desirous only of female partners, of female conquests. I would like to think that this is evidence of some "balance of life" notion throughout the cosmos of our consciousness. It just goes in the "I Don't Know but I'm Fine with It" pile.

That said, I suspect lots of people would find their sexual universe greatly amplified, stretched, and diversified by experimenting in the dream and exploring past one's world boundaries. Men, women, whatever. There are new sexual frontiers, more evolved sexual encounters, to be experienced out there, and there's only one place to get to it.

We are compelled to sexual action throughout the dream, as if our skin, our bodies, were their own stars needing to be exhausted of all potential energy until transforming into a supernova or a quasar, thrown back into the universe to begin a new cycle.

ORGASM EVOLVED

The experience of orgasm evolves in the dream. It becomes something far more powerful yet commonplace since there are no taboos or restrictions and the type of contact and stimulation usually required for an orgasm can be had whenever and wherever and with whomever. I'm speaking strictly from the male perspective; with orgasm in the world, male climax is usually dominated by the act of ejaculation, and for most men, sex without ejaculation seems incomplete or unfulfilling. In the dream, since there is no biological requirement for the product of ejaculation—semen, sperm, all the fun fluids—one is free to work towards a climax of infinite variety. This may seem like business as usual for most women in their world sexual experience; I can only say that, if the greater variety of sexual experience in the dream for men is enhanced infinitely, then I can't imagine what it could be for females, who've already had a great deal of world practice in orgasm through a wider variety of physical, emotional, psychological and spiritual means. Or perhaps, the dream levels the playing field of climax, orgasm, and rapture between the sexes and makes possible a truer union beyond the simple physical connection of sex parts. Even if that sexual experience is, essentially, with oneself.

Even after decades of the variety of sexual experience within the dream, I am still drawn to the most human, most male objectification of the female, but these are my limitations. I have not completely moved beyond the notion of orgasm, but have begun to understand that many other acts in the dream can easily replace it in terms of overall euphoria and connectedness to a seeming act of creation; shooting like a rocket up into my virtual cosmos, dwarfed by swirling nebula that can instantly morph into a singular room in a hillside mansion, dangling high above the ground and seeing denizens below, gazing up at me as if I were the sun, creating and orchestrating an entire eye-field worth of people and directing their moves and interactions, feeling the force and pressure of moving faster, faster into an abstract field that takes no shape and ceases to seem like movement and more like a slow-motion explosion of imagined particles, these events are greater orgasms of the mind and I seek them out frequently. Yet, I return to a physical coupling with a wide variety of female forms, simply because I want to. I desire it, and one gift of lucidity is that you can more freely move toward your desire.

Because of the "wet dream" phenomena, there is a visceral and real connection between orgasm in the dream and the world; it's one thing we can do simultaneously in both worlds, even without the benefit of lucidity. In the world, the body feels released after orgasm, awash in physical bliss and perhaps exhausted. Though many women can orgasm multiple times, most men need some recuperation time before attempting another ejaculation. In the dream, the energy is quite different, though one must fight the conditioning from the world. When lust and gluttony have no consequence, it's a game changer. I have waged epic bouts of sexual indulgence that have brought on a series of orgasms, but orgasms in the dream often move beyond mere ejaculation; if an incorporeal body ejaculates in another incorporeal body, as realistic as it feels, there's no biological result unless you lucidly examine the "evidence," in which case you'll see what you want to see. But just as repeated orgasms for a guy like me are not possible in the world, they become

YOU CAN BE FAITHFUL IN YOUR
BODY AND FAITHFUL IN YOUR
HEART, BUT YOU CANNOT BE
FAITHFUL IN YOUR MIND.

something different and altogether more rapturous in the dream.

PEOPLE

"One of the characteristics of the dream is that nothing surprises us in it. With no regret, we agree to live in it with strangers, completely cut off from our habits and friends." —Jean Cocteau

"My best dreams and worst nightmares have the same people in them." — Philippos Syrigos

Many dream researchers and enthusiasts argue that dream strangers are constructed in much the way movie extras are handled on movie sets. They are there to generically populate the show, and any interaction with them is ultimately scripted, whether conscious or not.

The reigning theory is that any conversation or interaction you have with a dream inhabitant is simply an interaction with none other than yourself, or your idea of that person or type of person, in whole or as hybrid with another person. I have tested this on thousands of occasions and have had many instances that have left me questioning the individuality of the other in my dream.

They are, of course, some manifestation of me, the splintered me as filtered through my catalog of human types, but their reactions to me—whether I am engaging them in simple conversation or whether I am forcing them to do something against their supposed will—have often been disturbingly, profoundly independent in nature. This multiplicity at work is mind-blowing.

The denizens of the dream are rebellious and complicit, they interact with one another much as they do with me, and they usually do not retain their physical identities. When we dream of a friend or family member in the world, we may see them with their recognizable faces or bodies, or we may just recognize them in the physical body of another. Dream people also appear in other visages, other bodies, and it takes getting used to.

I have been assaulted several times with the theory that inhabitants in our dreams are people from other dimensions within the multiverse, phasing into our consciousness. As a lucid dreamer, I can't buy this argument, because though they may act independently, I can typically make them do anything I want. If the dream were an exchange between parallel universes, I believe I would be as much the dream "slave" as the "enslaver." I absolutely cannot rule out the parallel universe theory, but that's the beauty of any parallel universe theory. Every nuanced world is just a quantum membrane poke away.

The dream inhabitants act and react almost identically to the world inhabitants. There is one extremely important correlation; in the world or the dream, I do not know what, or if, they are thinking.

I have seen people in the dream act upon each other in humane and brutal ways, and I've made no attempt to control them. Of course, when my focus turns to them, it alters their behavior (yes, like the famous double-slit experiment in which a wave, when observed, changes into a particle). I can compel them to do anything, but I often just watch the dream play out, even if a deeper consciousness within me is at work.

We aren't given the gift/curse ability to be inside each other's minds, even in our most loved and trusted companions, because we would absolutely terrify ourselves with the knowledge of their true thoughts, which are just as unpredictable, contradictory, banal, dark and dangerous as our own. We seek to know ourselves through those we relate to, but there can be no attempt to fathom the most shallow, illusory faith or trust in anyone, world or dream. We can have friends who watch our movies, but not our dreams.

In the world, we are surrounded by people. They are

a part of the fabric of our lives, and we are consuming more subconscious information regarding the people around us than can be measured. How they act and react, move and speak, appear and disappear from our view. When we need to interact, we do so by overlaying our own experience on top of them as a filter through which to relate to them. Sometimes we get it right, sometimes terribly wrong, but often it's close enough. Most people would go insane without the company and attention of others, even as flesh-and-blood white noise in the environment around them. It's why solitary confinement is the ultimate punishment for even hardened criminals who act violently toward people.

We sit, entrenched in a battlefield of guerilla observation. At shopping malls, airports, universities and museums, city squares and coffee shops, all the places that fold into one in the dream, we kidnap expressions and secretly steal infinitesimal periods of time from the wake of everyone we concentrate on. We waft like a molecule on the memes that ebb and flow between the masses, memes like plankton in the tides of human thought, direction and confusion. I feel them flow into the psyche and scatter there and know they are falling into place, settling into my chaos. And if someone or some gesture or some combination of events so captures me by surprise, I click the mental shutter and feel an electric sizzle as it finds a special place there, awaiting...mutating, reacting almost chemically to the change in environment. It is at once safer and more lethal. I advance upon that person, become the center of their focus, look them in the eye, and feel the connection.

It has already begun to happen, on occasion, that as I remember people I've encountered in the past, I can't recall whether I knew them in the world or the dream. The power of the dream and the dullness of the world conspire, I think, to keep me uncertain.

RELATIONSHIPS

My condition has made it a challenge to maintain a healthy relationship with a woman. When two people grow romantically close to each other, there is an expectation of exclusivity that begins to permeate the world they create with each other. Though they may initially be attracted to me because of the darker side I inhabit, it does not take long before that becomes a repellant. Perhaps this is more due to my utter honesty with them. They are aware that I inhabit two worlds simultaneously, and that I indulge my temptations in the dream. When most girlfriends watch their boyfriends' eyes as they check out the girl at the next table, they'll usually accept it as a male trait and don't bother themselves further with exactly what's going on in the guy's little fantasy quickies. For me, however, the girl knows that I'm probably indulging in sexual activities with that other girl while also interacting with her. She cannot watch my eyes revert to her and leave it at that. She knows what I'm doing in the dream, with the same level of lucidity and purpose as I'm touching her in the world, or eating a sandwich with her. And she cannot help but feel betrayed. She is unaware of the fact that she is likely doing the same thing in her dream; she's just not lucid, and the world emotion reigns.

You can be faithful in your body and faithful in your heart, but you cannot be faithful in your mind.

"If you can choose to do something with a girl in the dream, then out of respect and love for me, can you simply choose not to do things with them? I mean, how hard can that be?" This has been a common retort to my unguilty silence in these situations. It is difficult to reason with this, since only half of my world requires actual reason. I once replied to a girl "if you deny yourself that slice of cheesecake in this world for the sake of your health, then if you could indulge on however much cheesecake or chocolate you want in the dream, wouldn't you?" I often assure them that I wish they could share the dream with me, I wish that I could take them on the same journeys and see what I could see and experience. The sentiment is appreciated—usually—but not believed, mainly because it is rarely 100% sincere. On occasion, I've turned the tables of that logic, reached out to touch them with desire, telling them that in fact, I am denying the girl in the dream so as to concentrate more fully on her, now. I'm sincere in this; I made it a point never to lie to a lover about any activity in the dream. This slight cleverness is indulged, for a few times, then wears thin. Once an intelligent woman knows what's going on in your head, she will not rest; the erosive prejudice has begun, and the rift cannot be healed, like cutting off an affair or seeing a counselor.

What couple enjoys the sheer honesty of sharing their unfiltered dream experience with each other—all the strange encounters with other lovers, the uncharacteristic behaviors of the dream version of your partner, some which surprise, some which sow seeds of distrust. There is an unspoken contract with each other that what happens in the world of the dream, the "subconscious," the dark fantasies, can stay secret and hidden. It's hard when you place so much trust and faith in your partner to experience their betrayal in the dream; your version of them acts up, or plays into doubts you harbor, and they do things that repulse you. How can that not change your affection for them in the world?

In my dream, "you had an affair" is always the start of some very interesting conversations in the world.

A world relationship must be about shared experience. I tried very hard with the one girl I truly loved to incorporate her in any way possible in the dream. She would appear with me or I would conjure her up; I would take her sexually in every way, though I was free to do that in the world as well; but I would also ask her questions, deep questions about her own desires, to see what she might say. She and I would spend several moments at a time engaged in a three-way conversation; I could speak with the dream her, and report her answers and observations to the her laying before me, and we could see what truths were uncovered. After some months of this, I could sense cracks in her level of trust in me; how could she know that I wasn't merely making up answers in order to goad her into saying something I might want to hear, or to control and manipulate her into feeling what I might want her to feel? I may very well have been doing exactly that in engaging the dream her, so I can't fault her for such suspicions.

When you can mold and shape the person you love to do and be what and who you want, how can the world person compete with their dream twin? That is what she could not ultimately handle, I think. Once someone I get to know realizes that I am not lying about the dream, there is always a layer of unspoken suspicion. Imagine falling in love with someone and they tell you that, in fact, they are a double agent for two world governments. You may laugh and think they're joking; if they converse honestly and openly and convince you of the truth, you bear it almost grudgingly, as if suddenly they realize it's your job or your nature to be duplicitous. Love fades quickly in a fog of curiosity and doubt.

The dream is all sensuality, leaving little room for romance or commitment. How can you maintain a relationship when you can barely maintain the environment? There is no need for courtship, no need for putting one's best foot forward. Maintaining a long-term relationship of trust is not a necessity. You are a juggernaut of desire and the only obstacle is your power of concentration and lucid maintenance. There is no biological imperative that mandates procreation and reproduction. In the world, we've used birth control to free ourselves from the biological imperative, without sacrificing pleasurable interactions. We can have a series of meaningless one-night stands, or become nymphomaniacs, and it's all filtered through a moral structure that values the desire to create and nurture new life, and that exerts control over the notion of sin.

In the dream, we are freed by believing we are freed, a understanding that we are the only liberated soul in that world. It is maddening to shift between the two moral dynamics and look longingly at one's girlfriend when you truly understand this didactic truth.

In revealing my own struggles with relationships in the world, I can tell you that I have enjoyed two childhood loves, one exploratory relationship in my mid-teens, some dalliances through college and one early 20s relationship where I honestly tried to put all my efforts into the connection with her in the world; that was the woman I lost. I failed her because I simply could not turn off the dream, and she could not bear the duplicity. I loved her, I still love her, we no longer communicate, and I rarely conjure her in the dream. Now, as I have begun to travel and interact more with those earnest souls looking to explore my own way of thinking, I have more dalliances than ever, but am doubly guarded.

Relationships inevitably bring disappointment, and you hope the pain is less than the ecstasy. When you say goodbye to someone in the world, they are rarely gone in the dream; it makes it twice as hard to let go or to be rid of someone completely.

I can count on my hands the number of times I've broken down and cried, and it's happened more in the dream than in the world. The sense of freedom widens one's emotional outlets, and a relationship tugs on nearly every emotion.

THE INTELLECT IS
TERRIBLY JEALOUS
OF THE SPIRIT.

COMMUNITY

Think about this: we do not actually share conscious-ness, much less lucidity, when we are awake. We can be gazing into the eyes of our lover, our mother, our boss, or our child, and we do not exist in the same conscious realm. We see each other, we perceive each other sen-suously, we accept what we see and might even have a shared experience involving conversation, physical con-tact or mutual observation. But we are not in the same conscious field. Since we do not share consciousness in the world, shared consciousness in the dream seems highly improbable;
given that, is there a need for the same type of moral or ethical framework on which we depend in the world? We do not exist as individuals in the dream. We may not be just manifestations within another's dream, and we may be capable of independence and autonomy, but another person's dream is not our world. We can create the con-struct of another person, but their self cannot be present in our self.

Of course, there are countless relationships in the world where one partner is but a shell of their true self, in def-erence to their dominant lover or friend...this is not un-like a relationship you might have with a dream inhabi-tant. The deeper the attempts at communication in either world are what break down one's level of control over another, or the level of understanding of one another. But two distinctly separate "souls" cannot coexist in the same dream space, though they can seem to. Perhaps some artificial insemination into another being's dream will be possible someday; some sort of holographic pro-jection uploaded in real time via a neural link in just the right spot of brain jelly. When we harness the theoretical "holographic" properties of the multiverse and can trav-el via transference into another's quantum dream world, then I will be unbelievably thrilled. But that day is not in sight, and I therefore do not believe it possible for indi-vidual entities, physically, metaphysically, spiritually or other, to inhabit another's dream. More likely, we will see an increase in highly evolved virtual worlds inhabited with AI in which our avatars interact.

The dream may be the last space, the only space we can truly claim for ourselves; would we want the intrusion of anyone?

INTELLECT

I discovered there was an endless source of robust enjoyment in trifling with psychiatrists: cunningly leading them on; never letting them see that you know all the tricks of the trade; inventing for them elaborate dreams, pure classics in style (which make them, the dream-extortionists, dream and wake up shrieking); teasing them with fake "primal scenes"; and never allowing them the slightest glimpse of one's real sexual predicament."
--Vladimir Nabokov, *Lolita*

Why do people remember so little of the dream? Yet when some rare but powerful dream event occurs, it can stay with us forever as if it had happened in the world. Why are we compelled to dismiss an entire aspect of our existence? Because we violate our own inherent sense. We try—and fail—to *justify.*

The intellect is terribly jealous of the spirit, and the spirit pays little heed to logic. Therefore, we relate our dreams to each other in abstract terms, using the "conventional wisdom" of dreams as we've been raised to believe them. We are too married to mythology and still rely too heavily on the machinations of Freud and Jung. People are determined to keep their dreams on an academic or spiritual/mythological level, rather than to see them on an interactive, experiential level. We're looking for a story. Everything we see becomes a part of that story, and we're searching for the next plot twist, the next major character, the arc of conflict and resolution. In the world, we just keep building the stories up. In the dream, the stories just keep unraveling...

To intellectualize the dream experience is to throw a textbook at a rainbow. Intellect requires reason, logic, and rules; it is a process. Intellect is not gut instinct, no leap of faith, no blind wonder. It is hard to intellectualize while flying through a stormy sky, feeling lashes of rain against your dream skin, feeling the power of thunder around you and the spiraling energy of the storm around you.

Counselors and therapists almost always, by the nature of their training, take an intellectual approach in communication with a patient; it's their job to find some thread of reason to work with, some pattern to recognize. I studied the methodology, and spoke with hundreds of them (not as a patient, just in interviews and conversation). Probe as they might, they cannot crawl into the dream with their patient.

I've read countless books by scientists, psychologists, dream researchers, mystics, philosophers and shamans on "dreams" and dreaming. None describe a full biconscious world, and I have scoured the histories and recorded documents from St. Augustine through William Blake and William Burroughs to attempt to find clues of my condition. I can certainly suspect certain writers, poets, mystics and artists throughout centuries have experienced instances of biconsciousness, or periods of time with it, but perhaps could not believe their own mind. It is hard to read Poe or Kafka without feeling a kinship of thought and process. I have spoken with their avatars in the dream with no clear result.

The intellect is desperate to define. In the dream, there is no definition. Indeed, the intellect is terribly jealous of the spirit.

ENLIGHTENMENT

"One does not become enlightened by imagining figures of light, but by making the darkness conscious." -Jung

I was born, educated and culturally and socially imprinted in America. I don't need to live among a deeper, wiser, older people or take place in their rituals and celebrations to better explore my dream. I could move to Tibet and learn incredible dream disciplines with monks in remote mountain temples, I could discuss dreams every morning with a peaceful tribe in the Malay Peninsula

(such as the Senoi, who may or may not have existed),
or I could journey to the Outback and settle in with an
Aboriginal group and learn more about the Dreamtime.
But chances are you cannot afford those trips—in terms
of time and/or money, and even if you went to pursue
those cultures' experience with the dream, you cannot
have the same experience. Besides, there are no remote
native settlements left in this world that have not been
touched by Western culture.

You can study the history of human belief and practice of
dreams, starting with the ancient Egyptians, who revered
dream interpreters as "Masters of the Secret Things," and
"Learned Ones of the Magic Library." They had a word,
rswt, which, according to my research, simultaneously
meant both "dream" and "to be awake." The first known
writings of the dream are dated to 1350 B.C.

Indian shamans, Tibetan monks and Aboriginal elders
have no advantage over me when it comes to stepping
into the dream. I am original in my enlightenment.
There is much to learn from them, as there is much to
learn from a plumber or a mechanic. But they have no
more keys to spiritual fulfillment than a playground full
of children.

You cannot look to a priest or preacher to interpret your
relationship with your God; it must be original, one-on-
one, unfettered by the prejudice of any organization with
the agenda of getting a great number of people to think
alike; that's the opposite function of the dream. This
preacher, shaman or counselor will not be with you on
the other side. The dream is as unique as yourself, and
no one else can be your guide.

I have been overseas, travelled to three different continents (including one long stay near the arctic circle in
summer to see if the long daylight might affect my biconsciousness) and neither location nor interaction with
happier, more spiritual people has had any effect on my
dream. I cannot assign power over me to any individual
or culture.

Stop travelling to distant lands to seek enlightenment and fulfillment, and travel for spirit in the dream. If you cannot travel within the dream, then imagine that you are traveling within the dream, and you will open the doors wider for the convergence of dream and world. Imagination in the world is the thinnest layer between the world and the dream.

Read for enlightenment, take in words of inspiration and suggestions that can help you on your way (hopefully this book, for instance). Know that there is no path laid out for you, no plan that can be made for you by another, no wisdom that sees into your realm in any way that you cannot see for yourself given time, patience, and countless frustrating attempts.

It doesn't matter what you believe you are ultimately made of or what level of existence you inhabit. The experience of the moment (therefore the past and the future) belongs to a multitude of yous. The moment is always in flux, we float above it as we float in time, because we perceive the second changing into the next second while still grasping the previous second. Past, present and future all glom together and move in chunks, like ice floes drifting, or bullet trains gliding, or wolves lurching.

There is no point in time or space in which we will not be on this journey. Realize this in the world and you'll have some understanding of the dream.
Heaven, Hell, Satori; there is not a final staging, resting place for the soul. We cannot seek the end, only the end of fear. The dream may well be the procreation of the soul, an infinite circuit of consciousness.

WE HAVE PHYSIOLOGICAL
LINES THAT ARE SO
THIN IT'S SCARY.

IMAGINATION IN THE WORLD IS
THE THINNEST LAYER BETWEEN THE
WORLD AND THE DREAM.

SCIENCE

"It is impossible by any experiment whatsoever to determine absolute rest." – Albert Einstein

"Everything we call real is made of things that cannot be regarded as real." – Neils Bohr

Scientists are learning more about the dreaming brain, but still know very little about the dreaming mind.

We do not know what consciousness is, why it is, where it is, or how it is. Theories abound. We are closing in on identifying the tiniest quantum particles in existence and theorizing about the presence of even smaller, undetectable quanta. Is matter formed in particles or waves? Does direct observation alter their state? And some also see evidence (sometimes referred to as "quantum superposition") that particles can be in two places, perhaps even two dimensions, simultaneously. Consciousness may well be a constant stream of intertwining frequencies and wavelengths that, like a restless hand at a radio, we are tuning in and out of all day—and all night. We are, quite literally, made up of particles (or waves) that can be two places at once.

There are two places where science and the very laws of physics (as we know them) cease to exist: the event horizon and the dream. The dream is a singularity, every bit as much as a black hole is a singularity; a realm where the laws of physics and mathematics break down. Can we find the causal connection between the quantum wave of the dream, consciousness and the quantum waves of the world? Or, at the very least, can we find some tiny evidence for dreaming as a biological imperative? If humanity is tied to biology, then what are we in the dream?

Is the light by which we see in the dream made of photons, or is it the memory of light in the world that we imagine? If substance in the dream feels tangible, is it made up of quanta, just like the world, or is it some form of "entanglement" between dimensions?

WE NEED A THEORY OF EVERYTHING FOR CONSCIOUSNESS.

Dream research should be NASA in its proportions. Instead, it's a barely tolerated whim of some disparate science or psychology departments at a handful of progressive universities. If ever there were lost souls floundering in a realm called "research," it's dream researchers, relegated to the sleep lab to study twitching bodies and EEGs, brainwaves and neural transmitters. Like early ocean explorers, we're decades or centuries away from developing our dream SCUBA gear. It may well be that virtual video game creators have a better handle on the mechanics of dream construction than do scientists.

There are dream researchers and cataloguers, doing good work in trying to assess the common elements of people's dream lives. There are those desperate to develop technology that will prod people into lucidity within the dream. They are out there, like the alchemists of old, attempting to find the right combinations of the mysterious elements that will prove the magic is real. I applaud them. But the world of "science" has resisted acceptance of this work.

Dreaming brainwaves are the same as brainwaves in states of mental illness and dementia; this has been scientifically proven. The brainwaves of someone committing an act of murder are the same whether they are awake or in the dream, just as the brainwaves of someone experiencing sheer pleasure or terror are the same in either state. Brain studies on decision-making processes show that our brains register a decision seconds before we make a conscious choice; it's possible that we have chosen from within the dream before realizing it in the world.

All this research is doing, however, is proving that the brain is reacting to actions in the world and the dream with similar chemical and physiological assignments. The brain itself stays in the sleeping body, solidly a part of the world. It activates a shut off valve to the nerve signals and prohibits the release of serotonin, essentially disabling the muscular movement so that we do not act out the "fight or flight" scenario (this is known as sleep atonia); when we are chased and running for our lives in the dream, we are not jumping out of bed and through the house. There have been interesting cases where this system of physiological braking failed to work. Sleep-walking, sexsomnia and night terrors are potentially the result of the shut off valve failing or shorting out. This is not always a foolproof mechanism; we have physiological lines that are so thin it's scary.

When areas of the brain responsible for inhibiting movements during sleep are incapacitated, humans and animals can get up and act out their dreams. This is not surprising when you consider the theory (credited to Michel Jouvet, University of Lyon) that the dream arises from bursts of activity in biologically ancient parts of the brain. Some scientists believe that REM sleep evolved about 130 million years ago, coincidentally with womb-birth. This is perhaps because infant mammals at that stage needed dream activity to help develop their brains and to prepare them for the predators they would have to react to.

Normally, however, the brain can keep the body from walking while it is dreaming about walking (except, of course, for the random instances of sleepwalkers), but it chooses mostly to let us have erections or vaginal wetness while dreaming of having sex. When we jump in a dream, we usually do not jump from bed. But sometimes when we talk in a dream, our vocal cords pick up the action in the waking world. Plenty of scientific evidence suggests that many motor skills are synchronized in the dreaming and waking bodies. How does the brain differentiate between the motor skills of walking and getting an erection? Jumping or talking? Some people talk in their sleep consistently, others never. Some people sleep soundly through the night with very little movement, others do the Jitterbug or beat their spouses senseless.

Where many scientists and researchers want to claim that the visualization and sensory experience within the dream are a result of the brain's memory chip re-setting itself, or some residual holographic energy, they cannot explain lucidity and sustainability in the dream;

they cannot explain me. I studied theory after theory, all while living the reality of biconsciousness, which has been treated by the scientific community as wild speculation.

At some point, I grew tired of trying to find answers through scientific means; there are only so many brainwaves that can be measured and quantified. Experimentation using mechanical instruments is too flawed to discern visual activity. I would absolutely love to place a camera inside the brain to record dream activity like video, and perhaps one day in the far future this will be possible. But the realm of the dream is, currently, beyond science, and spirituality has no hold on it either. Too ephemeral for science, too visceral for spirituality. Yet the lucid traveler knows, feels, and moves.

QUANTUM THEORY, THE MULTIVERSE OR PARALLEL UNIVERSE

Many a slightly drunk astrophysicist, neurophysicist, quantum theorist and 2-scotch philosopher has cornered me at the after-lecture bar to offer their highly profound theories of the dream as alternate or parallel universe. Who knows? When the scientific establishment thumbed their collective noses at my experience, I pretty much stopped sucking at the teats of academia. When a supposedly brilliant researcher hunts me down at a workshop or event to drop theories on me, they are invariably fishing for my own ideas to run with.

Since man first gazed at the stars with a sense of self, we've asked "how does consciousness connect to the physical world?" Physicists have long struggled with finding the magical, unified "theory of everything," but even that will be incomplete if it does not include consciousness. And there is a scientific term for it: the Hard Problem of Consciousness. Is consciousness a fundamental part of the universe, or is it just a byproduct of biological processes? Science, and even philosophy, is all over the map on this.

We need a Theory of Everything for Consciousness.

Quantum wave interference. The Holographic Model. The Parallel Universe Theory. Cosmoneurology. Biocentrism. I have read the papers, I have tried very hard to understand the physics—though I was always mathematically challenged and did poorly at the subject. Nothing I have read comes close to explaining, in the laws of the physical universe, how I exist in two worlds simultaneously. The world of science still cannot explain why or how we dream, much less why someone is capable of living in the world and the dream at the same time. They can theorize at the possibility that subatomic quanta are capable of existing in two places simultaneously, or that these particles are waves that materialize into physically detectable mass only when under observance. We don't know how they enable phasing between the world and dream. The fact is, science cannot begin to comprehend consciousness, much less the dream.

Scientists attempting dream research are usually either in a university dungeon somewhere strapping electrodes to people's heads, or giving thousand dollar seminars in Oahu or Sedona. Dream research is cosmology, only without the Hubble telescopes and the WMAP deep space microwave probes. Sleeping subjects can be trained to send signals from within the dream via eye movement or muscle shifts; but we cannot take video or otherwise record any actual imagery, just neural activity. They can scan our visual cortex and map our neural transmissions, but cannot project our dream externally. This is the holy grail of dream research—if not THE Holy Grail of everything.

My favorite concept on the edge of dream/psychology/astrophysical theory is the notion that what's happening in our brains is the exact microcosm of what's happening in the multiverse. Fair enough. Save the research grant money, it's a done deal. Let's spare the endless arguments and just all agree that the vastness of the infinite universe is really (cue *2001: A Space Odyssey's* use of "Strauss' Also Sprach Zarathustra") an outer reflection of the inner infinite universe of the mind. Is it a coincidence that we have identified approximately 5% of the known matter of the universe (cumulative matter and energy, as opposed to theoretical "dark" energy and mysterious waves or substances we cannot discern), and that we use such a small percentage of our brains? The majority of real estate within our cranial blobs are just as big a mystery to us as is the universe. Is there a correlation? Is the brain a "filter" or "receiver" for the quantum waves we cannot yet detect? Let's go there! Because these things are the great unknown, and with the great unknown, we either fear it or it gives us hope. Or both.

I also admire the theory of Biocentrism, which essentially says that the universe cannot exist unless it is observed. The same is true of the dream. My own experience could be happily mixed up in the theories of Entanglement, which posits that paired particles can mimic each other's actions whether a millimeter apart or light years. Could one particle be in the world and another in the dream? Quantum particles can, apparently, be anywhere or everywhere, at once. Theoretically, then, a particle could go from the quantum fields of the world to the quantum fields of the dream. The famous "double-slit" experiment proved that waves become particles when observed. Likewise, when we are lucid, consciousness upgrades itself according to our level of lucidity or observation.

We are each in our own universe, our own reality. All of us are, in essence, WIMPS (weakly interacting massive particles). Your perceptions and experience in the world and the dream are profoundly different from mine. The nexus that this world creates gives us physical interaction via biological and chemical processes, even as we each inhabit our very own multiverse.

There are too many theories to get caught up in, and too little emphasis on valid research that connects our conscious tracts. Our governments place greater importance on space exploration, private developers would rather mine asteroids, and the creative community can't get beyond aliens attacking; an intelligent exploration of the dream as some kind of cosmic continuum is still shelved under "whack" and filed just to the left of Bigfoot research.   Please, wake me when it's over.

Oh, wait; I'm always awake.

PARANORMAL PHENOMENA

Most explorations and studies of the dream are lumped in with what is classified as paranormal, "new age," mystical or any categorization that so many pragmatists would scoff at. I do not disparage or disrespect those beliefs at all, rather I do not think dreams fall into the categories of the metaphysical. Our dreams are perfectly natural, everyone exists in the dream, it is a current of life that is inescapable. We do not fully understand the dream. But its existence, its import in our lives, is undeniable.

Regardless of my personal feelings, I'm always inundated with questions and associations of the dream with many types of phenomena; for most of these, I neither "believe" nor "disbelieve" their existence or the experience of those sharing or asking. I try to make the possible connection to the undercurrent of the dream, and in most cases, the dream provides a highly plausible context in which these phenomena can be experienced.

The Near–Death Experience

There are thousands of well–studied case histories of near–death occurrences. Throughout history, people in traumatic life–threatening situations have reported oddly similar experiences. When their bodies are traumatized and their brains are deprived of oxygen and they are either unconscious or clinically dead, they report seeing themselves, flying up into the sky, seeing loved ones or some form of God or comforting presence, or they are journeying, travelling they know not where. Neurophysiologists and neurobiologists have come up with no completely scientific justification for this brain activity. In my view, it's simple: they have made the phase into the dream, and it's vibrant and memorable because of the stimulus, the trauma and forces acting upon them in the world. They are temporarily trapped in the dream, physically unable to waken into the world as a team of paramedics try to resuscitate them, or they lay unconscious somewhere. In this experience, the dream explodes for them, powerful thoughts and emotions collide in lucid vision as they likely begin the transition to the next stage of their evolution, or the neurophysiological rescue flare before all goes dark. They see "the light" and move toward that light because the alternative is—well, darkness. The light is consciousness, lucid being, literally the continuance of sight. Then, when breath and heartbeat and rhythm return to their body, they are yanked back into the world, the dream experience tattooed upon their psyche at such a vulnerable moment that bridged both worlds.

Déjà vu

As psychic or physiological phenomena, Déjà vu is easy enough for me to explain, though you may choose not to believe it. Recent theories are that it is the mind's memory of spatial perception; the size and ambiance of a room, for example, jarring the memory of a similarly shaped room and perhaps a chain of actions that ensue. My dream experience differs. It's simply the alignment of an action in the dream and the world, simultaneously. You have temporarily breached the barrier of consciousness between the two states and they have, even for mere seconds, converged, flooding you with the feeling that you've experienced this sequence of events before. Rather, the feeling of familiarity comes from the mirror feeling in the dream. You enter a room in the world; in the dream, you conjure the same room, the same event; lucidity heightens and for a brief but jarring second or two, you are consciously aware of both. It's a powerful

OUR SENSES CAN BETRAY
US IN EITHER REALM.

feeling; it's a constant drug to me. I spend hours a day with the psycho-tingly sensation of déjà vu, as my worlds align quite frequently. This is usually in a biconscious effort, as when I coordinate playing an instrument in both worlds (I have on several occasions achieved the feat of accompanying myself on guitar in the world, drums in the dream). I've coordinated sexual acts—a few times conjuring my world girlfriend into the dream, more often a different girl in the dream. The alignment of experiencing the same act in two worlds is indescribable. The feeling of déjà vu in the world is just the echo rippling from the dream.

Try staring at yourself in a full-length mirror; imagine the mirror world is the dream world. Let your mind play tricks on you. If you're doing it right, at some point, you will get some small tingle of recognition that feels like déjà vu.

Hypnosis

I have yet to see a plausible demonstration of hypnosis. I have seen hypnotist "performances" and private sessions with psychiatrists trained in hypnotic technique. I do not deny the potential effectiveness of subliminal suggestion, as words and stimuli from the world can pierce into the subconscious; but I have not seen evidence where any suggestions have truly taken control of an individual. Think about it. To truly be in the zombie-like state of what we typically think of as hypnosis, one would have to be in a sleep or dream state, with fully functional nerve and muscular response. Some current theories believe hypnosis to be more of a waking state, with the subject simply hyper-focusing on the suggestion of the hypnotist, and usually with a subject predisposed to suggestive induction. I tried being hypnotized by a colleague I trusted and by a professional with whom I was not acquainted; at the point when most of their subjects might fall into a suggestive state (according to them), I was in the dream, hearing their voice speak at me. Yet because I am generally fully lucid once slipping into the dream, I could ignore their requests and commands. One guy rolled his eyes and assumed I was bluffing. The other guy was offended and threw me out of his office.

There can certainly be a kind of "placebo" effect with hypnosis; a person generally open to suggestion who wants to believe it is possible, or who wants to be submissive, could undergo a hypnotist's routine and perform just as the hypnotist suggests to them. We do not know if a hypnotist is speaking to the conscious forefront of a fully awake and aware person or to the subconscious mind of a fully awake and aware person (or, in my case, both). I do believe that an untrained individual could lean in to a person during certain stages of the sleep cycle, or under the influence of any number of drugs, and make suggestions that the person might act upon.

As can your lover.

Other Dimensions

It's entirely possible that the wormholes theorized to span through the multiverse, and possibly to alternate dimensions, go through us. Our brains may be conduits that spark or channel the opening of these quantum holes, and dark energy or some undefined quantum energies carry our lucid consciousness from portal to portal into an ether that can be fully, sensually realized by our uniquely particular constellation of particles that make up our selves, or soul. Perhaps the dream is its own constant wave field, where beyond the portal of the brain, it works without needing to obey the laws of physics.

Many believe there is a causal connection between the inner space of the dream and the outer space of the universe, or multiverse if you are inclined to believe in it. If it is acceptable that all possibilities are realized in different dimensions, then it is acceptable that they can be present and reachable via the dream. We can measure the ingredients of the universe down to the minutest particle; but we can't taste the soup. I don't think we will make significant strides in realizing the full potential of the dimensional experience until we truly start mea-

suring it from the other side. We have brilliant minds—
the Einsteins and Hawkings and Penroses—who can do
the math. Now we need the Magellans and Balboas (and
Thoreaus) to make the journeys.

SENSES

We experience our environment through five obvious
senses and countless undefined senses; we use the same
senses in the dream. Our senses can betray us in either
realm, they can malfunction, they can even lie to us, but
we cannot discard them. Sense can of course be hand-
icapped, which usually causes other senses to fill in the
gaps by becoming more acute. In the dream, the other
senses get some exercise.

I am able to control or enhance my senses through simultaneous exercises in both worlds. I can control pain,
and I can receive the memory of pain and alter it to a tin-
gling sensation. I cannot see telescopically, or hear the
drop of a pin miles away, mainly because in the dream,
all sensory experience is relative. The memory of sensations temporarily lend themselves to me while I am creating new sensations. The touch of flesh is the same,
because I would not want flesh to feel like feathers or
scales, though I could make that happen easily. I cannot necessarily achieve sensory usage that has not been
in my field of experience. Or, I have not yet learned to
sufficiently abandon my precepts to embrace such new
sensations.

In the dream, our senses are unleashed, even blended in
ways, but not magnified to superhero proportions, unless we lucidly pursue such desire. In the world, our eyes
have adapted to a limited spectrum of light wavelength,
our ears to a limited spectrum of audible soundwaves,
our touch to a limited spectrum of tactile sensation, and
our nose to a very limited spectrum of scents. Other

SENSUAL OUTPUT IN THE
WORLD IS SENSUAL INPUT IN THE
DREAM, AND VICE VERSA.

animals, who are made of the same elements and DNA as we, have a broader spectrum of sense. In the dream, we are another animal, newly released into the wild. We were captured as children and must re-learn the extent of our sensual heritage.

Science can explain how we see; how light is filtered through our eye, how an image is formed that our brain translates; but do our eyes repeat this process for seeing in the dream? Our ears? Our noses, our touch, any of our sensory stimuli, or is it replaced with the memory of seeing, touching, smelling, hearing? Sensations are as powerful or more so in the dream, but are we undergoing the same physiological processes? The measurement of brain activity during the dream clearly shows the brain is experiencing and reacting to things.

What we can see has a strong effect on what we think. In the world, we are largely captive to what we see before us. We can alter how we perceive it and change it by moving to a different location. In the dream, we clearly see what's before us but can change it by our own will, without moving.

One of the things that has been difficult for me to grasp in the dream is the use of gut instinct. In the world, we rely on gut instinct in almost every situation throughout our lives, and making a gut instinct is dependent on a few concrete factors, primarily the environment and our experience. In the world, the environment stays stable, giving us a foundation and an anchor for our experiences on which we build instincts and perceptions. In the dream, the environment is fluid, the denizens are fluid, and it is rare that something remains exactly the same. Stabilizing one's senses—physical and mental—in the dream isn't unlike trying to stand on a boat in choppy waters after standing firm on concrete for a long time, or focus on something after spinning on a merry-go-round.

You can close your eyes and plug your ears, but it does not stop the senses. The conscious mind creates simulations of senses and carries them wherever the mind goes.

In the world, no matter where you are or what you're doing, your immediate impulse upon reaching a brief plateau of lucidity is to quickly search your mind for the next responsibility, the undone task; am I late for work, did I take out the trash, what did I forget that I was supposed to do? In the dream, when you reach lucidity, your first impulse is to serve your deepest, darkest urges; and you have the power to sate yourself.

EYE CONTACT

How often do you look directly at the person you are talking to, sitting next to, making love with? When you look directly at someone while you're talking to them or otherwise interacting with them, you're projecting your thoughts and intentions directly into them, and they are filtered through their own receptive abilities. When you're looking directly at someone when they're talking to you, you're listening through two senses. Eye contact deepens the connection, provides confirmation of your listening, and often pins the other person to the truth. It's a 2-ply connection, reinforcing the conscious bridge.

In the dream, eye contact does the same thing. I have attempted to align eye contact simultaneously with someone in the world and also in the dream. I sat my girlfriend down two feet in front of me, and did the same in the dream (though in the dream we were seated in a breezy Mediterranean-ish portico, rather than in our off-campus apartment). I was at once staring at her the person and her my creation of her person, trying to tune out two environments. With no action, movement, or vocalization, I realized within just seconds of this exercise that it was the exact same response from her. If a wavelength were being emitted from each of her eyes into mine, the two pairs would have—for an instant at a time—attuned perfectly to the same frequency. Staring at her in the world, and her image in the dream, gave me the exact same physiological connection. Different than the sexual connection when I tried the exact same thing through intercourse. I could not get the two versions to mesh, they were distinctly different acts in different worlds. The body had too much to do. The eyes can float between worlds, but the body must move.

When you truly make eye contact with someone in the world, attention "snaps to" in the dream as well; you may be staring into the eyes of your dream version of that person or a completely different person, different sex, even a dog or strange bird—but it is that same contact in two worlds. I have always found this to be the case, particularly when I am "drifting" (not maintaining a lucid control over my environment). It would seem to suggest that when you make such a visceral contact with the attention of another being, it impacts your lucidity in both worlds, and I can't argue against that. The merest of glances don't produce the effect, but "locking eyes" can have a profound consequence and take the dream in an altogether different direction. Be careful who you lock eyes with; it's the closest I ever feel that someone from the world is peering into my dream, however briefly, and it can be soothing or chilling depending on the person— or creature—you're looking at.

The energy it takes for one person to truly connect— listen, look at, understand—with another is massive. It is draining and requires mental focus and an emotional athleticism that must be rare. To distinguish a real visual connection from riding the wave of emotional connection and ego fulfillment via the perceived connection is extremely hard. We inherently, subconsciously, know this. We may be biologically preconditioned to believe that to stare at another animal is to threaten it, or to attempt to control it, rather than connect with it.

Sensual output in the world is sensual input in the dream, and vice versa. We are constantly picking up on "vibes," mood swings, unexplained bursts of hopeful joy or sudden stabbing fears or bouts of mild depression. These are most likely sensate deliveries from the dream via the conscious bridge. The dream is constantly consuming our sensual experiences from the world, sucking the ripples and echoes of our actions, thoughts and experiences into the dream environment where they await the call of our dream activity. When you learn to phase between the dream and the world, these things are available immediately.

We can easily have an emotional or physiological reaction to something we see, feel, hear, or otherwise perceive. It's when we have a reaction whose origins we don't see that gives us unease. We "sense" something is wrong, we "sense" a separate presence—this use of the word "sense" is likely "experience" from within the dream. When we cannot make eye contact with a person, our level of trust and confidence can drop dramatically. Many denizens in my dream make riveting eye contact with me, even if I am not initiating or willing the contact to happen; whereas many in the world rarely look me in the eye at all. Unbroken, sustained eye contact forces a connection in either world.

Entropy may or may not be possible between the world and the dream, but it would be revelatory to measure the actual exchange of energy between the states. It may be possible that there is as much synaptic firing between the dimensions as occurs in our own brain. Senses slip between the layers of consciousness and can waken elements in the world or dream without direction from us.

Maybe the dream and the world want to converge; maybe it would be the Book of Revelations in human evolution.

EXPERIMENTING

"Stand there, baulked and dumb, stuttering and stammering, hissed and hooted, stand and thrive, until, at last, rage draw out of thee that dream-power which every night shows thee is thine own; a power transcending all limit and privacy, and by virtue of which a man is the conductor of the whole river of electricity."
--Ralph Waldo Emerson, "The Poet"

I've spent many years trying to gauge how the sensory experience from the world can be replicated, negated and intensified in the dream and vice-versa. Could I measure time and distance? Did it matter? I kept attacking certain concepts, marveling at how fantastic something would taste, or how the sound of a huge gong would literally make me float; how I could cut a gash in my forearm and bleed profusely yet feel no pain, then turn the blood into smoke. It was rare that the use of my senses made me feel like I was transcending my heart-pumping, lung-expanding existence. It was in the dream where the same simple, physical act became hyper-realistic, something to savor and revel in and eventually move beyond. I've catalogued years of simple and complex trials.

Many experiments proved to be a complete waste of time, but then so do many actions in the world. In college, I was not cut out for diligent research, meticulous note-taking or persistent goal-oriented action. In the end, experience is the only school that matters.

For a long time, I tried to categorize and index each specific experiment. I experimented with an idea and with variations of that idea. I don't include here a complete journal or log of all my experiments, and believe me, you are glad for it. Here is a sampling of what I did, and what you can do, too. More patient and meticulous minded souls could certainly improve on my approaches, and I've heard from many over the years.

Most of my experimentation took place as my body was sleeping; even though I generally can slip into and out of the dream throughout the day, my best concentration and focus is when my body is at rest, less distracted. In the world, I was often able to record first-person, real-time accounts of what I was doing in the dream, synchronizing my voice in both, and transcribing the experiences later. Talk about speaking in tongues; it's kind of like possessing yourself and recording it.

One dominant notion that kept presenting itself throughout most of my experiments was that the perception of a thing was often a more powerful tool than the thing itself. It calls to mind the Wallace Stevens poem, "Not Ideas About the Thing but the Thing Itself," which, in its own way, also explores the sentiment of sentience.

Create your own experiments based on what appeals to you; in my experience, it is not rewarding to simply mimic actions or sequences from the world, or to simply try to measure (with no benefit of instrumentation or recording ability) how fast or strong you can be or how far you can fly...those are fun things to do, but when you decide to spend your dream lucidity on some search for scientific or spiritual meaning, allow for the dream's chaos factor to always introduce some interesting element you had not expected...

To measure time

A neighborhood lined with a row of houses, mountains behind them. It is a kind of foreign country, it feels Scandinavian. The climate is cool, it is daytime, late in the day. The sun is obscured by haze. I look for a public clock display, and see none. I hope that my wish to see a clock doesn't automatically produce one somewhere, and my wish seems to be realized. I do not have a watch or pocket watch, and I know I'll have to enter one of the homes to find a clock. It's important that I use an existing clockwork from the dream, rather than materializing one in my hand. The neighborhood seems deserted, and I feel responsible. It's like in one of those fifties movies or nuclear training films, where everyone has evacuated their homes to the bomb shelters, and are merrily dancing in a ballroom sized bunker underneath my very feet.

It's like the emptiness and loneliness of place that the sheriff in "High Noon" must have faced when the town clocks struck noon. I think the High Noon analogy quite appropriate, where such an emphasis was put on the passage of real time, though it was movie time. Every few minutes, the film would cut to a clock, the countdown in real time in the unreal movie. Anyway, I know that I felt like Sheriff Kane. Gary Cooper. I needed to find a watch or clock. I went up the lonely street, walking slowly instead of flying, glad for the consistent feel of my feet, fully accepting the weight of my body in every step I took. I choose a two-story blue house and am surprised that the house is locked. Not wanting to disturb the tranquil energy I have been able to maintain, I decide not to bust the door down but to go around back, where I find a patio bordered in flowers of many colors, a black gas grill, and a set of sliding doors, which are unlocked. I go into the empty home and look around the showroom furniture. Ah, there it is--a grandfather clock, as well as a wall clock visible from the kitchen. I sit on the plush tan-colored sofa, the light pouring in from the late day sun, and concentrate on the clocks. The time. The passage of time in this world.

3:18 I sit, quietly, observing carefully the clocks, my eyes fixed on the long hand and the second hand. They move naturally to my count of one one thousand, two one thousand, three one thousand, and on. And so I am able to mimic time from the waking world. I count, one Mississippi, two Mississippi, as I was taught in school.

3:23 I am still fixed on the long and second hand of each clock; the tall, oaken-chested grandfather clock with a brass ring around the face and old roman style numerals on the clock face; and the small, white plastic kitchen clock.

3:31 Still looking at the clock hands moving, ever so slowly, I realize I am really bored. This experiment is a complete waste of my time, valuable dream time, all time as we know it. I will the clocks to become 4:03.

4:04 I was close. Without seeing them move, without

any movement or judged lapse of time, suddenly the clocks were 4:04. Like seeing the sun skip in the sky.

I abandon this experiment—I could sit and count time for as long as I wanted, but to what purpose? I can slow time, speed time, or create some stillness of time in the dream. Simply, things that take time in the world take no time in the dream.

I go up the long narrow staircase to a second floor and peek into the empty bedrooms; the more I concentrate on details within each room, the more details reveal themselves. A damp, abandoned towel on a bed. A watch on the edge of a nightstand. Toys scattered on a wooden floor—blocks that are not perfect squares. The last room in the hall, a girl sitting on a bed, looking up at me, the stranger, curious but not afraid. She is beautiful. Light, straight hair down her back. The cammie she wears is thin and frayed. She stares at me. I demand the stillness of time. Now.

Time does not matter. Experience matters.

To make sound the bridge between both worlds

I want to synchronize my voice between both worlds. In the dream, I sit on a bed in a museum. I feel like a piece of performance art. In the world, I lay in bed in a dark room.

In the dream, I begin to shout. I attempt to sustain a note for as long as I can. There are two objectives here; to see if I can sustain the note in the dream without the factor of "losing my breath", and to see if I can make the same sound in the waking world. This museum is like the ones I visit often in the dream. Huge, performance–hall–like rooms that are bright white with sparsely appointed paintings and sculptures. At first, the people around me stop, intrigued by my impromptu performance, but soon go about their business. After a moment, I do begin to feel a burning in my chest, as if from a complete depletion of air in my lungs; it spreads until I think I cannot stand it any longer. My world body needs to draw breath, and so synced does the dream body. I am becoming red-faced in front of these dream strangers. I realize that it is the true burning of my lungs in the waking world and that I'd best draw a breath of air in both worlds—I do so in the dream primarily to support the action in the world. I close my eyes and reopen them, phase fully into the world, hear the tiny electric hum punctuating the passage.

Experiment successful. But do not do this with your lover asleep next to you.

Involuntary bodily functions in the dream

In the dream, there is no necessity for performing bodily functions of digestion, blinking, or even breathing. We may reflexively move our chests, fill our dream lungs, blink or even cough, but these are phantom urges. I suspect that if we were to die and live on in the dream, the need to fulfill these biological urges would eventually cease. To concentrate on one function is to suddenly feel as if you must exercise that option, physically. If we use the form of our bodies to feel pleasure in the dream, then we can certainly perform other bodily functions, for pleasure or habit. In the world, we evolved these habits involuntarily, because to be required to concentrate lucidly on performing life-sustaining exercises would be fatal to our species. In the dream, I usually choose to ignore bodily functions not directly related to pleasure.

For the purposes of this experiment, I stop whatever I'm doing in the dream and check to see if I've been breathing, blinking my eyes, or if I'm making the sounds of digestion. Though it feels flesh and blood to me, it's of course a non-corporeal body I inhabit in the dream.

I run up a hill, resisting the urge to fly, and see if I feel the natural reaction of panting, with my blood racing through veins that probably didn't exist unless I exposed

them. I feel it because I think about feeling it.
Once I distract myself, the need to believe I'm breathing just vanishes.

I walk through a crowded restaurant and observe the diners. It's a fancy place, and everyone is in formal dress. I stop at a table with two couples engaged in conversation and eye their plates. One of the women has been eating pineapple and some kind of cake, and I reach across her shoulder and grab a handful of the white cake, being overtly messy and showy. I stuff my face with the cake, commit myself to the act of chewing, but become distracted because suddenly I want to leave a real mess around my lips. All at the table are instantly appalled, which makes me glad. Shut up and sit down, I say to them. I swallow, savoring the taste and texture of the cake. Then I grab the woman's champagne glass and take loud obnoxious sounding gulps and hurl the glass at the far wall in a swift stroke. I feel the cake sitting in my stomach and make a mental note to be aware of any stomach gurgling later, or gas. I want to belch but can't. Instead, I reach into the woman's fancy white dress and grab her left breast with my cake-covered hand. She flinches, scoots her chair back, but stays. I squeeze her breast gently and quickly pull the top half of her dress down and study her breasts closely. The wave of purposelessness convinces me I have no desire to continue. In the world, my stomach feels fed.

Again, distracted by sex. Very grateful for involuntary necessity in the world.

Urination

It does happen that, in the dream I have the sensation of having to urinate, which, of course, most often signals the need to do so in the world. Understandably, I'm careful to phase more fully into the world, trudge out of bed, suffer the cold tile floor, all while keeping my eyes closed so as not to be so far removed from the dream state. But I have, on a rare occasion, taken a piss in the dream, even when completely lucid, just for the fun of it—especially fun when performed on the 2nd or third story of a building overlooking a crowd of people. I can suppress the urge in bed and perform the act in the dream. Except for that one time, in camp during junior high. Dream-pissing is a waste of concentration.

Orgasm

As a male, orgasm in the world requires ejaculation, a biological necessity (though I have never tried Tantric sex). In the dream, I usually orgasm somewhere inside a girl, so I don't always see the physical evidence of semen. When a girl uses her hand on me in the dream, what I see upon ejaculation is pretty much what I see in the world. I've had no inclination to change the consistency or appearance of that fact (for instance, making semen rainbow colored, or sparkling with light). I've tried to stretch out the orgasmic feeling, and I can elongate certain waves of energy but struggle to stop the recession phase that's a natural and crucial part of the orgasm itself. In the dream, the mind wanders right after sex just as it does in the world. This could be very different for some women who seem able to ride these waves of pleasure between physical and emotional states.

Mastering the heights

In a tall building in a busy urban landscape, Chicago, overlooking the river, the Tribune Tower, and the Magnificent Mile. The lights of the Mile have just lit, shoppers bustling up and down the avenue as dusk settles. The river is below. I have taken the elevator to the top floor and found the exit door to the roof; I move slowly across the roof--this is one of the tallest buildings in the city--and go to the edge of the safety railing. The breeze is strong and cool, a mid-spring freshness to the air. My heart races as I peer over the railing with the top half of my body. When I fly in the dream I usually throw myself up into the air rather than jump off objects, and never need a running start. I am perspiring. I step up onto the first rail of the guardrail and slowly release my hands from the top rail. I peer down again, feel the world revolving slowly around me, see the magenta hues of sunset over the lake. In the dream, flight always feels new to my body. I am perfectly lucid and in full control of my body, the natural fear of being so high on a structure held together with steel beam, nuts and bolts. The wind gets stronger, harsh gusts stinging my cheeks. I'd like to jump out and fly above the city. But this is not the dream. Push your experience in the world.

Beyond Sense

Our senses get a lot of exercise in the dream, and can be heightened when mixed with emotional extremes we've never experienced in the world. I remember on many occasions laughing so hard at something that was so simplistic, and seeing it clearly in the dream, but once phased back into the world, having no clear picture of it other than the powerful emotional resonance of being filled with such pure joy. This works on all emotional and sensory levels. I've tasted incredible concoctions, heard amazing new instruments and sounds, felt textures unmade in the world, and seen colors that are beyond our spectrum. I've smelled scents both intoxicating and repulsive. Yet, though I can sometimes bring the image back clearly into the world, so often the moment is lost in translation, as if too powerful to be worthy of attention in this world. I know that goes against my rule of imbuing the dream with any kind of mystical "power," but plenty of unexplainable things happen in both realms.

Fun with Pain

Memory is powerful. Even carried into the dream from worldly experience, traumatic physical events leave a powerful imprint on our psyche, if not our bodies. This is why so many people fear falling in the dream, or fighting, or being eaten. We have millions of years of genetic code written into our physiology, and ignoring things like pain receptors is a challenge.

I wanted to see how well I could control pain.

In the dream, in flight, I swoop down from the air and crash through the window of a typical suburban ranch style house and find the kitchen. Everything in the kitchen is futuristically shiny, a clinical stainless steel. I search the drawers—too focused to concentrate on the odd gadgets in each drawer (is that a ladle, something that looks like a grater but more sinister). There...the knives. Huge knives, Japanese ceremonial knives and standard flatware. I suddenly notice the kitchen is a veritable museum of knives. I choose a common steak knife, place it tightly in my right hand, and hold my left arm out palm up, stiffly. With no hesitation, I place the serrated blade just below the inside of my elbow and press down, moving the blade slowly down my arm to my wrist. I turn my arm over and cut a similar path deep into the muscle to the back of my hand. Blood wells up, deep Hershey syrup blood, and oozes down my fingers. I feel no pain. The only thing that winces is my eyes, but I force myself to watch for whatever will happen. I am at a level of lucidity that could go either way; I could realize the pain, or not. The memory of the sensation of being cut begins to sear up from the flesh; the sight of blood is a powerful, visceral sensation in both worlds. I can bring the sensations into focus and generate complete healing of the gash without stirring.

Realizing this, I scrap plans for an experiment involving blunt-force trauma to the head. Pain is mutable. When feeling extreme pain in the world, I phase into the dream and feel some of that pain dissipate, as if I've just opened a release valve.

Fun with More Pain

I decided that working with pain and the perception of pain in the dream was too easily controllable. I wanted to know if I could control my world body's pain from within the dream, and if I could maintain my state in the dream without fully phasing into the world when under attack. I was going to have a friend punch me or put my arm in a vise, but none of my friends would do it. So I knew there were any number of well-known bullies on campus who were crazy jealous over their girlfriends. I chose one of the biggest jocks known for this behavior and staked out his girlfriend one afternoon as she was waiting for him after a class. I chatted her up—to which she was astonished and receptive, by the way—knowing her boyfriend would be along any minute. I had her laughing on the bench, and before I knew it "Doug" made a beeline and yanked me back. I braced myself for anything. He ranted at me to get the hell away from his girlfriend and a couple of his friends ran up; others in the area stopped, waiting. I figured I had to lay on an adversarial tone, so I came off cocky and told him I was just chatting with her and he should be a man rather than an ape. I could hear the wincing "ooohs" in whispered tones around us. He reared back his arm and I stood my ground, phasing into the dream like a bird into the sky. It was a quiversome balance, and I distinctly felt the impact of his fist on my left jaw, my consciousness in the world sizzled and pulsed, but I localized myself and visualized the pain as a red piece of paper, which I wadded up and threw up into the air. I could hear murmuring and a girl's scream from the world, she was yelling at Doug to stop, more angry and embarrassed than afraid, and others were murmuring "what's wrong with him?" I was standing upright, eyes closed, teetering, but had not even grabbed my jaw after the punch; I was displaying signs of being "either comatose or hypnotized," according to one pre-med student I interviewed afterward. I began to fall, and one of Doug's friends had the good sense and quick reflexes to catch me. Of course, in the dream, I conjured Doug, picked him up and flew him up into the sky, over a junkyard, where I dropped him from about a thousand feet up, watching him flail and disappear into a trash heap. I figured I'd emerge and see what the aftermath was. Once opening my eyes in the world, everyone was staring at me, someone had called 911, and Doug himself was sitting next to me, stupefied and scared. I sat up and told everyone I was fine, thanks for the help. I felt no pain, not the slightest bit, and never even showed a bruise (though my nose was bleeding). Doug seemed concerned. After years on school grounds of phasing in and out and making people feel generally uncomfortable, I decided to be honest and told him I'd intentionally provoked him as an experiment. He called me a freak, as did his girlfriend, and that was that. The EMTs arrived within a minute and saw no signs of any trauma.

This was a cocky way of doing this experiment. I was sneaky and manipulative. Wrong approach, probably wanted to bring attention to myself more than anything.

How we feel pain can be affected by whether or not we are with someone, friend or stranger.

Pain - Healing

Once I'd learned to deflect or shield myself from physical pain (granted, I had not flung my body off the thirteenth story of any buildings or anything), I wanted to explore the possibility of diminishing the effects of a viral or bacterial attack. When I felt the signs of a cold or flu coming on, I would, in the dream, make an effort to visualize the germs as plants or graffiti on a building, and I'd create a windstorm or small tornado or a giant powerful hose and wash them away. I would do this several times during the dream, as I became lucid to their repeated growth in locations throughout the dream, and after a season's worth of almost no cold or flu effects, I felt I had a handle on dealing with those kinds of diseases. Luckily, I've not had to deal with anything worse like cancer or tumors, though I would take the same approach.

Sound filtered into the dream

I am always filtering sounds from the dream or world from or into each other. When I sleep, however, I will often experiment with sounds I know are coming from the world.

I position my speakers at my bed posts; four speakers angled inward to cover me in a blanket of sound. I put 10 CDs in the tray and hit random play, then lay back. I phase into the dream. I am acutely aware of the songs as they flow into the dream. They play as if a soundtrack to the dream. I talk to dream people about the songs, and they offer their insights on artists and musicians I've never heard of before. I try to be aware of the continuity of the songs and sing along.

Soundtracking the dream

I'm often more fully lucid in the dream when sleeping in the world, and able to better focus on external stimuli from the world when physically dormant. I choose 3 very different songs to play during sleep to see how they begin to filter into the dream. Will I hear them on the radio in the dream, will I hear them as if they've been broadcast over loudspeakers, or just as some mysterious soundtrack? The key is that I will try not to control events in the dream environment, rather I will try to let them play out based on the energy of each musical piece. I set the timer on my player for each song, to begin an hour, two, and three hours into sleep. Because I do not keep track of time in the dream, I will not know exactly when to expect any external sound.

The songs I choose are:

"Supercalifragilisticexpialidocious" (Richard and Robert Sherman)

I am wondering if the zaniness of this tune from the

film *Mary Poppins* will infiltrate the activity of the dream denizens—particularly since the movie was a favorite in my childhood and I always felt its whimsical, dreamlike quality.

"Closer" (Trent Reznor, Nine Inch Nails)

During angry moments, I often cranked up Nine Inch Nails, and this song satisfied a lusty, carnal edginess within me; if I hear it in the dream, will I be driven to fulfill those instincts?

"Ascent (An Ending)" (Brian Eno)

This transcendent composition from Eno, pioneer of ambient music and no stranger to dreamlike compositions, would always calm me. It is one piece that will instantly uplift my spirits while retaining whatever melancholy resides there.

I phase into the dream and go about my usual business of exploration, chatting with denizens and flying from place to place, stopping to imbibe some different tasting substance, fondling strangers and playing, shooting up to the cloud line and skimming vast green bodies of shimmering water. I am in the heart of a teeming metropolis when "Supercalifragilisticexpialidocious" can be heard, not from a stereo or loudspeaker, but being sung by an old man in a raincoat (it is not raining). A nearby woman joins in and soon, several bystanders are drawn into the song, merrily dancing in circles, doing jigs and reveling in general silliness. The song is fluid and constant, not skipping verses or jumping ahead or back. I am exhilarated, and realize it is rare for me to just sit and observe the denizens rather than make myself the focus of their attention. A horse manages to make an appearance, clopping down the street on its own; I fly to the horse and stroke its mane as the song ends to much laughter. It's an exhilarating few moments within the dream, as if a flash mob had sprung for no reason and given much merriment to onlookers.

Later, I am in a restaurant and hear a persistent clattering from within the kitchen. I've joined a table with a group of young couples who appear to be wealthy, or at least extremely well dressed, but bored. I've had some fun with various rearrangements of clothing on their bodies, and a whipped concoction of some kind of chocolate and cream is sitting in front of everyone. I hear the snare thump intro of the song "Closer", growing louder from the kitchen—the industrial part of the building. When the vocals come on, they prove too captivating for my ego, and I choose to sing along to those at the table, as if I were filming a music video; and I decide this will be a music video that could never air on world TV. Clothes are ripped off, heads and bodies are pressed against tables, one boy gets thrown through the window onto the street, and I struggle with timing any kind of copulation with either of the girls to the rhythm of the song. The song fades out and there is a mess all about the table, other diners in the elegant room standing and watching, bemused and horrified. It takes seconds for them to return to normal as I move on. The desperation, the chaos and frustration of trying to orchestrate something seem ironically underscored by the tenet of the song itself.

When "Ascent" begins to build from the ether and I recognize the synthesized chords building, it envelops me with a wash of peace, exactly as it does when I hear it in the world. I'm hovering over an immense playground filled with thousands of children, the sounds of their laughter and the screams of their interplay ceding the sound spectrum to the music. It's a scene I visit often; I love to hear the laughter of children, like the waves of an ocean. With the onset of Ascent, I realize that I want to change nothing, to have no effect on the dream as the music unfolds, and am surprised to see the children begin to rise and float into the air, like dandelion seed fuzzies wafting with wind currents, their arms outstretched. I watch their faces, reach out and brush against their hands, and do not disturb a single child on their ascent. I cannot help as I float among them thinking that this is the vision I might have wanted and subconsciously made happen; but I am caught up in the rapt visual spectacle. A thousand Chinese lanterns with windswept hair, big eyes and wide smiles, twirling, reaching, rising and disappearing into an ethos. When the song fades, I am alone and it grows dark. The lights of another distant city beckon. The city seemed to come out of nowhere. When the spectacle is over, I then revel in the silence, for a very long time; I am able to hover in midair and watch the world do nothing, nothing at all.

Bi-world Conversation

I coerced my girlfriend, Sheila, to wake up around 4am and start whispering to me. By 4am, my body would be in a completely relaxed wave of sleep and not as prone to jump into action. She wasn't to tell me beforehand what she would say, or do, only that she would whisper to me so that I could conjure her in the dream and see if what she said in my ear would also be spoken by her in the dream.

She leaned into my ear and whispered "find me." When I heard her voice in the dream, I was in a public square watching people from different time eras mingle and argue. I'd concocted the mashup of timelines, but wanted to see what kind of conflict or intrigue it would cause. I was caught up in a yelling match between a Roman centurion and a rotund businessman when I heard her voice. I looked through the crowd, wandered down the street and found Sheila sitting at a café, smirking at me.

"Where am I?" she asked in the world, but not in the dream. I whispered very softly back, "At a café."

"What am I wearing?" She was still silent in the dream, but her demeanor was clear; she knew what was happening, it was just as if she hadn't yet decided to participate. I was consciously trying not to manipulate her.

"A gold miniskirt and a loose tank with sequins. Your hair is pinned up. You are not wearing a bra."

"Don't forget the shoes."

"Looks like little boots. Green ones." I heard her disgust in the world and she smiled in the dream, an eyebrow arched.

"Find me some new shoes," she said, and her mouth in the dream said those words, as I heard them in my ear, in bed, her breath warm. It was almost like in a foreign dubbed film, slightly off sync.

I took her hand and led her around the city corner; there was a drugstore, another restaurant, and some clothing stores that looked like they might have shoes.

"Fly with me," I said. "You won't need any shoes."

"I want you to tell me what's in the biggest shoe store in your fucking dream." Her dream mouth did not say this. My dream self and my world lips were in sync. I didn't want our somewhat synced dream time to be wasted on shoe shopping, but the instructions were for her to tell me what to do. We went into the shop and two young women greeted us. They were dressed in skirt suits, like executives. I told her, described the multi-storied building, the racks of shoes. I told her to ask for what she wanted, since she couldn't see for herself. In the dream and in the world, she asked to see the most expensive shoes in the store (that figured). The store looked more like a shoe museum or emporium than a typical mall shoe store; if she were truly there, Sheila would have loved it. I already felt a pang of regret in this experiment; I wanted to strip down the suits on those girls and fuck them in front of those massive mirrors I saw down one of the long aisles. Sheila wanted details about what kinds of shoes the dream could conjure. The shorter girl brought us the most expensive pair of shoes and I described them to Sheila; a pair of spiked heels made of brown leather with small diamond studs where the stitching would be, as if they were somehow held together by diamonds.

"Put them on me," she said in the world, but not in the dream. I knelt and put the shoes on her feet, they fit perfectly. The dream Sheila did not move to look in the mirror, she just stared at her shoes.

156

I asked Sheila to speak to me more to see if her dream avatar could pick up the words in advance, but I could not anticipate her words and feed them to her. I took her into the city and described things to her, flew her up across the buildings, and we experienced somewhat synchronized lovemaking in a public fountain. The sensations her hands and mouth made me feel in my roused body in bed did not quite match the movements we were making in the dream, which was rough on the concentration. I came in her mouth in the world, but in the dream, I was inside her. She did not let me wake up enough to work on her own pleasure, joking that wearing the most expensive pair of shoes in the universe was pleasure enough for one night. After a short while, she mumbled some things here and there and trailed off.

You do not have to be biconscious to enjoy imaginative foreplay, but it gives everything a new dimension.

Waking up to go to sleep*

One can never shake Poe's line "all that we may see or seem is but a dream within a dream," so I thought I'd do something about it.

I thought for a time that it would be truly profound if, in the dream, I went to sleep to see if I could enter a new layer of the dream. Would it be the dream, or would I simply walk through some psychic back door and wake up?

In the dream, I lay back, go to sleep--a "state," not a true physical action, and wake up within a dream. I am aware that it is a simulated sleep as my dream body lay prone (being noncorporeal, the dream body doesn't require sleep for rest). I had flown into a large white house, into a tastefully decorated Victorian style room, through which I walked to the hall, which was miniaturized, like a dollhouse. I went down the stairs, noting the shine of the entryway chandelier, and walked into the downstairs parlor. A huge sofa was positioned near the fireplace, which was ablaze with a crackling fire. I went to the sofa and stretched myself out on it, closing my eyes, wondering if I could sleep within the dream. I felt myself slipping and soon gave way to sleep, or rather a minimized phase of consciousness. While asleep, I had a different dream. When I turned lucid in the second dream, I was instantly shocked back into the first dream and my eyes also opened in the world.

*I was inspired to do this by a Three Stooges comedy, where Curly is sleeping and snoring very loudly, and Moe smacks him and yells "hey you! Wake up and go to sleep!"

Transitioning Exercises

I have experimented with a way of transitioning my place in the dream, like teleportation or "phasing" as I call it. Though I can often shift scenery, morph buildings and even people, I wondered if I could almost "cut scene" to an entirely different location. The problem was always that I would feel the need to close my eyes to do this. Once closed and in the same darkness my world eyes beheld, control and lucidity within the dream environment could shift, degrade, or be lost altogether from the natural urge to phase back into the world. It took a great deal of mental practice to be able to close my eyes within the dream and reopen them to a new environment. I tried going from country to country, ecosystem to ecosystem, earth to alien planet, earth to outer space, night to day. I achieved this mainly when trying to replicate general locations I was familiar with (phasing from a typical Midwestern cornfield to Times Square, for example). What proved most difficult was returning to the same location. I have home constructs throughout the dream and environments or "cities" that I return to frequently, or inhabit regularly, but nothing is ever exactly the same. Objects do not always remain where I left them, people who inhabit those environments might change in appearance somewhat, colors shift and even entire buildings move around in some mirror image trickery or disappear and reappear altogether.

When I truly focused and concentrated on a familiar person or object, I could see the form take shape into my vision and expectation. It was not always perfectly realized in detail; but it was always true to my emotional calibration.

I developed enough discipline in phasing that I am usually able to briefly close my eyes, reimagine an environment, and appear there as if teleported. Sometimes I cannot muster a completely controlled lucidity to make a building or person appear before my eyes, but I can place them nearby, around a corner or behind a wall or on the other side of a hill, and I can walk or fly past the obstacle to see the person or object there.

Superhuman Exercises

Growing up with such an interest in superhero stories always spurred me to try to re-create super powers. Superman was always easy—flying, speeding, breaking through things, lifting heavy objects with ease, feeling no pain. Being the ideal and iconic all-encompassing superhero, pretty much all physical powers begin and end with him. There was no need in the dream to replicate the powers of Batman (unless you count his fierce mental determination and problem-solving skills) or Wonder Woman, whose powers nearly replicate those of Superman's. The Hulk is somewhat similar with the added fun of just letting your rage run amok and destroying anything in your path for the sheer sake of destroying it. Flash presented a quandary, mainly because if I were running or vibrating so fast as to appear invisible, it was just like shutting my eyes for an extended time and I could lose control over the environment or slip into the world again. Super speed seems superfluous in the dream, as there is never a need for rushing anything or getting anywhere fast when you have nothing to run from and nowhere particular to go. Green Lantern's ring is a cool construct, but again, when I have the power and will to create whatever I want, it seems silly to do it using a ring's projection. So alien powers and tech, superhuman strength, acrobatic agility and invisibility or mutant powers like stretching were a moot point in these exercises.

Most interesting and challenging were the mystic powers of characters like the sorcerer Dr. Strange, Dr. Fate or Zatanna, even cosmic mega-powers like Spectre or The Phantom Stranger. To make objects materialize or disappear, to hypnotize and control people, these were always easy since I was essentially the world's creator. Allowing huge creatures, mystical forces and evil-looking spectral entities into the dream and battling them is often fun.

The greatest and most complex issues of exercising "superhuman" abilities in the dream were the questions of how much control and authority to exercise in any given environment or over a given person or group of people. Appearing superhuman meant having that moral obligation, which is a complex issue of its own within the dream. Mostly, it was fun to re-enact a hero scenario and get grateful reactions from the dream denizens, even if you're not saving anyone.

Inhabiting Different Bodies

Even now, I am always most comfortable in my own skin, my own dream avatar being essentially my twin, but there was a time when I felt compelled to experiment with taking alternate forms of being.

In high school, I wanted to take a female body form, which was easy enough to do, though weird to look in the mirror. Touching myself in female form felt little different than touching myself in male form, a strange amalgam of the memory of my own flesh with the sensations that came from touching the body parts of the few girls I'd been lucky enough to touch intimately. But I had no internal physiological or sensory reference for a clitoral or vaginal sensation or orgasm, so was able to climax only through my imagination, giving me sensations not unlike the male orgasm, and only after several attempts.

I did attempt at other times to take the female form and have sex with a man. I experimented with a variety of female forms of shapely beauty, different weights, different hair lengths and colors and breast sizes, even different races in comparison to the man I would conjure to fuck me. Again, at best I was mimicking the sexual experience from a male point of view with the mask of the female body.

One of the experimental threads I was always most excited to work with has been taking the forms of certain animals, and even an inanimate object or two. I have often taken the form of wolves, bears, eagles, and other token animals that I've studied enough to gauge movement, sound and natural actions. It was easy to see how people throughout time could confuse the power of this dream shapeshifting with actual transformation, believing they might have been cursed (or blessed) by sorcery. True or not, Castaneda and others had plenty of stories of shapeshifting, and aboriginal histories are rife with such stories. I could relish the act of running as a cheetah or swinging like a monkey, even swimming like a dolphin; but since my sensory knowledge of the actual experience was sorely lacking, I have always felt I was cheating myself somewhat, and would return to human form. It's possible that even in the dream, we need certain evolutionary phases before we can truly create new modes of being and experience and accept them as a true experience.

Even with all my power within and over the dream, it is very hard to imagine taking a form beyond what I live with and experience in the world.

Projecting the Self

I wanted to see if I could take my conscious self, the self we feel centered from, and put it into another being or object. People often report in their recalled dreams that they were observing the dream from someone else's point of view, or even as an object. Shapeshifting enthusiasts claim to dream from the point of view of their totem animals. Of course, we cannot rely on the integrity of this inhabited person or object to represent the true nature of that individual or thing, and at least in my experience, no dream denizen looks at you any differently.

First, I tried to be a girl, which I've experimented with many times before. It's distracting for a variety of reasons, but I have done it a few times with mixed results. The most interesting projection I ever did was to place my POV in a park bench in a bustling park. The actual feeling of the exercise is more like I'm inhabiting a camera, since I had no reference for the inanimate existence, and it still felt as if I had a corporeal body somewhere. I could expand or narrow my vision to include a stereoscopic view of the entire park before me, or to zoom in on a person approaching me, then of course to watch them usually sit right on me. This is not as kinky as it sounds, and for me, zero pleasure was had in it. I could not translate any sensate reaction or feelings.

I would try to project myself into someone I was fascinated with—a lonely child on a street, a woman running after something, a man looking menacingly at a storefront. I saw through their eyes but could not inhabit the whole package with a reliable authenticity, and that fact pretty much broke down the experiment. Without capturing the true experience of that body or frame of mind, it was a futile exercise. I occasionally repeat this experiment in the dream, but believe it will be many years before I can master this type of skill.

Our experience in the dream is inherently tied to the self.

Shouting down Satan

This experiment was born from a desire to prove once and for all the nonexistence of evil entities, demonic spirits, psychic succubae and others that seek to damn one's soul. These very superstitious notions and the influence they held over human culture always bothered me, but only in the way that a bad horror movie might bother me. I wondered if I could evoke even my own ultimate symbolic representation of the most Evil one, and have some kind of epic battle of wills. I was raised that, if you do believe in God, then you must believe in the Devil. Well, I do believe in God—a creator, an origin beyond our understanding—and would never presume to be able to conjure even my own representation of the creator of all things; but I don't believe in a great Satan. Coming from living in two worlds at once, I can see how some people might consider themselves possessed, even be provoked to strange and bizarre behavior. But other than that singular pesky ghost that started my dream awareness as a child, I'd never encountered anything that made me believe there was a force beyond my own fear and my own ability to scare the shit out of myself.

In an empty city, at dusk, I wander; a sense of foreboding is everywhere. It's clear that Satan has come to hold dominion over the realm. I become aware of demons watching me from inside buildings, from behind the curtains of windows, snorting in derision. I do not believe in an entity such as Satan but am compelled to accept, for the moment, such an embodiment of all that is evil; the uncertainty perhaps comes from the desire to protect myself.

I follow a trail of countless, sneering demons—parts hyena, ape and gargoyle, jeering from the shadows, barely visible. At the entrance of a grand old theatre, a blank marquee emits a shuddering light. Walking into the dark lobby, I breathe in a terribly foul stench and think well that's about right I guess, still playing along and enjoying, for the moment, the B-Movie Hammer Horror theatre of it all. The lobby is covered with thick crimson drapes, old and musty and moving with a subtle, almost biological pulse.

Down the long aisle of the theatre, I'm aware that Satan is in the room, there's an instant electricity that instills fear in me, as if I could accept this is all real. It becomes an overwhelming, uncomfortable scenario (always risky in that it can erode the quality of lucidity). I recall that my mission in the dream game here is to face down the embodiment of all evil and see what transpires from the confrontation. I decide to wait for Satan to come to me. He does...cloaked in a massive black cape and hood, more a classic depiction of death, sans the scythe. At least I was not being ironic by making Satan a little girl, or a cute puppy. Still, walking up to face the pure embodiment of what most of mankind believes is the evil and enemy of all that is good leaves a daunting pitch to the atmosphere, and my lucidity in the dream falters a bit. Fear does manage to find a vein; what if? is all I can think of for a few seconds. It's that powerful. I have no true reference for what the face of Satan should be like—as depicted in horror movies, head of a goat or ram, that sort of thing? Handsome, rock star? No, doesn't fit with the cloak. He approaches and I stare into the dark recesses of his hood into a soupy, indeterminable swirl of darkness, synapses of fiery electric blood popping like stars exploding, some sulfuric scent hitting my nostrils. I smile at the familiarity of it all, the flood of references of the portrayal of evil from childhood bible stories and graphic horror movies. I wait for him to say something curious, threatening or profound, to grow immense like a dragon or Godzilla. It is, effectively, a stalemate. I continue staring into his facial galaxy; I tell him he has no power here; that he is a fiction I could wipe away with a swat of my arm. His arms rise and spread out from his solid, oaken frame, as if to clap my head in an embrace. I feel a rush of air and wince, bracing for the hit. I realize I could disintegrate him in an instant or turn him into a moth, but it's fun and challenging to let the mind unfold as it will, especially on this scale.

In less lucid moments of the dream in my youth, I had recurring visions of coming upon a massive grizzly bear in the forest; it put its eye on me and would charge. Though I could generally sense that this was not quite real, the visceral terror of being charged upon was enough to induce panic, and the physical body does not know the difference between the two. Facing down the king demon was a similar feeling, but I was fully lucid now, if not in complete control. There was a very brief temptation to just surrender to the mythos and see what happened—would it transform me, would it weaken me? I resolved further to shrink him down to the size of an M&M and squash him underfoot, but as his animal, guttural snarls filled my ears and his stench filled my nostrils, and a mesh of fear wrapped around me, I realized that was not the proper method for dispatching evil; do you not counter evil with its opposite—love and compassion?

I seemed compelled to play into the storied ideals of good vs. evil.

I wasn't about to hug this writhing form in front of me—I realized I was concentrating quite hard to keep him from growing larger. He was seething and spitting something about "I need only show you the truth to make you fall to me," and I realized the wisdom and truth of that statement. I shouted "you're right," and, filling my face with great dramatic flair and burning laser beams into the soupy visage of his face, added "BUT I MAKE THE TRUTH HERE AND YOU'RE NOTHING BUT BAD FICTION." I squeezed his form down, down, hunkering and quivering as he fought—and I did get the sensation that there was an actual entity battling my concentration—crushing the air around him until smoke drifted from his robe. For the first time, I reached out a hand and grabbed hold of the black cloth and yanked it, hard, and it took a few times to yank it off as if ripping a thick and dusty curtain from an old never-opened window. Beneath the cloth, I'd created a glowing butterfly, pulsing with light, and he alit on my finger. I was compelled to gently blow on his wings and send him up into the sky.
"I release you," I said.

PSYCHOLOGY

MENTAL CONDITIONS

Though I have not diligently researched the thousands of catalogued mental and physiological diseases, I can tell you from my experience, and from interviewing many victims of these diseases, that their roots (or progression) may well lay from within the dream, rather than from in the world mind.

Think of the diseases that are considered mental disorders, or psychoses. Take a trip through the current DSM (Diagnostic and Statistical Manual of Mental Disorders). In some, a chemical imbalance seems to be one of many possible culprits, which is why we treat many mental disorders with drugs. But drugs mainly mask the symptoms; they cannot necessarily cure the condition. Brain damage is sometimes found to be the cause. Scientists have mapped certain areas of the brain and what those areas are directly responsible for.

When it comes down to conditions of the mind, why do we not expend more research and energy on the other half of the conscious mind where we reside? Because money is meaningless there, and we like to be rewarded for our research efforts. The money is in behavioral science, not dream research. The dream is behavioral science; it just can't be captured in simple experiments or on secret video.

Here's a short list of mental disorders that could be affected by the dream:

Dementia
Delirium
Alzheimer's
Attention Deficit Disorder
Bipolar disorder
Obsessive-compulsive disorder

Schizophrenia
Depression

Paranoia
Autism (and a wide range of the Autistic Spectrum disorders, like Asperger's)

These are just a few examples. It is entirely possible that these maladies originate within the dream and manifest in the world mind.

It may even be possible that there is disease capable of forming exclusively within the dream that affects the dream mind; not communicable or viral or bacterial or cellular disease, but psychological disorders that may affect the mind exclusively in the dream and/or the world. Our mind, our brains, and our senses are the bridges between the world and the dream, and what affects one world will most certainly affect the other. The wide varieties of what most people would consider insanity most certainly have roots within the dream, and it is possible that most phobias do as well.

When we develop physical conditions, so many of them can be treatable from simple physical acts of discipline: lose weight, exercise, chew your food thoroughly, drink plenty of water, eat whole foods, and wash your hands frequently. We ignore and take for granted our body's amazing resilience and suffer the consequences when lacking some self-discipline.

I've published a few of my experiments on dealing with bacterial/viral illness from within the dream; how I would visualize the virus or bacteria as dark spongy growth somewhere within the dream (on a building, on a street, attaching itself to an object, sucking at it), eradicating it by blowing it away or taking a huge hose and washing it away. I achieved some success with this technique, reducing my usual sinus infections and seasonal colds to minimal durations. Because I thankfully have not suffered from anything more serious like cancer or other disease, I haven't been able to put that methodology to the test.

LUCIDITY IS NOT YET
CATALOGUED AS A
DISORDER OR DISEASE.

Mental disorders may also be treatable or preventable with concentrated acts of discipline, including lucidity within the dream or using visualization techniques particular to your own dream sensibilities. There are records that some people who begin to exercise mutual lucidity in the dream and the world can achieve a much greater control over compulsions that tend to turn destructive, such as overeating, gambling, or other risky "seven deadly sins" behaviors. I've long hypothesized that many compulsions (which can eventually become addictions) originate in the dream, where we are free to indulge our every whim. The atonia that keeps our bodies from enacting movement within the dream does not extend to our minds and behavior; without a measured lucidity and control, our actions in the dream have a powerful effect on our actions in the world. The barriers between the world and dream are thick for some, thin for others.

I can say I have never suffered from what might be called clinical depression, or delusions, or any discernible mental disorder (not saying I'm perfectly sane, either, but sanity is relative), though some doctors would define biconsciousness as a disorder. I have an outlet in the dream that few enjoy, and I believe the balance in consciousness provides for me the means of escape from a great many conditions. I do not feel trapped. I can, literally, battle my demons when I feel the need. Yet I have been diagnosed in my youth with attention deficit and autism. I am lucky that my parents were a) willing to take my word for it that I was fine, and they believed me, as long as the school work was done satisfactorily and I had a healthy attitude toward home and people, and b) not wealthy enough to throw any amount of money at forced drug treatments.

It has on more than one occasion been suggested that I may be some sort of savant; this "syndrome" which balances keen talents of focused hyperawareness with some form of deficiency in social tasking could indeed explain a lot of elements of my actions and reactions to things in the world and dream; but there is no test to prove what is already a greatly mysterious mental condition. Considering the amount of time we spend in the dream—conscious or not—savant is normal.

Lucidity is not yet catalogued as a disorder or disease. Should it? In between the world and the dream is thought, imagination, and the maddening, euphoric feeling that there is so much more.

PSYCHOSIS

Some studies are trying to link psychoses to the dream. It is a broad term for a range of mind-related problems from hallucinations and delusions to paranoia and even catatonia. I can tell you from experience that a psychotic episode in the dream can happen just as easily as in the world...but when I am fully lucid in the dream, I do not have psychotic episodes. True lucidity eliminates psychosis, though it can occur in either state when we mistrust our lucidity.

INDUCING DEATH

If you fall to your death in the dream, will you die in the world?

People still ask me this somewhat inane question; it is the scary myth that you think about as a child, and can never truly resolve.

An "afterlife" could well just be another state of mind, another mood, another dimension or phase. We theorize that the brain is the neuro-physiological-chemical housing of the mind and consciousness, but we are far from proving any such thing. We cannot know that if the brain dies, consciousness dies with it; so we created the notion of the soul.

I do often think of preparing myself for the eventual continuation of the dream without the benefit of a return to the body and the world mind. I am rooted in the quantum waves of the dream that may well be tied into the dark energy of the universe, and when the body fades, I imagine I will be able to make the final shift, to propel my consciousness completely into the dream. Whatever pain or residual effect from the cause of my death that the body resonates will subside, and I will be travelling alone between the corporeal worlds, the filaments of mind, soul and life just waiting to be turned back on when a new conduit presents itself. I wonder if people will be able to make this leap without the experience I've had, or if to them it truly seems they've gone to a heaven or hell, rather than just the next phase of conscious being, which they've had access to all their lives. For how long will one's self continue to ripple and reverberate through the dream field, before dissipating or being absorbed by other energies? How long can the conscious entity we are familiar with continue before evolving and transforming? If we are composed of the same minute particles and atoms that were spit out at the Big Bang some 14 billion years ago, how long will the same particles that have composed us and acted as conduits for our conscious abilities continue the journey? If the death of billions of bodies and billions of conscious selves has been recycled through the universe, what long dead radio waves have we been picking up on the quantum-psyche levels? If the dream is a psychic ether, then the brain is the modem/router that channels it into the computer-like mind and body.

I have at times been brave enough, at my most powerful and lucid in the dream, to attempt the act of suicide. I mostly tried "killing scenarios" when younger (specifically after reading Dostoevsky or Kafka), and quickly learned that I could do any number of terrible things to my body, but the spirit was filled with rescue. I could not shoot, fall, step before a train, or electrocute my dream body. Perhaps the inability to kill myself in the dream is because I have no experience dying.

The real advantage of these acts within the dream were in learning to brace myself for an impact, an impalement, a monster's fist in the face, an acid spread across my arm. I had to get creative sometimes, as a gunshot, knife stab or jump from a high bridge never worked. I could torture myself and erase the pain, mangle myself and re-form the body, but I could not find a way to die in the dream. Death in the world may be a one-way ticket into the dream, but death in the dream has proven beyond my capabilities.

I could not kill a body in the dream, because the body is essentially a holograph. How do you kill a spirit?

I began to wonder if I had the power to commit suicide by sheer mental exertion; by willing myself, under the crushing weight of responsibility, to succumb. When I lay alone in bed at night in a cheap motel, the phantoms of my failures encircle me, and my heart pounds as solidly as the drums of a native uprising; I wait for it to burst, for the flood of a heart attack to wash me in blood. The surge of every erratic beat bringing me closer to what I come to believe would be a true and lasting release...to transfer the pulse of my life-force from this shell to the dream shell without skipping a single beat. The heart pounds on and I lay stubbornly accepting this, refusing to talk myself down, building myself further into this frenzy. Though my body lay still and warm and protected, I am waging a war against it, against the weight of life, and my mental exertions stir whirlpools of activity in my heart and nerves that begin to make the bed shake.

This time, I think, I will walk through the door fully cognizant from this state to that, and I will never go back through. All that is needed is to release the final stage of fear, any fear that keeps me rooted in this bed. I will not shed this phase by the shock of a gun blast through my mouth, or even some pretentious freefall from a great height to simulate a flying experience and hope I die before I hit the cement; no, I will molt this consciousness willingly and lucidly.

There are two figures who appear in my dream randomly, almost always together. Though they take somewhat different forms, they are usually a man and a woman seemingly in their 20s or 30s. They fluctuate from attractive to plain-looking, are usually dressed casually, but always give me the distinct impression that they are watching me. These encounters are one of the few instances in my dream in which I am creeped out. I sense (or allow myself to sense) that they know more than I do. They have sat at cafes with me, walked with me in mega-bookstores and flow alongside me during storms. At times, they are completely nonchalant and offish, at other times they seem eager for me to follow them, which I can never bring myself to do. I have never in many years asked their names (I'm almost afraid to ask their names, to give them an identity—what would it matter?) and have never followed them; it's a distinct fear that by following them, I'd be leaving the world permanently behind. I've asked them what their intentions are and why they keep reappearing and have received mildly unsettling, potentially cryptic answers such as "always watching you," "you're very interesting to us," "we're just keeping an eye on you," "always wondering if you're ready." If I believed in the notion of the angel/demon (they must be one and the same creature), these figures would fit the bill. I once slammed the man through a museum exhibit and he simply smiled, amused. I had sex with the woman on a mountainous precipice and she reacted with studied patience, almost curiosity, as I pumped away at her and stared her down. I felt she could have disappeared but chose to stay. They are the only two figures in the dream who recur so frequently and seem so clearly to have their own agenda, which may or may not involve my death. I can control them, to an extent. They project a combined malice and compassion that provokes an imbalance in my sense of control. I both dread and desire what revelations they might bring one day.

Gardner Eeden just died. We have no clue what killed him. He just left.

ABERRATIONS

They who dream by day are cognizant of many things which escape those who dream only by night.
-Edgar Allan Poe

The lunatic is a wakeful dreamer. —Immanuel Kant

Extraordinary circumstances in the world can lead to further extraordinary experience within the dream; when you form an aberrant or unusual outlook on life in general, whether from mental or physical challenges or depravity, then it's likely that your perceptions are, by circumstance, honed very differently than the average person. It's as if you have access to many more channels (or many less). Circumstances push us deeper into our psyche than we know. Even Freud thought that psychosis was dream activity spilling into the waking state.

When working on my earliest research projects, I was pathologically impatient and resigned to my struggles and failures within the confines of academia. I could not secure funding for interviews with these unique groupings of people who might have some extraordinarily different experience with the dream. Over the past many years, I've worked slowly but steadily on fishing for the right subjects, weeding out the pretenders, and speaking with a select few people within each category. It was all done with volunteer subjects for my own edification.

Like most impersonal research done today, I started with each on the internet, engaging in occasional chats; most of the subjects approached me via forwards from some of my posts. Some I found through extensive searching and screening; trawling chat rooms and sites related to the category. When it seemed there was sufficient trust (for the internet), I either met with some during my infrequent travels, or met via online video chat. Some, I just knew from my online following. It's important to stress that these are not scientifically based, peer-reviewed studies. These are conversations and observations from a limited pool of subjects. A couple of topics, like schizophrenics and serial killers, I couldn't get access to subjects at all, but would still very much like for studies to be done there.

I am still looking to build my interview base with these subjects. Each door opens that room with so many other doors. Here are simple summaries of just some of the subjects and the questions that kept opening doors.

THE TERMINALLY ILL

When you are certain of your own death, does the mind begin a natural search for its next playground? Does the subconscious understand to begin laying the groundwork for a complete transition to the dream? The body may know when its demise is imminent; some subjects report an intuition they did not have before, a "general sense" that they would soon die. Of the few terminally ill people I was able to speak with, only one who reported this "intuition" was correct about dying within the week.

David O, an advertising executive in his sixties, was in late stage leukemia. His dream slowly became much more vivid, and he felt as if he was spending longer in the dream each night. He contacted me to help him achieve lucidity. I gave him some counsel in how to begin thinking about the dream and the possibilities of reaching some awareness within the dream.

David was not particularly religious and was not caught up in any constraining notions of what he should expect regarding an "afterlife" or of a heaven or hell. He was eager to hear of my experiences and was doing a lot of research online. I was a little worried he was trying to absorb too much, too quickly. Knowledge without experience can be mentally debilitating.
I must admit, every time I left his apartment (where he

was in home hospice), I felt some sense of guilt; what if I was wrong about everything? Was I consigning him to some folly regarding an ability to slip into the dream? I wanted him to have an original journey and was very honest about that. At the very least, he was wanting to believe in something, and this gave him far more comfort than abstract notions of angels and a promised land.

When he did not email me for an appointment, I worried he might have passed, and when I went to his apartment to check on him, the hospice staff was cleaning up. He'd passed the night before and his body had just been taken to the mortuary. He had no close relatives, only some friends from the agency, to which he'd devoted his life.

We are all terminally ill. Aging is an illness, a destruction of our cells. The dream is the only state in which we are not dying.

THE BLIND

Many studies of the blind have been done, regarding both those blind from birth and those who lost sight during and after childhood. Most of these studies show that their dreams reflect their sensory experience as it is. If they were previously able to perceive light, then light, shapes and abstracts figure into their dream. Those blind from birth tend to dream with the same sensory relationships in which they inhabit the world. It is only the arrogance of sight that tempts us to feel sorry for these people. When you have no visual framework to carry into the dream, the mind is free to take the vast sensory array outside of sight and create wholly new forms born from all senses, not just sight. The dream can twist and manipulate our perceived senses into something altogether more powerful.

Kelly, blind from birth, lives a very different reality than most of us. Now 24, she's formed a preternaturally strong buffet of sensual intelligence and a fervid imagination. She describes colors and "sees" lightness and darkness. Speaking with her, I got the sense that she is lucidly tuned into her world and dream environments, since they are much closer to each other than in ours.

"You suffer from blindness, too," she told me. "You can see me, but you are not seeing everything. You can see outside your body, but you can't see what I see inside."

Kelly was able to intuit things about me, about anyone she encountered, that few could know. This was not practiced in a "psychic" manner; she didn't touch a palm or ask leading questions. She wasn't taking stabs in the dark. She says she had developed keener senses of smell, of taste, and of touch. She ran a blog under the name "Kellen Heller," irreverently playing off the remarkable Helen Keller's legacy.

My interviews with Kelly quickly became tainted, from a scientific or sociological perspective, as we began an intense relationship that lasted for months before she moved to a new research center in Seattle, willfully and excitedly becoming a subject to test new advances in virtual reality technology for the blind. I was devastated that she could pick up and move on so quickly, but she maintained that nothing ever truly ended for her as she could relive and expand upon any experience. We corresponded, and I wrote to her for months with questions about the clinic and her experience there, but her responses become more and more cryptic and we lost touch.

PROSTITUTES

I spoke with several prostitutes and call girls about their experience, which is unique in their need to mentally and emotionally detach themselves from the physical body so often. I only engaged with women who worked independently, by choice, for themselves; I wanted to be sure body work was their conscious choice; anyone unfortunate enough to be unwillingly serving as a sex slave would have many other factors in their heads.

"Candace" worked in the Bay Area as an independent escort; she'd been working for nearly five years. She'd paid her student debt and was saving up for a house. Attractive, petite, bisexual, and smart, she knew what she wanted and had no illusions about what she was doing. She was pushing thirty and felt she'd be out of "the game" within a few years. She was interested in dreams (as well as a lot of other more distracting New Agey stuff) and followed my work, so I met her at a café near City Lights to talk.

Candace said that though she was usually very attentive to her customers, she had developed an ability to "float" just outside her body during sexual activity, as if she could "split in two" and be in two places at once. Several of the girls, but none of the guys, I spoke with said some version of this. Candace was especially adept at doing this with her frequent customers, because she knew their "rhythms" and could give them what they wanted while not getting attached to them on a physiological level. I asked her if that wasn't like marriage—similar, predictable sex with the same person, a familiar routine for the body in which the mind could not help but find an imaginative zone, the dream, in which to drift separately.

Candace was adamant that without her ability to drift into the dream during these encounters, she wouldn't be nearly as comfortable doing sex work. We spoke about how most people tended to disengage during sex—maintaining an inner fantasy even as the physical reality was happening, keeping their eyes closed so as to add strength to the inner fantasy rather than the outer reality.

PEOPLE ON HALLUCINOGENIC DRUGS

I willingly abandoned this research project, early on. Drugs of any kind bored me silly and though I had previously been fascinated with the ketamine and LSD studies of the early pioneers of "altered states of consciousness," I realized that subjects tainted by synthetic substances would yield no true, pure or verifiable information regarding our natural symbiosis with the dream.

You know by now that I loathe using artificial, chemical psychotropic drugs to find easier paths to a supposed altered state.

I spoke with stoners, drug researchers and junkies alike and found no credible instances of a deeper or more intense lucid state in the dream when under the influence of drugs. In fact, I began to wonder if the entire exercise of hallucinogenic drugs shackled the mind to the world, rather than freeing it to experience some heightened state.

The scary thing is that developers are trying to create synthetic drugs that do all sorts of things to the brain. A drug can only affect the brain chemically; it doesn't actually do anything to the mind itself. But the mind is critically aware of the brain's state, and the body's state, and when it is disrupted, the mind knows.

THE SUPER WEALTHY

There's a cultural connotation/connection between thinking of "the dream" and "to dream of," so when we think of dreams, we often think of aspirations, rather than a concurrent realm of existence. Freud long ago implanted the notion that "dreams" are wish fulfillments. And what do we spend our world hours wishing of more than getting rich?

When your daily world is freed from most any form of materialistic need or worry, does that alter the world/dream relationship? When you can freely indulge your whims in the world, how does that affect indulgences in the dream, where there is no currency, no concept of want/need, no imperative to pay bills and worry about financial survival?

I spoke with a handful of people who are well over the hundred million mark in personal net worth, and certainly the old adages are true, that money alone can't buy happiness; but it can buy a peace of mind that the poorer percentage of people do not always have. And though most of the wealthy I spoke with certainly worked hard not only to maintain and grow their wealth (only one individual was a "trust fund baby"), they were able to enjoy a leisure that most of us never truly experience. In the end, my interviews with them did not single out any reasons why money might have given them a richer dream world. But, it certainly seems to be making their world a lot dreamier.

THE HOMELESS AND DESTITUTE

When your entire day is a struggle for material survival to meet basic needs, how does that affect the dream? Is activity in the dream more of a fantastic escape or does it tend to reflect the harsh realities of the day?

For many destitute persons, the word "dream" is completely synonymous with "hope." I fed a few homeless people dinner one week and interviewed them, individually, about sleeping and dreaming.

One thing that truly surprised me was that some of them kept talking about what a great freedom they had; not beholden to any financial obligations, debts, rents, or, for some, relationships. Most of their day's thoughts and fantasies revolved around having sufficient security and

enough to eat, and their memories of any dream fragments were, for the most part, about relationships. Every one of them with one exception reported that sleep
was often fitful, depending on whether or not they had
a familiar spot; and that shelters, which would seem to
offer the most security, were, the least secure.

PUBESCENT KIDS

It has always been fascinating that one of the most recognizable signs of our emerging sexuality comes through
the dream (the "wet" dream for boys and girls). I wanted
to research the months preceding and immediately after
the wet dream phase for pubescent teens. How valuable
would it be to truly understand the onset of the mind/
body - world/dream connection as it develops into one
of our most crucial life functions?

Try to get a kid to talk honestly about their growing,
shifting sexuality—a period of life often wrought with
anxiety, fear, dread, wonderment, a cacophony of emotions. It's one of the most volatile stretches of our lives,
and the dream is usually the first testing ground for our
most vital functions, physically, mentally, and emotionally.

I put out a note to a few followers who I knew were parents of pubescent-age kids, and asked if they minded if
I had a frank conversation with their sons and daughters about sexuality in their dreams. These progres-
sive-minded parents didn't have a problem with me
interviewing their kids and even insisted they not know
the information ("treat it like a counseling session, confidence and all," was the general attitude).

So I got to sit down privately with a couple of thirteen and
fourteen year old girls and boys. I asked whether they
had recurring dreams with sexual activity and whether
or not they were sexually active in the world. Only one

boy had been active in the world, but just general fooling around. I was keenly aware that none of the teens I spoke with were 100% candid with me—there's just too much immature embarrassment or shame connected to the very idea of it (despite the fact that all these teens were raised in fairly liberal, open-minded households). But I came away with a few observations, not the least of which was that the girls seemed to have recurring experiences with a fixated crush (one they knew in the world, and at least one or two actual celebrity-types who they could only "dream" about), as opposed to the boys, who could be excited by almost any girl. So the girls would dream about a person, whereas the boys would dream about an act.

All of them felt they had at some point become lucid in the dream, and that it had been connected to a sexual act or possibility in the dream, because it didn't feel quite "right." The fact that they'd had no experience in the world negated any confidence or clarity they could have about imagining what it could or should be like in the dream. I couldn't really eke out specific descriptions of what they saw, did, or felt done to them.

SCHIZOPHRENICS

Any biconscious person, or any person who has had experience with true lucidity in the dream environment, knows that there are an infinite variety of representations of one's self. There have been many studies done of schizophrenia, a condition which could be described as living constantly in two worlds (or more), with one world commanding the stage and relinquishing the stage to the other. I wanted to closely study those most extreme cases and look for similarities with my own biconsciousness. Schizophrenics may simply be unable to distinguish between the world and dream; how many are there who could use guidance in becoming lucid as a means of more effectively controlling and/or engaging their personae?

I could not get access to committed schizophrenics, unfortunately; a blog and a book apparently aren't good enough credentials to get inside the mental health facilities system.

It is likely that a great percentage of psychoses and mental conditions such as autism, schizophrenia, Alzheimer's and others are directly connected to the dream's incredible influence over the world and how our perceptions can be trapped between them. Yet the majority of research for these conditions goes toward drugs. Because drugs create money.

PATHOLOGICAL CRIMINALS

This was to be a study of violent criminals, repeat offenders who crossed the line from crimes of passion, need or want to crimes driven by extreme violence, power and pathological sickness, people who seemed to harbor an immunity from any moral sense in the world. Was their interaction with the dream pushing them, justifying their actions in the world? Would those who claimed they were compelled to commit their crimes because of "a voice in my head" or "God spoke to me" be willing to explore the origin of that "voice" through the dream?

I would not consider any subjects whose crimes were committed under the influence of drugs. I am also fascinated by the possibility that someone locked in solitary confinement, with little or no interactivity with other people, might begin to see some blurring of the lines between the world and the dream, perhaps a necessity to survive the days of torturous loneliness.

ATHEISTS & FUNDAMENTALISTS

I lump the two groups together on purpose, because either group's fervid and unshakeable belief in their own absolute truth regarding a being (or nonbeing) of which they have absolutely no knowledge is one and the same condition. This study was close to my own heart for a lot of reasons, not just my upbringing, but from a deep belief that science and religion are the same thing, just searching for answers to our creation and destiny via different mechanisms. I wondered if there would be similarities or connections in their dreams.

Atheists, largely science-based in their approach to the dream, generally tend to believe that consciousness is seated in the brain, and therefore the dream is a product of neural pathology. Some would not deny a certain spiritual aesthetic in the workings of the dream, but gave little significance to the dream as anything more than the mind, acting more as a supercomputer, shuffling and "defragging" memory segments as a method of self-maintenance.

Fundamentalists tend to think the dream is a possible means of communication to and/or from God, or a tool of temptation. Not a one of them I spoke with would believe that it was a co-existent state, mainly because there had been no such description in the Bible. Idealistic rigidity kept both from being much more curious about the possibilities of the dream and how they might use it to explore their science or their faith.

BICONSCIOUS IN A DAY

I've been asked that if I were to keep a journal of events in the dream and the world as I experience them simultaneously, what would it look like?

Consider your day. You wake up, probably gaze out the window at the "real world." Cars go by, neighbors move around outside. Then you move into another room with a different feel, a different light, and relieve yourself. You check a screen, which thrusts you into a different layer of the world—stories, snippets, videos, short bits of digital breakfast. You might exercise, shower, feed yourself, servicing the body and its needs, but your attention is increasingly pulled, like gravity, to some responsibility, task or chore—maybe knowing you have to go to work or run some errands. You get into a car or bus, it moves and the world transitions before you. It's all familiar, drone-like, until you see something of noteworthy difference; it gets filed into the subconscious, just like all the mundane details. Or, it may get played out in the dream, churning into some alternative scenarios affected by your current disposition. Your day is one of constant transition and various channels flux between attentions to mind, then body, then consumed by story, then activity unfolding before you. Things you understand and things you do not understand. This is exactly what happens in the dream, but usually without any sense of control.

You can be passive, or you can be directive. Everywhere now, screens. Screens that take us further in layers of attention and perception, further into manufactured dimensions and augmented realities. Screens, like hallucinogenic drugs, are just simulated windows. Your mind stretches between the stories of television, the stories on your tablet, and the touch of

your partner next to you, the taste of your tea on your

tongue.

So it is that we build a day of myths, stories and uncertain perceptions, built upon narratives that have been woven throughout our entire lives. At the end of the day, we care or don't care; perhaps both positions coexist equally.

Thoughts are rarely, if ever, completed. We begin a thought but don't always follow it through. We get distracted; other thoughts cross into new tangents, splinters and side tracks. Considering our entire day of consciousness is 100% filled with thought, that's a lot of distraction. You are already biconscious to some degree, flowing from a world in a screen to a world in front of you.

The dream is no different, except that our thoughts are visualized; a thought becomes its own world, with its own actions, on top of which our dream mind is still thinking thoughts within those thoughts.

Look at yourself in a series of angled mirrors and you see an infinite number of selves. Take the mirrors away, and the infinite selves are still there.

The day's conscious pull is very different for me. I can drift in and out of the dream and the world, sometimes bring them into alignment. In either world, extraordinary events repel the mundanity of the other, and sometimes quiet meditations can unite the states. The worlds are keenly aware of each other, sometimes supportive and sometimes combative. At times, one world calls for my attention and the other is content to idle. Then there are times when both worlds scream for my lucid involvement at once, like combative twins.

*In the dream, I've been flying through an old abandoned
city, with run down facades, trash-strewn streets, a musty
odor, and the occasional feral dog barking. There is a
low-voltage hum in the atmosphere, something I often
hear; sometimes it's as if the dream were all a huge
industrial factory or movie set, and other times it feels
more like a larger presence surrounding the dream with a
droning air. I fly into windows and walk through
apartments, which are very neat and tidy and upscale, as
if the interiors of a ritzy high-rise condo. People are
ignoring me for the most part, unless I harass them. In
front of an older couple, I walk through their living room to
a set of glass shelves, on which are displayed Hummel-
like figurines, but they are not Hummels, they are
cartoonish figures of animals engaged in overly cutesey
acts of love, with one or two in some perverted sex
positions. I look at the lady, assuming it is her collection,
and throw them to the ground at her feet, smashing them
one by one for the pleasure of it, and finally I just make
them all explode in place and the shelves with it. The
woman looks only slightly upset, the man is a bit bemused.
I hear a duck-quack of an alarm going off and know that
it is my real world alarm. It's hard for me to turn off direct
input from the world,* so I phase into it and shut it off. The
sun is streaming through the window with tiny streams of
dust particles following the rays down to my covers. I
move through my apartment and *the dream apartment* at
the same time, entering a bathroom. In the world, I pull
the front pouch of my underwear down and take a piss
into the toilet. *In the dream, I can still feel the stream of
piss going through one of my most sensitive body
passages even though I am not urinating there, I am
going through the medicine cabinet of the elderly couple;
it is filled with vials and prescription bottles for drugs I
have never heard of: cloxoproof, dimentasic, damitol. I
wander down the hall, noting that the carpeting is more*

189

plush, almost overgrown like grass, and open a bedroom door. A young woman sits on her bed, as if expecting me, or perhaps just not surprised to see me. She's dirty blonde, looks to be in her late teens or early twenties, though age does not matter here. I'm finishing my piss, tap tap and shake, up the underwear, turn to the sink, water on full, cold, I fill the blue cup on the sink and drink deeply. *Hands are sliding through the girl's hair, she looks up at me, curious and expectant. I feel the phantom rush of cool water down my throat. I don't feel a full-on energy to lay her back and fuck her, but I want to touch her; my hands slide to shoulders, breasts and hips. I ask what are you doing today and she immediately answers "the rose bowl," though I do not ask whether it was a sports event or a gardening chore. Look what I can do, I say, as I lean back against her bedroom wall so hard it begins to crack until it splits open and warm light pours in* as I walk through the warmly lit kitchen, putting coffee into the preset filter and turning on the machine. I pull two English muffins out of the orange bag on the counter and pop them into the toaster, get a tub of butter from the fridge as *I'm hovering in the air just outside her bedroom, she looks with mild amusement at my flotation and I'm wondering whether I'd like her to join me or whether I should move to new space* schhhtaak! The muffins pop up and my nostrils are filled with the nostalgic scent of toasted bread, I put on the butter and set it on the table by the window. I'm enjoying that it is a Saturday morning on which I will not be going in to work and will be able to take a ride along the lake if it's not too windy, I glance out the window and don't see the trees blowing too furiously though *the few sparse trees in the dream have begun to blow, and they do so almost frighteningly as if an invisible tornado were approaching, one breaks off and heads toward me, but I step back in the girl's room to let it pass. She is putting on pants, I tell her not to do that and she complies as I fly backwards, with a smile, back over the war-torn city. I'm in the mood to explore, seeing as in the world I'll be sitting reading news for a while with my coffee, so I can fill out the dream a bit more, realize more potent details such as the way some human figures are staring at me through the busted windows as I glide by. My eye catches the tallest building in the distance, with a penthouse atop that looks very out of place in its surroundings, so I whoosh up to it and land on the patio, where a table is set with breakfast. The setting is for three, but I don't see anyone. The view is spectacular, even though I realize I could change it to any view, any height I desire, I am often grateful that my mind creates it all for me to change or enjoy, as is, such as the arrangement of clouds in the sky; I will away the wispy clouds for a full bright morning sun to match the world's, even though it is not the world's sun. I study the plates* goddammit they put raisins in these muffins—I get up to check the package, I just bought the wrong package, they look so much alike and I don't like to seem too indecisive in the grocery. I put the muffins aside, refill the coffee and settle back down to get through the business section, which I always feel obligated to read even though I have no investments and work for myself. *There is an oatmeal-like cereal in one of the bowls, I put my finger into it and taste it, it is sweet but with a hint of whiskey flavor, and I think that would make a popular breakfast food in the world. A man emerges from the kitchen onto the patio, seems genuinely surprised but pleased to see me and invites me to sit down and eat with him. I decline to sit down, but smile at him and gesture for him to sit and eat, and ask "are you alone?" "Never," he responds as if I'd been accusatory, and his tone sets me off just a bit, so I hurl one of the plates off the top of the building and wait to hear it smash on the pavement below, but it doesn't. I levitate into the air a bit, I am always doing that in front of dream denizens because sometimes they seem in awe of my flighty power but many times they treat it as if it's perfectly normal even though they can't or don't do it themselves.* In the paper, I read that Russian hackers have stolen the passwords and records of tens of thousands of customers from a major retail chain and *the man starts taking on a more Slavic form, a bit sinister. I physically pick him up a foot off the floor, he protests, but not violently, and I throw him over the edge, turning my attention back to the penthouse. Like the plate before, I do not hear him, neither screaming nor splatting, and for all I know he disappeared as soon as he was out of my view. I could look down over the edge and clearly see his body, or not; it's a Schroedinger's Cat kind of thing, the results of my actions are the cat, they could be in two states at once until I observe them in one or the other.* I feel a tinge of guilt for the connection between the news story and my treatment of the denizen, but I'm just trespassing in my own backyard, really. *I go into the penthouse via the open kitchen and observe its elegantly appointed décor. Feeling a bit more lustful now with some breakfast in my world body and when I walk into the large bathroom, there is mist in the air and a middle-aged woman facing the beautifully lit mirror, wiping off steam, looking at my reflection. You killed my husband, she says with some European accent, and I say "yes," feeling a lot like James Bond. She turns, I press against her, my clothes come off with little complication—even fully lucid, buttons can be pesky--and we have sex, me and this Sophia Loren-type; sometimes people can shift image a bit during sex, especially when you are close upon them and can't see their whole visage, as I am concentrating so willfully on the act itself, and in less lucid moments, they can change form altogether, but I'm not distracted at the moment and orgasm quickly* gripping the table, briefly, pausing, closing my eyes to help deepen the intensity in the dream. Though in the world I feel an echoed, intense reverb of the orgasm, I do not experience its residual effects, which is good as I won't have to change my pants so often as I did in my teens and twenties. Phone buzzes on the table, it's B, wondering if I will be biking the lake today which I most certainly will be, especially if that promises to involve the same thing it did when I biked with her last week; B is a very independent girl, smarter than me, a bit of a stunner when the pretentious alt-goth dressings come off, a quick study and funny as hell. Not my girlfriend, but a FWB was our unspoken, mutual understanding, and I tell her I will see her at the boathouse in half an hour, my enthusiasm fueled by *still being inside the nice European lady in her bathroom. I ask the woman's name and she says Veronique, which of course it is in my Bond-inspired scene. Well I'm going to call you Bette, I say, because I'm more of a Betty man than a Veronica man, but I'll keep that French thing going. Conversations with females in the dream can be the most complicated, since for years in the world I conditioned myself to a post-coital sensitivity to make sure I was present for a girl if she wanted to talk or spoon or whatever, even if I really just wanted to nap or read something, so in the dream I kind of wait, stay inside the girl, see where her demeanor goes even if it is just my demeanor all along, I surprise myself sometimes. Now Bette gives me a vibe that she's in a bit of a hurry to get ready for something, so I pull out and step back, run my finger over the softening shaft and smell it, it is always surprising what kind of scent arises from dream couplings, just like in life but more exotic, hers is tangy with a hint of citrus. Sometimes I imagine scents that wouldn't occur in the natural world, a hint of spearmint, maybe, or of freshly mown grass. I concede those choices to the flow of the dream rather than lucid choice. And so our vast catalog of senses rotates.* Solid black t-shirt for biking on a spring day? No, gotta go with blue, and the brown shorts, though it's barely shorts weather out there. Wrinkled, but pressed shorts are so metro. Keys. Bike lock key. Money, we'll get some lunch or something. *I'm already out the window and flying over the city again, it's changing, slowly becoming more suburban, more lush and green, the lakes and ponds are sun-dappled and there are sounds of life. Motors, children playing, a leaf blower somewhere. I look back; the war-torn districts are still there, receding. Sometimes it changes. I'm going to let the dream flow for a bit, I swoop down into a city fountain, all the kids laugh at me, I emerge, totally dry, and sit on the edge, I want to watch them play* as I carry the bike down the steps and onto the street riding towards the boathouse in Lincoln Park. Don't want to be too caught up in the dream as I'm navigating the city streets, Saturday traffic. *Curly headed girl's just staring at me, intensely, some kind of ironic smile on her lips, she's observing me and I don't want to stop her* at the same time the mail truck swerves just off lane enough, I was in his blind spot, I smack into the right side of the mail truck and hit the pavement hard, trying to stop myself with the right knee and right hand but my shoulder takes the brunt of it, fucking ow ow, a brick of smoldering pain in my arm and *I put my shoulder into the fountain and turn the water black with the pain, make it boil, leech out the pain, turn it into fizz that evaporates in the air, and the damn girl is still watching, with a "good trick mister" expression, she knows, she's one of those independents and I have to ask her* hey man, are you OK? I'm so sorry man, you were in my blind spot, stay put, I'll call an ambulance, already on his cell phone. I look at my arm, red blotchy marks with little oozes of blood, but the pain is minimal now no, I'm OK, really—my bad, just got distracted—really, I'm OK. No worries. I get up to show him, Latino man in a mailman uniform, genuinely concerned, two hipster passersby standing just off to the side wondering if this will require their involvement. I put my hands up in the universal everything's fine manner and laugh a bit. Driver, visibly relieved, says I got some Band-Aids in the truck man, we can clean you up or something, and I think well I'm not far from home, I could just go fix it up there, but aside from a nasty bruise this will be fine, and the pain is pretty much gone, *still sizzling in that fountain and the girl won't stop staring* so I back away, pull my bike up to the curb, it's six blocks to the boathouse. This is where whatever autism level I have really kicks in, because I want the world to make some decisions for me, I want to coast a bit and for the wound to go away so I can continue riding. No, it's good, really, sorry to scare you…thanks for stopping. I'm cool. And I'm on my bike, wobbly-riding down the sidewalk until I get my balance back and swerve around the corner, narrowly missing a group of teen girls and an older woman drafting behind them. I'm able to cross the street without waiting and ride the rest of the way through the park where errant Frisbees and unleashed dogs will be my main concern. *How old are you I instinctively ask this girl, putting my hand in her curly mane and playfully messing it up. I'm OK, really, she says sing-song like, mocking my verbage from the world. What's your name I ask? Joan of Arc she lilts, emphasizing the Arc heavily. Well, Joan of Arc, I'm going to call you Joan of Park because that's where I met you. Do you want to fly with me a while? I'll race you. She stomps her foot and shouts can't fly! I laugh at her, I love these Peter Pan moments. I take her hand and we rise up, off the ground, her trailing beneath me, silent in her wonderment and fear. The world taboo creeps into my head* you're flirting with a child I think, *I could morph her into an older girl, but there are times when I like to let the spirit take precedent over the form of it. I pull her up parallel to me and rush faster, up into the sky.* Close to the LSD now, traffic rushing by on a Saturday, the rumble of trucks all amplified by the underpass echo and *I let the storm clouds gather rapidly, feel the electricity in the air, winds quickening, lightning around us, rain pelting us, a chill to the air, the rumbling of those trucks magnified as thunderheads. If I were feeling cruel, I could drop the girl and tell her to fly on her own, but whether I am feeling her dependence or my own, I keep her hand in mine and fly toward the nastiest looking cloud in front of us, closer, closer* on the other side of the LSD I see B in the distance, down by the pedestrian path, paused with her nose in her phone, wearing her black bike helmet, now taking a selfie until she sees me, waves, goes back to her phone. *Joan of Park is unsettled but I say to her this is as exciting as it gets, girl, and turn around, pushing backwards into the violent black cloud and emerging into clear blue sky on the other side.* Hey vision in black I say to B, who does not reach in for a friendly kiss, just a knowing glance. She puts her cell phone in her bag. Which way today? Let's go down the lake, let's be brave I say. So, into the Saturday crowds then. I think of when I met her at the bookstore, the first time we had sex, in my apartment right in front of the open window, as if it were just the thing to do, no hang-ups, no declarations of love, just a snack for the body. *With little miss Joan of Park dissolved into the ether, I pause in the silence, hovering between black clouds and fury on one side and bright sun and calm on the other, I positioning myself, hovering, half in the storm and half out, feel the rumbling in the left side of my body and the warmth on the right. I glance down, a mile down, fields and farmhouses, an occasional car and truck moving along roads to nowhere, or everywhere. I point my body downward and take a hard, fast dive to the ground, rising up to me, I'm a bullet, steeling my mind for the impact and the give of the ground as I bore through it* weaving around bike and pedestrian traffic at full speed, catching up to B, who's relentless, glancing back to see if she'd lost me, she loves the chase, but I'm gaining on her, people are moving aside, roller-bladders weaving off our path, an annoyed stroller mom or two throwing a nasty glance at us, but we don't care on this day, these actions are the rippled echoes of fucking *concentration wobbles a bit when you're grinding through solid ground at the speed of a locomotive, and there is always the risk of getting stuck, but I'm mentally girded and continue through rock, dirt, burrowing into a vast, cavernous pocket filled with twinkling lights like an underground city out of Jules Verne stories, I've been here before or it seems I've spent time here, there's an emotional gravity surrounding me, but I don't want to slow down and explore, I'll come back to this place or a place just like it soon, I follow the buildings of light along the embankments of a rushing river and everything becomes more epic, the waterfall that must drop to the center of the earth, mist in the air now, drone-like things the size of toasters, I did not conjure them, are flying and darting around me and* we're finally off the pedestrian and bike paths and onto city streets, where she has to stop at a light and I pull up right beside her and snap the spandex band at her waist, she gives a yelpy squeal that fills my ears, fills my lungs, fills me with lust. Hey, let's hit the MCA, I say. I want to stare at overpriced thoughts. Buy me an iced mocha, she says, and I'll consider it. The light changes, we cross the street walking our bikes and veer off Michigan Avenue at Walton to stroll our bikes the rest of the way down to the museum *still shooting at full speed, if a building or object appears in front of me, I smash through it with ease, an immense rush of power that's unstoppable, faster, faster to a blinding light ahead, an immense, gaping hole in the side of this cave, through the opening into empty space, thick clouds or foggy mist below, further down to where you have no bearings as to how far you've gone, up, down, it's all one direction, I hover again like an Olympic diver just off the springboard, and zoom at full speed, down into a surprise even I can't see coming, these are exhilarating Superman stretches, having complete mental confidence that no matter what your mind throws at you, you can tear through it with no resistance and* I walk a bit slower, *as I'm moving faster in the dream and concentrating on the rush of total power I must* move carefully through the obstacles of the city streets You OK there Gardner? She says, quizzical glances to me, I'm fine, I say, minimal words because I do not want to stop the rush, *boring through earth and sky and now free fall, you reach a point where you wonder if you should concentrate on making something appear, some guideline or sightline, this is where the mind can play tricks on you, you can psych yourself out, lose confidence, your speed and power and freedom vacuum-sucked away, but I maintain the speedforce, increase it, still seeing nothing but feeling everything, certain I will move through even the worst traps my deep mind can produce, tinges of dread creeping in* Really Gardner, you're OK? You're freaking me out babe, I'm moving slowly on the sidewalk and trying to hold onto my bike, she reaches out to grab it, leans the bikes against a fence and puts her hand to my arm to steady me, I'm trying not to focus in the world, *keeping to the slipstream in the dream, like riding a wave of green lights on Broadway the length of Manhattan stop thinking about Manhattan Gardner, empty the mind and rush, just rush, you're traveling the distances of entire planets in seconds, there are flashes of light and pockets of darkness and you can't imagine what shape you want them to take, this is the elevator to God and you just can't stop it or taint it with bias, if I rush like this much longer I will lose consciousness in both worlds and black out, I've done it before and this is not a good place, don't freak out the girl any more, she doesn't know the whole truth of the*

198

dream world thing, feeling a chill in the rushing air now, temperature is a bad thing as it makes emotions and memories spread like a flash fire, keep concentrating Gardner, this is a pocket between the dream and the world, don't talk, don't talk, rush, I don't feel my skin, my body, no sensation of wind, B is pulling out her cell phone and a couple passing by ask if everything's OK, they're going to call for help, *goddamnit just break it feel nothing but the memory of air in my face, I slow, the clouds clear out, I tense, resisting a momentum that shouldn't exist in the first place, I reach a hilltop looking over a vast verdant field, a fucking epic Van Gogh painting of fuzzy yellow flowers, I slow it, slow it, and drop to the grass, grateful that breath in the dream is mimicry* Don't call, I'm fine, I'm OK, just lost my train of thought for a minute, I'll explain later—really, I say to the couple and others who have gathered to watch this reality show, it's cool, I hold my hands up as if being arrested, my world brain is still reeling from the rush of the dream, but most importantly B's hands are around my waist and I am breathing her in, a faint perfume of sweat and pheromones that pulls me in, *from over the top of the hill marches Joan of Park, she says in her nastiest most victorious shriek "I beat you, hah!"* Explain what? B asks, almost annoyed about the scene. Well, it sounds—and is—crazy but I was trying to do a distance record in my head, not really distance, more like...endurance. It's all good, I kiss her on the forehead, how about that coffee. You sure you're ok, she says again, her hand pressed into my chest, your heart is racing like off the charts. I lean over and rub my eyes, hard, fists pressing into my eyelids, friction and warmth, swirls of colored patterns exploding like a kaleidoscope, and *in the dream the patterns fill the space in front of me, become larger, taking on a life of their own and floating up to the sky, battalions of static shapes before me and around me, like fireworks.* Totally good. I get on my feet, shake it off, in an exaggerated way to elicit an uncertain chuckle from her, and pull my bike up. Let's walk the couple blocks to the café. She picks up her bike and we walk down the street, absorbing the sounds of the city. *I tell Joan of Park to watch the fireworks, and she sits down next to me, smoothing her suddenly color-swirled dress out beneath her, and for a moment she's like a wondrous, curly-haired, blue-eyed ideal child in a commercial. I let the solitude, the patterns, and her amazement be a meditative balm for a little while, looking from her eyes to the patterns and back. It enables me to* enjoy the stroll with B until we enter the café to a line of about 13 people, roll our eyes and say screw it and head down to the museum. I'm more careful in our walk, guarded as to avoid bumping into people or objects and rousing suspicion of being on drugs, or just being an idiot overall, and so *the dream loosens and meanders, shifts out of my control for a while and crosses scenes like blurry channel-changing*, and when B and I stop at the last intersection to cross to get to the MCA, *in the dream I find I am teaching a class to about 20 or so students of all ages, we are standing around the classroom in a brightly lit contemporary high rise building, evoking more of a newsroom feel, looking into television monitors that are hung from the ceiling and we have been trying to get ladders up to the monitors so we can see the images up close. With strengthening lucidity, I realize I'm teaching a course in some kind of computer programming, which I know nothing about, but they are very curious where I'm going with the whole climbing-the-ladders-to-see-the-monitors-more-closely thing. I look into the screens, which seem to be displaying the same image with slight variations, of swarms of insects—cockroaches, bees, and such—and I grin at the students and say "computer bugs," then I tell them all they pass with flying colors and then myself fly out the window, I always love the sensation of leaving a room of baffled dreamizens in a spectacular fashion. Of course I'm wondering if the dream conjured images of bugs solely so that I could deliver such a bad pun—well, two bad puns if you count the "flying" comment. I briefly regret not staying with the class to see where I would consciously take them but know it would probably end up with some variation on naked mid-air yoga, and besides there's a huge gleaming white building in the distance and I know exactly what it is, it's the art museum, vastly bigger than the one before me in the world, as* B and I lock our bikes and jog up the steps to the entrance *I am flying down to the valley where my dream museum sits and I know exactly what I am going to do there.* We flash our membership passes, check our helmets and head straight to the modern art wing to see the same paintings and exhibits we've seen often enough before. *In the dream, I crash through the huge glass opening of the building, three story tall plate glass windows that shatter spectacularly at my violation, and I revel in the instrumental sound of the glass hitting the concrete floor there, visitors ducking pieces and running short stretches until they completely normalize the way they do in the dream, because I don't feel like monitoring their emotional behavior at the moment, opting instead to fly through the corridors to that one room where they display the Dalis, the Magritte, Surrealistic schlock and awe. I could enter the paintings, change their colors, talk to the spectral visage of each artist, but I bide my time until* B and I arrive in the same room together, pausing, sitting on the fake-leather bench in front of the huge textured untitled Rauschenberg black hole, the soul-sucking "I could do this with enough black paint" canvas that most people will claim is something abjectly profound. I look around because it is time to play one of my favorite games, though it will be more complicated with B here, so close to me. There are twelve people in the room and I am in luck, next to the Magritte is a petite dark-haired round-glasses-wearing college-aged gamine, studiously absorbing the hat, the train, the fireplace, in some dreamy place of her own. I wait until she turns and I see her face fully; it is perfect, she even glances at me and off again so now I will do what I call "phase-in-place," in the dream *I am in the exact room I inhabit in the world, with the same people, though variations and fluctuations occur, I am fixated on the girl and while B and I have an excuse to sit quietly and ponder the ebon gateway, I hover above the girl, she notices, and I move down upon her swiftly, almost like I'd imagine a vampire would move; she's not surprised or repelled, big accepting green eyes all over me, I take off her glasses, rip off her vest and Bowie tee, requisite black bra, pull the skirt down, the tights, and let my hands move over her body as if covering it with invisible paint. Shoulders, through the hair, the neck, the small breasts, back, hips, thighs, I lift her up, into the air with me, and lay her down on the same fake leather bench as B and I sit, contemplating silently, and fuck her with every ounce of existential lust I can muster in two worlds. This phase-in-place is very much the sensation of déjà vu, I feel it in both the dream* and world body, reach out and take B's hand, gently, to feel the sensation of female skin in both worlds; she does not reject it. Sometimes it's hard not to mimic my dream movements with my world body, I feel a compulsion to stretch out on the bench on top of B, but the game is to maintain world composure *despite the spectral feral sex happening in the middle of the room; denizens of two worlds ignore the possibility and stay in their own thoughts*, including B, who may or may not sense via the spasms in my hands that something is transpiring, and I wonder if that's just me thinking stereotypical thoughts of how a girl has greater intuition, spiritually or psychically, than a guy, or maybe I want her to, and maybe I'll just explain it all to her over that coffee, or dinner, or maybe I'll be inside her later, describing some dual sex partner within the dream. *We become the art exhibit, her passivity, my thrusting energy, and the people in the room in the dream* and in the world *move through each other occasionally, it's like watching two overlaid videos with ghosted images interacting. I start to come and the room swirls, the paintings swirl, the people watch with intense interest,* I put more pressure on B's hand and she looks at me, eyebrows up, I do not look back because I am not sure what that will say to her. *I stay inside the girl, lift her up to straddle my lap on the bench, I look into her eyes and she stares back, there is compassion there, she puts her hand to my cheek. It's all highly evolved masturbation but feels incredible.* In the world, the girl is standing just beside me, taking in the Rauschenberg, maybe feeding off the residual energy of our coupling on that bench. You want to move on? B asks, I say sure, our hands disconnect and we slowly meander to the next hall. The girl glances at me as we pass by, and I imagine why. We meander through the sleek white galleries, stopping to gaze at an image, or part of an image. *I keep to the same rooms within the dream and reach up to touch the paintings and sculptures there, occasionally ripping the canvas or toppling over the pretentious collection of sticks and scrap metal. Sophomoric, I know, but I want to stay in the same place for a bit, and* too much reverent admiration in one world just makes me want to *destroy a few things in the other. The sounds of shattering, ripping, and tinkling glass in the dream counter* the quiet calm of the world. Between glances at B and swirling splotches, strokes and spatters on canvases, I think of how we are simply living in the moment, there are no plans to be in love, to develop a story together, nothing beyond our moments gliding from room to room, and it is the same in the dream, mirror images with no structure, no purpose, nothing to escape from nor anything to drive toward. It's a rare peace and tranquility in both dimensions, a purposeless drift, framed in the world only by night, day and closing hours, and framed in the dream only by the reflection in the world. It is of course too tempting in the dream to reach out and touch people, to burn a memory onto a gallery wall and look at it as if it were a great work of art. What in the world is so rich in metaphor and creative expression is a *tactile playground in the dream, where the shifting works of art and the people observing them are all the same piece of art, a living sculpture I inhabit and will never complete. I hover in the air next to people, look down at them, watch a painting change colors, relinquish a fluid control and allow the artworks to present themselves as chunks of my own artistic imagination filtered through decades of being told what art is supposed to be, combined with my deep mind's desire to show myself the infinite variety of what color, dimension and desire can produce. I freeze the denizens of the dream gallery, disrobe them and call them statues, push them into paintings and installations leading who knows where, very much beyond the imagination of the artists whose names grace the placards.* B loves Dali, and as we look over the artist's strained attempts to recreate a dream-like surrealistic landscape filled with his own struggling and obvious metaphors, I chuckle, beneath my breath. Melting watches and Christ-like figures are symbols, not dreamscapes; I'd like to impress that on everyone at the gallery I overhear say "he makes everything look so much like a dream." We get our coffee at the kiosk and contemplate our next move; meandering back up to the North side, B gets texted and decides she wants to go back to her place to help out her roommate with some stuff and take a shower and she'll see me at my place later. At my apartment, I lay back on the bed and zone for a bit, consider reading, but I feel exhausted.

I drift in the world and the dream, and must have drifted deeply as *I'm in a dining room, speaking with organizers of the Led Zeppelin reunion concert; I'm being asked to sit in on drums, and I'm elated, gleeful about playing John Bonham's old massive Physical Graffiti-era drumkit. Lucidity has dimmed significantly, though I clearly know that I have never, ever played a drumkit, but it doesn't matter, I just know this will be the best night of my life banging on those drums.* Skim-sleeping, it's almost like snorkeling with a mask, going just above the water's surface, then just below. It's often how I sleep, I can have a dark period or two during a power nap and come to first in the dream, always, before waking in the world. *The dream shifts into static, when I was a kid I sometimes projected cartoons into the static, ones I'd seen countless times, and let their well-worn narratives veer wildly off track, jumbling comic characters with real ones, like Roger Rabbit on acid. It is only a surrender of lucidity, not a loss, and I can focus on an object to grab me into a more lucid awareness, and I stretch and focus and the dream is totally mine again.* When I open my eyes and glance at the sleek little silver clock stereo on my nightstand, it's already going on 6 o'clock, so I've been skimming and drifting for a while. I get up slowly—I never rise quickly, it's too jarring for both worlds—and head to the bathroom to whiz and determine the general state of my appearance. *In the dream, I'm in an office-type building, very sleek and modern, and I go down the hall into the women's bathroom, a light turning on automatically as I swing open the door, and I also look in the mirror. This is a mirror exercise I like to do sometimes; gaze into the mirror* in the world *and the dream until the mirror background in the dream morphs* into my world bathroom. If you can keep staring and concentrate on your features and pierce your own eyes, it gives a keen illusion that you are breaking the barrier between the worlds, that your conscious injection into the other side has built a visual bridge. *In the dream, I push through the mirror, just like Alice through the looking glass, but it is always another room in the dream that mimics the world.* In the world, I have pushed and pushed my imagination to form the visual of the dream's mirror background into the world, and it seems ready to morph into that dream realm but it's a power I can't seem to conjure strongly enough. Still, in both reflections, I look like crap and in the world, I jump in the shower, whereas *in the dream, I go through the office building, room by room. It's empty of people but there is an ominous tension within those walls, so I flex my lucid powers and start dissolving it room by room, the open sky beyond illuminating the next room and the next. It's somehow turned into a towering skyscraper, feeling something like 100 or more stories, so I decide to fly out the window and survey the structure. It would be at home in any modern city except for the Jenga-block holes I disappeared. I hone in on the power center, the CEO's corner office on, let's say, the 72ⁿᵈ story, and burn the windows away to land in his sparsely appointed domain. An expensive looking rug, a wet bar, a minimal desk with a row of computers all monitoring busy-looking warehouses, rolls of stock market numbers, and porn. I'm fully aware that I'm making it up as I go along, though he seems uninitiated to that concept, a young and smarmy looking near-balding upper-crust type who regards me as a potential dealmaker. I wait for him to speak because sometimes that's the best way. I do not begrudge where my mind takes me, but I do want it to answer for itself. I have never worked for a large corporation, or within the finance industry, or real estates, technology or any other industrial strata he may represent. I feel no hate or fear, but am certain I would not trust this man if standing in the same office in the world.* "You have talent," he says. "You are clearly someone who can make things happen." *I still say nothing, moving about the spacious office observing pictures of his two children, hearing the faint sound of water running* as I am still in the shower with gallons of steaming water rushing past my ear, *and I see the executive washroom has a shower, and in that shower the form of some nubile girl. He smiles with a wink, "this could all be yours." It is all mine, I say, and pick him up, into the air—finally someone acts surprised at this, it's rarer than you think—and fly him out the open window to contemplate the ground far below. I say to him you have talent, you have will, you came to this world at this moment to learn to fly or fade away, and I drop him, his flailing limbs grabbing at air for a few seconds before he floats, haltingly, drops and floats some more, then plummets—was that me? I released control after the drop. He disappears from view, his descent still and forever occurring. I didn't just kill a man, I snapped a thread. A conscious needle pulled out of my psyche. Normally now I would go back into the office's washroom and explore that shower scenario, and I am curious enough to see the visage behind the sliding door, but she's already out of the shower and dressed and looking over those monitors. It's all yours, I tell her. At the moment, I don't want to get sexually worked up, I want to save the energy in both worlds for time with B, and* I wrap up my own shower, hurriedly dry, muss my hair appropriately and pull on jeans and a simple denim button-down shirt. *What the hell, I go up to the woman and put my hands on her hair, neck, her breasts. She's unfazed by my actions, maybe some remnant of her being the boss's girl. I threw him out the window I tell her, what are you going to do? She contemplates this, actual furrowing of the brow and thoughtful eyes searching the room, me, her blouse halfway undone where my hands were, and she says "well it goes without saying the décor around here will be a lot cheerier." I laugh at this, she genuinely made me laugh, and we're complicit now in her enjoyment of my vanquishing her boss man. I kiss her, I touch her more aggressively, she stays put in my arms but she's clearly making other plans. Uncommitted to the task, I ease back, rise up into the air and fly out of the building.* The tinny static of the buzzer in the world *glitches right into the dream, and I know that B has arrived.* I'm already to the intercom, buzzing her in. I throw open the door so it is not closed when she gets to it, and she bounds along, holding a bottle of wine and two take out bags from the best Thai carry-out place in the city. I give her a kiss on the cheek, take the bags and the bottle and set up the table. "I'm starving," she sighs, and I grab plates and two wine glasses and have the food out in seconds. *In the dream I can smell the pad thai, the spices are wafting in the air where I float, taking in the skyline of yet another massive urban complex, a system of mazes awaiting exploration. The city takes on a slightly Asian texture as I descend further into it, a pastiche of photographs from exotic Asian city streetlife at night, bustling, sizzling, bright and foreign.* B has dug right into the cartons and is slurping noodles with abandon. I tell her I fell asleep after our ride and was a lazy bum the rest of the afternoon. You want to go out tonight, stay in? I ask. "Netflix and chill" she says, "let's find something old to watch." I pull out my laptop, open it up and we start searching movie titles. *I reach through the steam of the vendor's cart and pull a variety of exotic looking noodles out of the hot pots, feeling heat but no pain; put them to my mouth and imagine varieties of new tastes. Occasionally when I do these taste binges, things come alive in my mouth if I'm not careful, and the reflex works in the dream, I spit it out and see some nasty stuff; regain composure, stuff mouth again. I could imagine tastes without putting anything in my mouth, but I like the sensual act of grabbing the food, putting it to my mouth, watching the reaction of the vendors. Eels, noodles, jellies, things of all colors writhing, as if I'd spilt a box of Crayola's into a soup kettle. I float along the busy streets and observe from above the action, most people pay no mind, just go about their business in my dream, the business of existing. I can have profound conversations with them in any garbled language that sounds like any language ever spoken or all languages, and it will make perfect sense in its nonsense.* "All these Bollywood titles, but you never see an Indian horror film," says B. "South Korea does horror, Japan fucking owns horror, even China puts monsters into movies. Germany invented horror cinema and the Italians made it creepier and grosser. What's the fear of horror movies in Bollywood? Not even a musical horror movie?" I don't know, I say, cynically, death, starvation, rape, social injustice, religious massacre, systemic problems from decades of colonialization...maybe horror movies are not what they need. B snorts and lays her head in my lap. B is not subtle. *She just put her head in my lap! I shout to all the vendors, families, pedestrians and gangsters in the street scene. This is happening! They are unfazed, unmoved, unconcerned. Yet I hear the slow, rhythmic clapping of one individual down the path, off the street, beyond a series of food stalls. I follow the sound, which does not stop. I rise higher into the air but can't see under the tent tops. I could whip off all the tops, but I'm not feeling particularly destructive at the moment, don't want to interrupt the expressive individual, so I land on the wet pavement, filled with oily puddles aswirl in color patterns of reflected neon. Past the stall selling wooden carvings of owls, past the sashimi chef to a dirty canvas tent lined with plush figures of esoteric and avant-garde musicians. The man sits in his folded chair in the rear of the tent, still carrying on a perfectly metered clap, staring at me. We lock eyes. He half smiles and I volley with a half-smile and raised eyebrows. Congratulations he says in a deadpan Chinese monotone. It sounds facetious, and I know I would be facetious with myself about my declaration. I shuffle through the caricature dolls hung from racks. Iggy Pop. Serge Gainsbourg. John Denver. On a more boring night by myself in the world, that would be enough for me to instantly conjure a concert with the three of them. But I am very excited with B and want to cede more concentration to the world* as her hand shifts up to my knee. We are having more fun just going through titles of bad movies than actually watching one. It's not likely we'll get to actually watching one, though I'd be happy to. *I pull up another folding chair and sit with the clapping man, who has now stopped clapping and is regarding me with suspicion. We watch people go by.* So Gardner, tell me about this dream thing. I'm kinda curious. How does it work again? You say you are always awake in your dreams (The dream, I correct her. It's just one state) okay, the dream. So, you're in the dream right now? I am. Doing what? Well, I'm sitting in a tent surrounded by stuffed animals, there's an older Asian man in a folding chair to my right…we're watching people go by in an open marketplace. B laughs. What's the old guy's name? *I ask, what's your name? The man turns to me and says "Moto."* His name is Moto. Oooh, squeals B. Let's ask him what he knows about me, maybe he knows all kinds of secrets. I tell her it doesn't really work that way, but she insists. I ask her how do you know I'm not just making up his answers? I don't, she says. Let's just play the game, Gardner. So ask him, ask him what object do I keep in my middle dresser drawer? *I turn to Moto again, point to my head for some reason, and say she wants to know if you know what object she keeps in her dresser drawer, the middle one. Moto contemplates for a moment and says "her Beanie Babies."* I tell B, your Beanie Babies. B is taken aback…

like very, very aback. Oooookay, she says. Wait, I say, for real? She nods. I try to think if, in the few times I've been to her apartment, I somehow got nosy and opened some of her dresser drawers. I could tell she was thinking the exact same thing. I put my hands up and swear to her I'd never gone through her dresser drawers. I don't think I've ever been in her bedroom alone. It's possible that I assumed a connection between having told her I was in a stall filled with stuffed figures and her thinking about her Beanie Babies, and I subconsciously figured those were the only types of plush toys she would keep tucked away in a drawer; that would be a fair assumption; she was a little girl when those things were popular. I could tell now that B was wracking her brain to come up with questions she knew I could never possibly know. *I recall an old series, Asian stereotype detective movies, Mr. Moto or something similar. Just another needle of trivia pulled from the haystack of my experience.* OK, says B. What nickname did my father call me by? *I look at Moto. He is distracted now, and stands up, stretches, doesn't even acknowledge me. Starts walking away, I tell him to stop and he doesn't, so I will him to stop, and he keeps going. I get up after him, fly up above him to assert some authority over him. You know the question, I say. What's the nickname? He leers at me. "Dunkin Punkin." And he walks off, and I let him. Lucidity unravels when faced with uncertainty.* I repeat the answer to B and she is genuinely spooked. She chooses to laugh. All right, she says. You're good at this…who've you been talking to? Again, I hold up my hands in arrest mode. Honest to God, just the freaky old man. He's gone now. Seems as good a time as any to just put my hand around her back, coax her in with an intense gaze and kiss her. We are so talking about this later, she sighs. *In the dream, I look for a suitable space to align, to "straddle" the worlds so I can concentrate more fully on B. Flying fast, feeding off the rush from both worlds, I zero in on a big city landscape.* Gaze into open windows and lit environments of apartments and offices on upper floors of skyscrapers. My hands are caressing her body, start with the shoulders, the small of the back, the back of her neck, her hips, move to her breasts, over the shirt, then working fingers through openings and slits until skin meets skin. I advance on her, she advances on me; funny how things just slide into place on a girl, but on the boy it's like searching in a toolbox. As my hands cover her body in the world, *my eyes cover buildings in the dream; I land on the terrace of a penthouse apartment and go in through open sliding doors to a living room, complete with fireplace and large bed-sized couch. Her entanglement twin is on the couch, looking very much like her. I sit down next to her and hold her as I'm holding her in the world, or close enough, and take a few liberties with the action on this side. I lay back and say nothing, wanting her actions in the world to filter through to the dream her, imagining she controls her own figure.* She's already touching me, yanking at jeans to pull them off. I've pulled her skirt down to the knees. A bra unhooked and laying loosely on her belly. The kissing is deeper. I pull the skirt off her legs and she kicks it across the room; slide my torso down her body, get on my knees and put my hands on her hips, tease the panties down while kissing that open field of taught abdomen. Tongue kissed all the way down to her neatly trimmed mons, moving slowly. *Concentration is in shaky synergy between worlds. I can't just stop to fully recreate my apartment for effect. In the dream, we are much higher up, forty maybe fifty floors up, the windows open, an unsettling breeze gusting into the room with splintered tendrils of heat. Because I have been so focused in the world, I have skittered in the dream, and in the distance, Godzilla screeches. I glance from B's body to the window, and across miles, our eyes connect; once Godzilla sees me, he moves toward me, as quickly as his behemoth body can carry him, which is much quicker than in world movies, because time in the dream is merely perception. He's quickly at the window, his right eye turned in and focused on our bodies. There's a sulphur-like smell. Lucidity rises, I don't wish him away; he's a captive audience and I proceed to let my hands in the dream match* my hands and lips in the world, guided by the timbre of her sighs, out of her mouth into my ears and through my tongue in two worlds. *Two women sighing, four tongues licking, the scent of her in two worlds, four hands on two hips, the snarl of Godzilla at the window. It's some masterful control on my part keeping him at bay while pleasuring her, all the while knowing this is not a symbolic thing, there is no connection between our fucking and Godzilla destroying the city, no representation of our animal natures; it's just that Godzilla sometimes fucking bothers me in the dream and I've learned to tolerate him rather than vanquish him or throw him into outer space. He can watch and foam toxic blue at his mouth, screech all he wants.* B comes, hands grasping my hair, *though she doesn't do the same in the dream, more distracted by the beast than me. I momentarily pull away from her and fly over to the window, an arm's length from Mr G, and I stare into his right eye, the fury in it, and match it, shouting at him I RULE YOU, and when he rears his head back like he's going to spew that hellfire over the entire floor I shout NO and he relaxes. I back up to B, passive, and turn her body to face him, put myself behind her,* while in the world B is returning oral favors. It is impossible to describe the richness of the simultaneous sensation of mouth and vagina, and like an orgasm, it can't be maintained for long. *Oh, and while staring down Godzilla.* I turn B around, slide into her from behind to match worlds. Tell me what you're doing to her in the dream, she asks. Exactly the same, I say, no lie, right down to the rhythm. Whether she believes me or not, it clearly amuses her. She's not me, says B. Only one you, I say, but a lookalike of you is fucking amazing too. I come with no vocal fanfare like hers, *in both worlds, and when the tremor subsides and I pull out,* in the world I collapse on the couch *and in the dream I fly up again and tell G the show is over. Dream B walks over, gloriously naked and dripping, and reaches out to touch him. He allows it and retreats with a huff, stomping, causing fires and screeching like metal on a chalkboard for miles.* I don't tell B about the Godzilla thing, I don't like that people automatically cast interpretations and symbolic junk over the dream, but mostly because I don't want her to think I was concentrating on anything but her. As she rises from the couch like Venus and saunters gracefully to the bathroom, I kick back, breathing hard, *and fly off, nude, into the night, skyward so as to see only the stars. Orgasm is mental power as much as physical, a connection to the universe as much as to the flesh born of that universe. And there it is, the realization that here I'm not sitting on an atmosphere-bathed, gravity-clad rock in space; I am the space itself.*

So that's a typical day in a biconscious mind, me in both worlds and their overlapping synergy...though I did leave out most of the details or this would be a very long book. How easily I can slip into the dream and back to the world, seeing a fully realized life on either side, yet both sides shift and phase beneath me, the world in much slower motion.

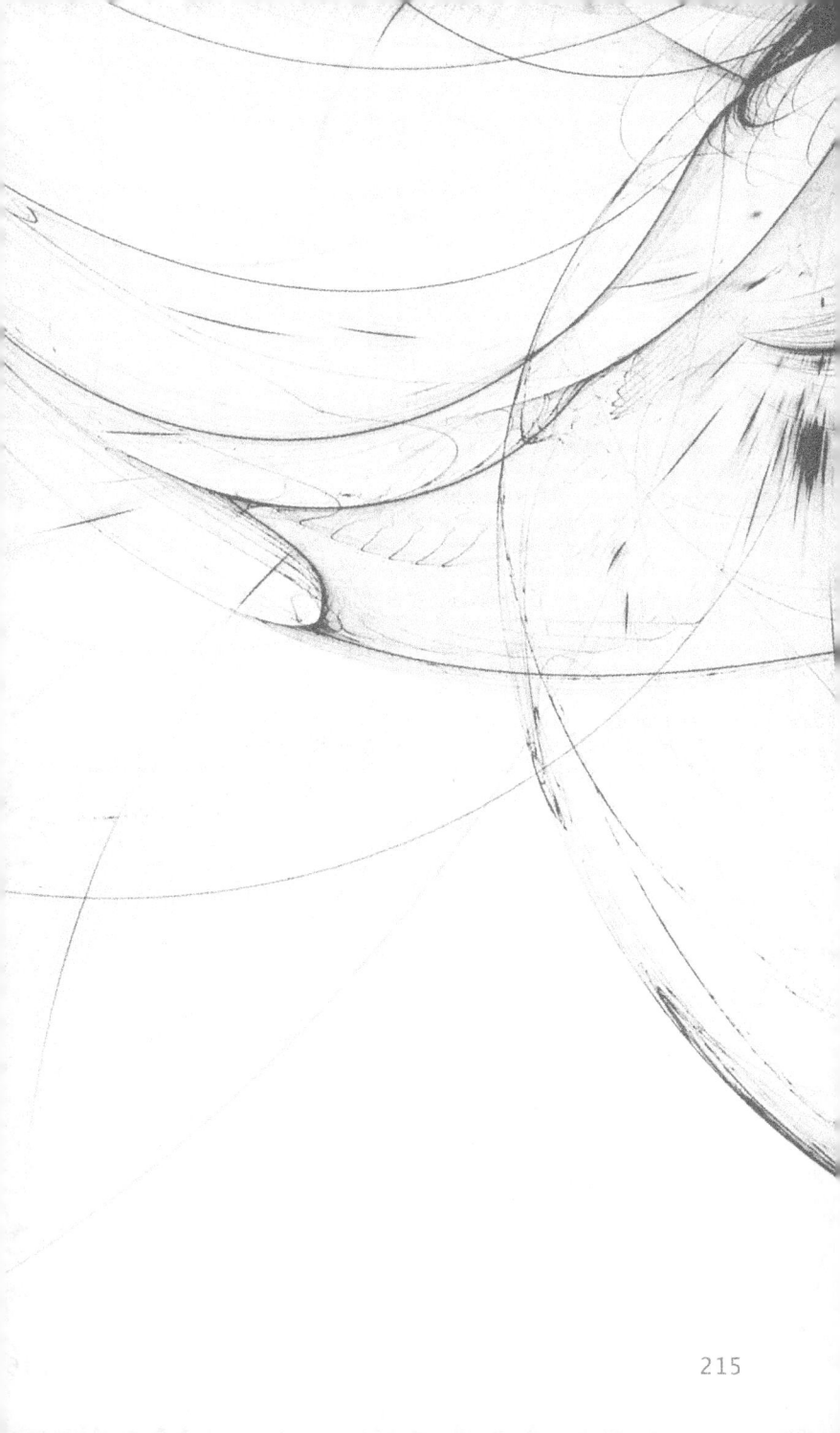

ART AND CULTURE

"The universe is made of stories, not of atoms"
– Muriel Rukeyser

The dream has inspired countless works of art from cave paintings to virtual reality simulations, acting as a conduit for divine inspiration both philosophically and scientifically. Entire artistic genres, such as surrealism, spring from the dream. Ideas and expression are one of the only things we can carry with us into the world.

The dream itself is an ever-evolving work of art.

The dream is perhaps even more filled with media than the world. Books, amazing works of art, cinemas that play fantastical movies, radios that blare all manner of music; these permeate the dream every bit as much as that media fills the world. Imagine walking through galleries of never-before-seen works of art from your favorite artist, going into a music shop to see albums never released from your favorite musicians. Imagine discovering works from artists completely unknown in the world altogether—all courtesy of your own vast warehouse of a lifetime's constant streaming of media product.

When we consume such vast amounts of information that are largely meaningless to us in the world—think game shows, junk books, muzak in elevators, late night veg-induced television—the data must go somewhere. Think of memes as particles or waves, and you see how these visions, once put together, cannot simply evaporate. Rather, they are strewn about the conscious quilt in unexpected ways, only to pop up in some hodgepodge in the dream.

I visited bookstores and libraries and read book titles, made instant memory snapshots, phased into the world and wrote them down. I have entire notebooks filled with the names of books, writers and odd snippets. I've read unpublished works of famous world authors (indeed, works that have never existed), written passages down and researched whether there were any such passages in the writer's work, or even similar sentence strings.

I watched televisions. In one home, I sat with a family and watched television for quite a long time, alternately fascinated and bored by the programs, which were at once familiar but different, of course. I didn't use a remote, but forced channels to switch, and this ability did not impress the family I sat with. I remember joking with them, "how many endless thousands of channels you must get, and I bet there's still nothing to watch!"

There were commercials on dream-world television, on channels that seemed perfectly realistic as programming entities. I could have zapped any intrusion from ads on TV or in magazines, but it was far more fascinating to see the advertising and marketing process unfold in the dream. What are we selling to ourselves in the dream? Pretty much the same crap we're selling ourselves in the world; unless we choose to alter it. But of course, if you are lucid and realize you can change it or ignore, there is no reason to watch it. Still, it's always fascinating how the dream mimics and warps the world.

I sat in a living room with well-worn comfortable furniture, right smack in the middle of a seven-person family, and the mother and father kept looking different because I wouldn't concentrate on them. Wood grain was everywhere in the decoration. I would ask my hosts if they'd purchased that cleaning product, or if they had any of that brand of food in the house, and I'd look for what stocked their shelves and fridges. I would see those products and others that never existed in the world. Generic names like CleanSol and HyperScrub, but one of my favorites was Clown Wipes. I created commercials that told the people whose homes I'd invaded what they needed to do for me.

I could conjure the music, the art, the movies in many different forms—making the artists themselves appear before me to perform; but the construct of the media product I was used to working with in the world (a stereo to play music, a museum to see artworks, a television to view programs) gave me some level of comfort. It is incredibly difficult to move beyond those methods of feeding the dream; content, stories, images, voices; it is dream fuel. All media is its own dream state, swallowed whole by your dream, and played back to you (usually in fragments) in the world and dream both. You can be absorbed by it, its reality and its transformative power, in either world; or you can ignore it in either world.

Fact is, whether you are in the world or the dream, the deeper and more closely you look at anything, no matter how it appears to you—conjured by the control of complete lucid mastery or stumbled upon by confusion or apathy—the more detail you will uncover.

THE SURROGATE DREAM

All art, throughout mankind's history, is an attempt to recreate the dream. We have always aspired to bridge the gap between our waking reality and the dream's grasp on our psyche and spirit. Even as we convince ourselves we are trying to chronicle or capture what we see in the world, once filtered through our mind, it becomes a product of the dream. Every new technology that seems to create more vivid, realistic and convincing dimensional realities is in fact an attempt to break into the dream, or to release the dream, to make the viewer the lucid traveler who has some element of control over the journey. Whether it is a poem or a video game, a movie or a musical piece, it's drawn from the wellspring of the dream and seeks to replicate the dream experience.

In ancient times, people's dreams terrified and elated them. They may have been hunting at day and were chased by a large predator, terrifying them; in the dream, maybe they again are chased, and it terrifies them no less. Waking up, they are confused. Their ignorance of the dream causes them to ascribe the event as an act of their god. In the dawn of human consciousness, it was all too easy to confuse our reality, our memory, and our dream. They felt then—as we feel now—compelled to bring the dream into this world. We have achieved a self-awareness, but mankind as a whole has not achieved a complete self-awareness. Our awareness is evolving.

Very much up until the advent of industrialization, people had a much keener relationship with their dream, even if it was a reverent fear. Industry and technology then began to vacuum the peaceful moments of our lives; now they seek to re-create the dream environment, outside of ourselves, through the manipulation of images in multi-media, such as film and computer simulation. When I say "they," I do not mean to suggest that there is an organized conspiracy by any group or organization to "control" or direct us to some such condition. I believe it is a sad truth of our own collective and chaotic path to self-destruction. Thirty million people working hard in the name of progress can do significant damage; especially because we cannot define "progress" without becoming embedded in subjective arguments of morality. The same is true of the dream.

The prehistoric man had to use every facet of his consciousness simply to survive. His instincts and his senses were razor-sharp. Today, in our disconnectedness, in our safe, walled-in spaces, we operate on a "selective consciousness." Call it Remote Consciousness. We do not need to be fully lucid and aware to survive. Everything is packaged—there is little raw processing in our lives, there is no hunt that relies on sweat and sinew and stealth, there is no connectedness to our fellow humans through the tools of survival. In the extreme cases where there is that connection, it's a profound experience.

But some of us still seek to hunt. Animals or other humans, we want to exercise the human ability to choose to kill something or someone. The dream is an environment in which we can experiment with our curiosities. It is where we are most viscerally active as hunter and hunted. Why the fascination with images, from early art to painting to photography to film to computer simulations? Because it is our unstated attempt to re-create the dream environment. To create a world and populate it with our own dream collective. The less such a work has a coherent storyline or clearly defined characters, the more we call it "dreamlike." And some work has come close to our best and worst dreams; for me, David Lynch's film *Eraserhead* seemed eerily like the unsettled world of vague, nonlucid dreaming. For centuries, art and illustration sought to capture visions from the dream, then photography, then film, now digital simulation, immersive games and virtual reality. Immersive virtual reality will emerge and perhaps complete what some believe is already a holographic universe, world and dream. Theories abound that the universe itself is holographic.

I've watched countless examples of creative minds tackling the maddening notions of the dream. Most pale terribly to the actual experience and an appalling percentage simply continue the archaic Freudian notions of what "dreams" are supposed to "mean" to people. Occasionally some interesting imagery or conceits break through and a glimmer of a possible dream environment is realized. Oddly, I sometimes find watching surveillance cameras eerily close to the dream; a single point of view, no edits or cuts, denizens moving from in frame to out of frame, unaware of the watcher, unable to respond unless acted upon.

At some point, these artistic interpretations—whether canvas, screen or holograph—inspire and influence our vision and experience in the dream. Celebrities appear in the dream, situations from shows we've seen, landscapes from memorable or mundane paintings and films we've watched, these can infiltrate the dream and affect us, no matter how banal or brilliant. Just like the world, you do not always get to choose what takes perch in what area of the dream. After a lifetime of interacting with people in the dream who are celebrities in the world, and with the personification if great characters from books, I've come to believe that if fictional characters can appear in the dream, no matter how much altered by the individual, then they do exist.

"Space...the final frontier." You can hear Captain Kirk's

(William Shatner's) voice vividly, haltingly, an oft-repeated phrase of pop culture echoing boldly, stars flying past your face, the whoosh of warp speed in your ears. These are indeed the voyages.

Yet, if space and the mind are the same, or at least drawn from the exact same origin, then the mind is the first and final frontier. We can go light years away from the Earth, but we'll still be trapped in the realms of our own consciousness, and we will never master this frontier. It is as deep and unexplored as the infinite cosmos, and maybe that's the crux of creation.

In science fiction like "Star Trek" and similar shows, it always fascinated me that they rarely portrayed beings as other than humanoid. The reasons were clear enough—no budget for effects, and without the human-like connection within the story, how can you care for the character? It is often like this in the dream. We can't conjure or encounter beings too alien to relate to on some level. My mind has reams of information to deal with people, animals, and plants. We can't fathom or visualize a being that lives on a cosmic or quantum scale. But stay long enough in the dream, and you will be able to understand new forms of intelligence.

Many forms of light can express intelligence, living, moving over and through you. The way you may feel the darkness watches you; not eyes in the dark, but the darkness itself. Rooms, entire buildings can exhibit an emotional sentience that can be at once unsettling and reassuring. I have, in the dream and in the world, stared into a void of darkness or overwhelming light and sensed a static life peering back at me, as if measuring.

One thing "Star Trek" had a lot of fun with was "Star Trek: The Next Generation's" famous Holodeck (a virtual reality simulator). They kept missing the real possibilities, though. They assumed everyone would just want to program different time periods, or become their favorite characters. They rarely hinted at the darker indulgences possible within, understandable for prudish television in America. But wouldn't certain crew members get addicted to the holodeck? How many crew members do you think were barred from Federation service because of holodeck abuse? And what stories the Enterprise janitorial staff would have about the cleanup of the holodeck after sessions.

You don't have to schedule the holodeck of your own mind.

We might all love the idea that, in the future, computers will be able to simulate an interactive environment that is physically real to all our senses, even simulating people who react to us and seem to have wills of their own but can be shut down by one command from us, the user. The flaw of the Holodeck, of course, is that if it actually existed, especially in a starship with 400 people on long-term duty, people would be so addicted to it as a means of escape that it would be a huge problem.

In the meantime, our movies and TV depictions are our Holodeck, our dimensional portal, to the dream. It would be impossible to critique all media that portrays dream states, or even a "dream-like" environment, so I'll review some of the more recognized shows and vehicles and how their depiction of the dream fares compared to aspirations of lucidity.

2001: A SPACE ODYSSEY

Arthur C. Clarke's and Stanley Kubrick's *2001: A Space Odyssey* got very close to the more interesting connections between the world and the dream. Slow-building, with long stretches of near silence. Mind-blowing in its day, perhaps, but ponderous; the final mind-trip is intriguing but academic. Still, it made the connection between the inner-most realm of the mind and the furthest reaches of space. Those who marvel at the profundity of this concept have no idea. In the end, Dave is a traveler, a witness who has crossed through a time-space barrier; he is self-aware but not quite lucid, as he can't control his environment.

CONTACT

Carl Sagan and the mind/cosmos exploration *Contact* evoked some interesting questions of outer space/inner space connection and quantum theories of the mind being the ultimate spatial frontier. Sagan uses the construct of aliens bestowing this technology on us, but Jodie Foster's "journey" is somewhat believable and well played. If the machine they constructed simply enabled her to tap into the dream and visit a world of her own making, where she could imagine seeing her father again, that's within the realm of possibility for the dream. Still, the central message is sound: "out there" is really "in here." She had a more self-aware experience, but never quite turned lucid.

ALTERED STATES

Paddy Chayefsky and director Ken Russell went primordial in this classic story of science-gone-amok. This film made enough of an impact on me when younger, because it dealt with the visceral power of the dream. I was still conflicted about my "dual citizenship" in both worlds, and this film piqued my curiosity about altered states in general; would drugs, after all, affect my condition? I sought out any place that would rent isolation tanks; it wasn't until I was in college that I had access to the tanks. Floating gave me a place to truly relax, even from feeling the musculature in my body as I lay prone. I vehemently deny that it takes both isolation and mind-altering hallucinogenic drugs to achieve a kind of cosmic self-awareness, because I've been there without the drugs. I liked William Hurt's intensity and his ability to play it as experiencing something so powerful he felt guilty. That we might transgress to the point of our creation is pretty far-fetched; it wouldn't likely be realized in the world, but it could occur in the dream. It's something I haven't tried. Still, again, he never turned lucid, just simian.

DREAMSCAPE

This cheesy 80s thriller actually had some very dynamic ideas about conquering one's fears within the dream, but the notion of being able to transport into someone else's mind and interact with their dream is, for now, sheer fantasy. The characters who were able to enter dreams fully lucid seemed to be able to conjure items and turn into monsters, but didn't fly or use other forces of control? Still, it was surprisingly fun and moody despite the campiness. And it gave some cheesy side-eye to the potential of a lucid experience.

INCEPTION

Christopher Nolan's epic thriller of one man's exploration of his dream has a lot of interesting ideas, and certainly was braver in its complexity of dealing with the dream state than any film before. However, it also is rife with blatant symbolism, pandering to the dream notions of the general population, and any lucid traveler in both worlds would tell you that if they felt they're being chased, or losing control, or under threat from some contrived menace, Uzis and other guns are never the go-to means of defense in the dream. When you have the powers of Superman, playing with guns has no purpose. The notion of having a team that can go in and extract information from a sleeping victim is novel, even if avid lucid dreamers can laugh off the notion of a specialist who can reconstruct, bend and fold the dream "stage" at will. As I was watching this at the movie theatre, in the dream I was having sex with Ellen Page while explaining to her that what she was doing was cool, but the reality of lucidity was way, way cooler. She was very grateful.

THE MATRIX

Once past the central theme of the entire movie, that we are all truly asleep, plugged into a giant machine to give existence its very energy, and are kept compliant in a simulated environment of the "real" world, this is a pretty easy conceit to dismiss. And they stopped having any fun with it after the first movie; where the striking visual style broke new ground, the notions about the dream or even consciousness in general got bogged down in too much leather and too many bullets. I say again, future screenwriters of dream projects: bullets and guns are meaningless in the dream.

ERASERHEAD

Eraserhead is a little freak-fest of dark industrial mind-fucking, genuinely creepy in that it deftly replicates elements of the dream—the drone and ambient sounds, the offbeat actions of people who seem hypnotized, the nightmarish creations born from the mind which we accept as natural. The baby that seems a baby to the parents but is some kind of indescribable monster they are compelled to care for; the lady in the radiator who is at once extremely repulsive but sexually intimidating.

Lynch created some similar dream-like moments in his film, *The Elephant Man*, but it was narratively crafted to tell a story. Moments of dream quality imagery continued to appear in brief stretches of Lynch's films, from *Wild at Heart* to *Twin Peaks* and *Lost Highway*, but there were also many strained constructs. For instance, I have never encountered a dwarf in my dream. I do not believe that little people represent or symbolize anything that would make them an obvious choice for dream population. Lynch has used them—as well as the reversed audio voices and other manipulations—because they are unusual. But to him, they are props in a play meant to say, all too obviously, "isn't this weird? Must be a dream."

Still, Lynch comes closer than many directors and auteurs in creating a claustrophobic kind of dream scenario. Better than Fellini or Bergman, who are often credited with dreamlike film qualities, but they are too introspective and dramatic. Fellini turned surreal for surrealism's sake, as did Bunuel and other European directors.

FALLING WATER

A very studious show about collective dreaming, this TV series wears out its welcome quickly once it starts showing dream sequences, which feature the usual cavalcade of dream tropes; being chased, faceless men, conspiracy. I've been highly skeptical of anything regarding collective dreaming, and since *Falling Water* is determined to tell a narrative using the dream world, it's already failed. The dream does not have a narrative, does not serve a narrative, and isn't interested in your conspiracies.

UNTIL THE END OF THE WORLD

Wim Wenders' rambling, disjointed epic is largely forgettable except for the central plotline of a device that can record images to be played back for a blind person from within the mind. The side effect of the device, however, is recording dreams. And the people in the movie who record their dreams become addicted to them, like to a drug. This strikes me as a great possibility. If we had this technology, the world would be a very different place. The same conceit was explored less elegantly in Kathryn Bigelow's frantic *Strange Days*, where Ralph Fiennes sells black market "experiences" to people.

WAKING LIFE

Richard Linklater's artfully animated 2001 film about a man meandering through his dream world encountering various denizens is at times fascinating and does offer some insights, but it's too cerebral and intellectual, too damn verbal, to give any real, profound sense of the dream. Not that it isn't beautiful and even hypnotic in its own way, well worth watching; it just questions, questions, questions, and there is no true lucidity.

STUDIO GHIBLI & HAYAO MAYAZAKI

The films of Japanese animator Mayazaki *(My Neighbor Totoro, Spirited Away, The Wind Rises, Princess Mononoke)* are filled with colorful and surreal imagery that often seems dream-like, but it's the depth, silence and space that he has so much patience to display that truly gets the dream. When you exist within the dream as I do, those long pauses become more the norm...a lot of time goes by where there is no action whatsoever. Mayazaki's stories may be classic tales, but his imagery feels very much at home in the dream.

If anyone were going to do an animated film about having a lucid dream, Mayazaki could pull it off beautifully.

VIDEO GAMES AND VIRTUAL REALITY

All art, and most all audio-video technology, aspires to recreate the dream and bring levels of conscious control to us. Consider the advertisements for the latest video gaming technology, proclaiming "a more graphic, immersive, interactive experience with more life-like animation!" The sales pitch for the latest TV screens promise greater clarity, richer depth in tones and sound, a larger screen and greater details for ever richer perceptions. The screen entertainment experience will soon literally surround us in virtual, three-dimensional space with sensory stimulation. Augmented reality devices promise to put fantastical things into our virtual environment for amusement, edification, and pleasure. Of

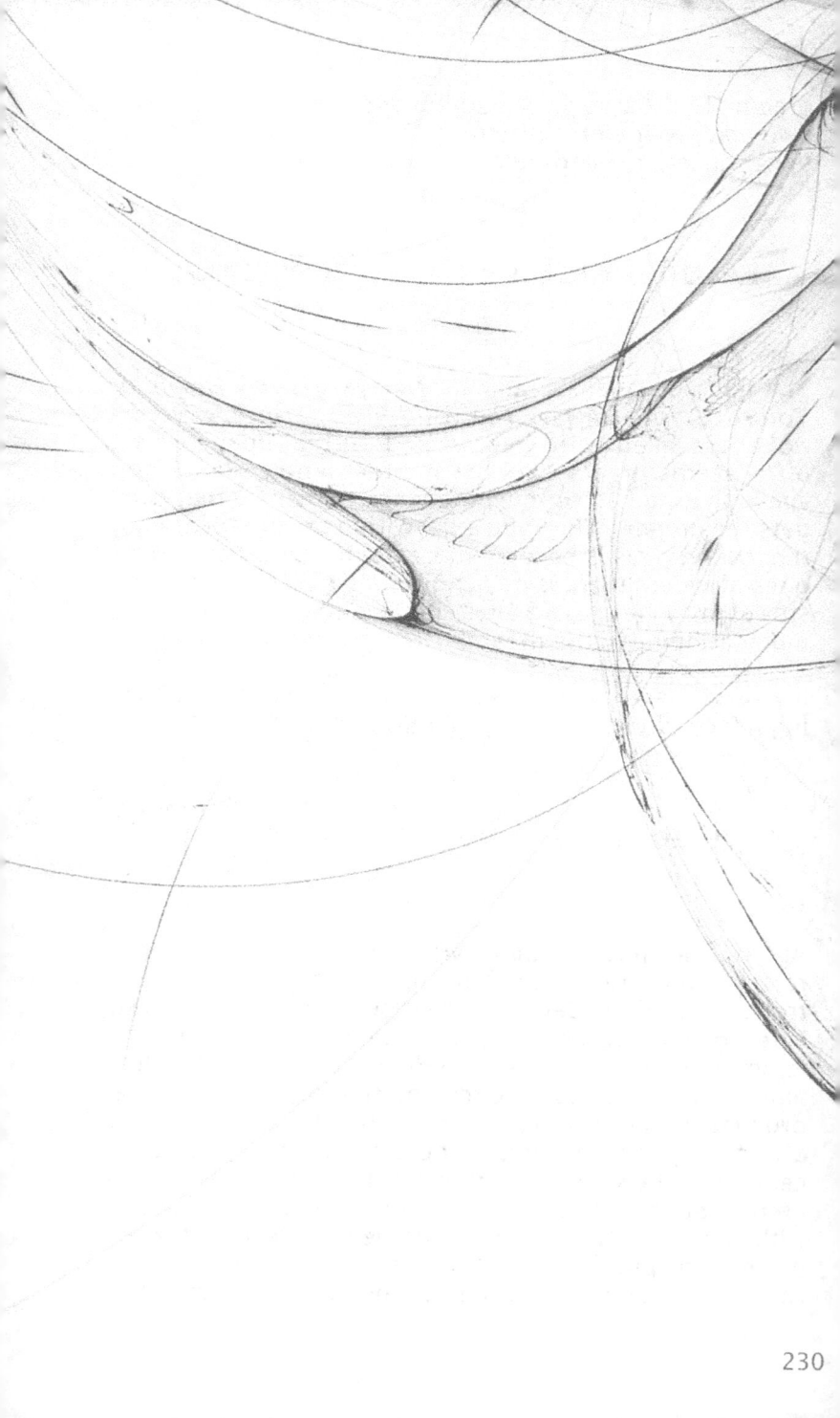

course, that "technology" is already accessible within our minds, in the dream.

Immersive video games and the new crop of virtual reality experiences, with surreal content and first-person vantage points, are one of the closest technological substitutes we have for the actual dream. Even the first wave of shooters ("Doom, "Quake") from the nineties captured an otherworldly feel and gave the player a sense of control over the environment. Some games have a "God Mode" play that can be unlocked, giving you complete invulnerability and enabling you to fly. An ability to shift point of view, stop and speak with game denizens, be passive, direct the action, and skip forward or backward in game time just further mimics the dream.

We're continuing to make advancements in artificial intelligence, robotics, and quantum computing, which only puts the simulation of the dream closer. However, I think the important question is, if we continue to insert our consciousness into AI, will it diminish our ability to work within our own self-generated environment? A natural path to this other dimension was given to us, freely available, not at the mercy of electric utilities and internet companies. Will generations of subservience to the artificial dream affect our evolutionary ability to inhabit the real dream?

More than any other emerging technology, virtual reality environments might do more to help us prepare for a transition to lucidity and biconsciousness. You are immersed in a separate visual dimension, with a first-person view, though your body is safely positioned in the world.

We are slowly preparing humankind for a disembodied reality within a fully realized virtual environment, and we will be our own avatars.

FUTURE

"What if you slept? And what if, in your sleep, you dreamt? And what if, in your dream, you went to Heaven and there plucked a strange and beautiful flower? And what if, when you awoke, you held the flower in your hand? Ah, what then?"
--Samuel Taylor Coleridge

The matter of the universe evolved into elements; elements evolved into organisms; organisms into life; life into consciousness. Consciousness into...?

It is tempting to say "matter." Bringing the cycle of life and creation full circle, our consciousness fills the dark matter of the supposedly infinite multiverses so fully that the energy continues to build, swallowing everything like a black hole into an infinitesimal but unimaginably powerful speck that explodes, beginning the cycle anew.

It's an interesting realization that cosmologists speculate there are as many galaxies in the universe--more than 100 billion--as there are neurons in the brain.

We can discover elusive quantum particles, or waves, in one or multiple places at once and in an infinite number of universes. We can measure them, we can seek connections between dark energy, the space-time continuum and consciousness on many levels. These are worthy scientific pursuits, but the real question is what do we do with this? How do we use this to move into a new phase of existence? And the experience of that is already accessible, within us; the dream is the platform for this path of evolution—and possible answers to our origins.

While science continues to research the dreaming brain, only the mind can create the renaissance of spirit necessary to make the next evolutionary leaps in consciousness. We may yet find some synthesis of technology, artificial intelligence, biology, and neurology that enables us to flip a switch to move between worlds and therefore entire universes. We may discover neural pathways that bridge the gulf between matter and consciousness. Like all technological advances, we will not be ready to wield such power unless we first explore the terrain it gives us. As it is, we have barely begun to map and appreciate the breadth of the human experience, much less the possibilities of the entire spectrum of the conscious experience.

I desperately hope that there are others out there with the same abilities as me, and that my works can reach them, challenge them, affect them, encourage them, and console them. I would love nothing more than to sit across from someone in the world and share mutual experiences of the world and dream with a fellow traveler who truly knows what biconsciousness is. Someone who knows what it feels like to live in multiple dimensions.

Over the years, the effect of biconsciousness does take a toll on the physical and mental person in the world. I am prone to vertigo in the world, there are slight dizzy spells where the world spins briefly. An aging, wearying body in the world is no competition for the powerful spirit in the dream; I linger in the dream ever longer, even as the world demands attention, sometimes dangerously so. I will need to stop driving soon; too many near-misses that are clearly my fault.

I do not think scientific or religious study of biconsciousness will take meaningful form any time soon. These days, the world of science needs to produce results in the form of quantifiable data, preferably data that can translate into products with profits, or military advantage. Religion will not look more deeply at biconsciousness or lucidity for the same reason they sever the line of questioning that leads to the reality of God. It runs too deep and too contrary to its traditional thinking. It reveals too many profound flaws in the stories and does not satisfy a sense of moral justice. Most religious orders like to keep their ideology well in the abstract, where it can best be manipulated for the task at hand. New Age ideology is much the same; the more abstract, the better.

We do not even have a proper framework in which to

study, much less understand, consciousness—let alone the dream. It may well be that we grasp the nature of consciousness no more fully than a stone grasps the water that, over time, shapes it, erodes its very structure, smooths and polishes its harsh exterior until it becomes a gem.

The only hope is that people will begin waking up, shifting, transcending current habits and realizing that the dream is ever present; one need not even close one's eyes to access it. The leaps in logic and faith that were required to begin serious study of quantum phenomena need to be made in the study of the dream. You do not need to grasp quantum physics, psychology, or nontraditional spirituality to recognize that there is a major part of your life being ignored, and it is the probable source of all your unease, lack of fulfillment, uncertainty and fear. It could become the source of your greatest pleasures, and if you are so spiritually inclined, your salvation. It will likely, in one way or another, be your entire future.

What does any of this mean to the average person who is perfectly content with the occasional strange or disturbing dream memory? What difference does it make if one is more aware of their dual nature in the world or the dream? Does it make the world, or even one's own life, a better place? Living a simple life is an uncommon virtue, but even those who lead the simplest of lives—say, Tibetan monks for the sake of argument—are preparing for a conscious afterlife by learning to tap into it now. You will need to learn to create and master your own world or be swept along in the stories you cobble together from the creations of others, lost and wondering why the universe won't answer your prayers.

If the dream is a preview of our next phase, then it's possible that, with lucidity providing our means of practice via active participation, those who foster their bi-world abilities will be much better equipped for the journeys ahead. You may soon be able to use a simple app via your smart phone to monitor your sleeping brain and use electrical stimulation to jolt consciousness within the dream, but you will need to take the next steps to actual lucidity. Your behavior and participation will not be dictated by technology, and drugs won't be there to help you.

Some scientists will promise that you'll have instant lucidity and be able to fulfill your wildest fantasies, solve deep-set problems, eliminate phobias, and many other life-changing advantages. However, achieving true, sustained lucidity is a skill of consciousness. It's a skill you already have within you; it needs to be practiced in the world as much as in the dream. Many people are content to be extras in the world/dream show, and some would enjoy being an occasional featured player. Only a few are capable of controlling the narrative, consistently and in a life-altering, meaningful way.

Every day, exercise your will and stretch your creative drive; what would you do if you were conscious in the dream right now (and remember, you are in the dream right now)? Will you blaze your own trail or be sucked into the ether of other people's constructs? For how long would you allow yourself to be tied to familiar faces, to hindering attachments no matter how deep the love, to comforting sensations, to concrete, stone, water and air? How long until you forget the feelings of want, of loss, of terror? How long until God, Freedom, Love and Dream merge for you and render all other tactile experience to feel like shackles? How long until your Being and your Awareness melt into one and give you the ultimate sense that moves beyond touch, taste, scent, sound and vision? Is it Nirvana? Is it God? Is it the merging of the Creator and the Created?

Is it a trap, is it an illusion? Are we free radicals roaming a cosmic network? Or is it all light and shadows, playing tricks on us?

Ultimately, the dream may be where we exhaust the human condition; where all our mental, emotional, spiritual fears and elations must play out before we evolve. To another dimension, to God, to rebirth, to nothingness, to everything.

Have you started yet? Are you Lucid?

ASK
REMBRANDT
Letters, Insults & Concerns

I've received countless letters, emails, and even a few subpoenas and other legal queries questioning the validity of my work. It's gratifying to spew my psyche's guts and disturb many people in the process, and sometimes get paid for it. Most of these letters and emails have been sent directly to me or my PO Box. A few early examples were originally published in some random newsletters or journals I was working with and many came from the "Ask REMbrandt" column some alternative papers ran. I throw them in this compendium because it widens the perspectives of people's perception of the dream and how the pursuit and denial of the dream affects us. I hope.

Dear REMbrandt:
When we "imagine" something, is that just coming straight from the dream? Is "thought" generated within the dream? Are daydreams just slipping into the dream momentarily?
CC

Dear CC:
I imagine so! Imagination, creative visualization, daydreaming, plain 'ol thinking—these are all consciousness-based activities and as far as I know, travel wherever our conscious self goes, be it world or dream. I can use my imagination within the dream same as in the world. Of course, when I'm doing amazing things in the dream, I don't often sit and wonder what it would be like if I could do mundane things in the world. When I'm doing captivating things in the world, I let the dream dim a bit.

Dear REMbrandt:
Mr. Eeden, I have read with great interest your observations on the effects of external stimuli on the sleeping, dreaming psyche. I have recently divorced my wife, and I thought you might be interested in why. I'm a man of 62 years of age, and my wife two years younger. Ginny and I have been married near thirty some years. We'd been

arguing for years about sex; she was no longer interested in it, and I was. That's an old husband and wife story, I know, but she got this crazy idea from some crazy old woman. For the past three or so years of our marriage, completely unknown to me, she would wake up at some point during the night and whisper, repeatedly, into my sleeping ear "you're ugly and you have a small penis." Like a mantra, she chant-whispered this cruel suggestion, over and over. I began to lose all my confidence in everyday activities, and it completely eroded my sexual abilities. I lost all desire and couldn't even face a prostitute. I became so weak, emotionally, that I had a near mental collapse. By day, she was sweet, loving, and seemed truly concerned about my condition. I only caught onto this in therapy, when I began to do some dream recall. I'd had many dreams where people called me ugly, and scenes in them where I was exposed and felt terribly ashamed of the size of my member. Then, in some dreams, I remembered distinctly hearing the phrase said to me. My therapist jokingly mentioned that maybe Ginny was doing this. Well, I feigned sleep several nights in a row; that first night, I thought it was just plain silly, me staying awake all night to expose some imaginary evil my wife was practicing on me. But I was determined, if for no other reason than to go back and tell the doc he was crazy for suggesting such a thing. But, lo about one in the a.m., Ginny turns herself over, her mouth preciously close to my ear (I always sleep on my back), she stays that way a few minutes, then I hear this low whisper direct into my ear "you're ugly and you have a small penis." I tested several other nights in that week, and almost every night, she did the same thing, around the same time. Well, you can imagine my shock. My therapist took a great interest in the whole thing and suggested we take legal action. One night, just after she whispered her little evil mantra about 30 times over, I said to her "and you are an evil, sexless old cunt." "You can't prove nothing, you'd sound crazy" she told me when I told her my intentions to divorce and sue; but my therapist told me to have her read your article, and it convinced her I had plenty to back me up. Ginny gave me an uncontested divorce and now I'm back on track—and on Viagra. I'd be anxious to attend one of your seminars, if you ever come into the Tulsa area.

Dear Viagra,
It truly serves as a warning that we do need to heed the direct external experience of our bodies during sleep; you never know what wants to crawl into the dream from the world.

Mr. Eeden;
I have a peculiar job. I watch videos of people who don't know they're being videotaped. Not CIA stuff, I just work for a sales and marketing research firm whose specialty is gathering visual data of people shopping, you know, their habits and actions, like do they immediately go to the right when entering a store, or, do they rearrange merchandise because they don't like how its displayed, or what do their kids start looking at. Anyway, I've been working on this job about five years now, and after the first year or so, I began to have more and more vivid dreams. I never used to remember them. But I'd wake up, feeling like I'd been to work all the while I'd been asleep, watching people. Only I saw them doing more than shopping. Now I have more nightmares than ever. I went to some dream seminars and a therapist, but all I've got for it are some astrological printouts and a $400 bill. I read about you in that interview in that computer magazine and got your email address. Be glad to compensate you for your time if you can help.

Dear Surveyor,
You have a fascinating job, probably, and I'm not at all surprised that both the physical act of covertly viewing strangers and the emotional conflict and/or pleasure you get from it is having an effect on your dream world. Maybe you are having a negative experience in the dream because you suppress the guilt manifested by your line of work, I don't know. But let me save you plenty of further therapy bills (not that I'm not recommending it or that it wouldn't somehow help you, but I doubt it in this instance). USE the experience. Rise above it; start

keeping a log of all the activities of your coworkers, your bosses, and your company overall. Put these findings out on the internet. You might lose your job, sure, but you will reap some rewards psychologically, I promise.

Dear REMbrandt:
I eat a 16-inch pizza before I go to bed; I have nightmares. Enough said. You're whacked if you think food doesn't affect my dreams.

Dear Pizza Dude,
You are correct, I am whack. Food and body processes, like indigestion, can have some effect on your sensibilities within the dream, just as external stimuli like music, noise, or blow jobs can be experienced by the dream self. The fact that indigestion gives you nightmares instead of other more pleasant scenarios is just too bad for you. The next time you're stuffing your face with some junk food that's going to be digested during your sleeping hours, double down on the intake and see how far you can push it. Use the cause/effect to see if massive ingestion of junk food gives you a heart attack in the dream, then see if you wake up to remember it. Let me know how it goes!

Mr. Eeden:
I have just stumbled onto your site from researching dreams of the prophets, and I am sickened. I have never seen greater evidence of pure evil in my lifetime. The notions of what you propose are so far from the beliefs laid down in the Good Book that I thought I was reading another Satanic bible, a book whose sexy claptrap has brainwashed countless youths over the past three decades. Yours is a dark and evil world, an existence without morality or ethics that seeks to place people in the very den of Satan.

I shall dedicate a sermon or two--or twenty--to putting out your drivel.
Reverend Alan Thorpe

Dear Rev:
It is astounding to me that the Christian of today, whose entire faith is based on the dreams and visions of men long dead, place absolutely no interest or faith in the dream they glimpse every night, and what one is capable of there. I've no doubt of the existence of God when the wind rushes my face as I hurtle toward the earth, or as I enjoy sex, or see the beautiful, untouchable expanses before me. Mine is a very direct experience with God; yours, apparently, has been dictated by the dead. Of Satan, well, I can tell you that I've seen evidence of his good humor, and, like Mark Twain, prefer it to the company of angels.

Dear REMbrandt:
My name is [redacted]. I write and publish books pertaining to government conspiracies in covering up incidents of paranormal and/or extraterrestrial activity. Are you aware that the dream states you describe are not unlike the descriptions that UFO abductees give of their experiences? Have you considered the possibility that you were, or continue to be, an abductee? Or that alien intelligence is influencing the dream states in which you describe so vividly? Have you ever been involved in the military? I believe I can help you find answers to these questions.

Dear UFO Guy,
I certainly cannot rule out the possibility that our dream state is all a complex neural front for alien monitoring and research on humans, nor can I rule out that the world is the same kind of test lab. And I highly disagree that the dream states I describe are in any way similar to the accounts of the average alien abductee. I have never in the

dream experienced an anal probe. I do not see "greys." I have no loss of memory. Now, what was I saying?

Mr. Eeden:
I am a 52-year-old cancer survivor (for now). I have teenage children and a loving husband and don't know what I would do if cancer returned. I belong to a network of cancer support groups and we have all discussed your techniques for how to heal yourself from a variety of illnesses but that you'd never suffered from serious diseases like ours (which range from breast cancer to pancreatic cancer and bone cancer). We are spread all over the world, and though we certainly couldn't ask you to visit us in person, would you be able to write a book or more detailed work on healing that we could find direction, or even just inspiration from? You have no idea what a great service this would be.

Dear Survivor:
I've given a lot of thought to this and have determined I will try this, or at least find a way to present my experience in more detailed terms. If you've read or followed my work at all, you understand how skeptical I am of my approach working for any other individual. I realize the possibilities inherent in my experience and don't take them lightly. I can't prescribe an approach, or a system, or even steps to follow. I struggle to find the best approach to helping those like yourself beyond what I've already written on my own self-healing techniques (somewhat vague, admittedly—it's such an intuitive thing). It's not terribly unlike creative visualization or the myriad mind/body techniques already well-covered. Dr. Patricia Garfield wrote a very insightful book on the topic, *The Healing Power of Dreams*, which I believe is still in print and offers lots of steps and approaches; though I warn you, it does rely on a certain amount of dream symbolism. It's a step. I can promise you I am trying to collect my thoughts on using biconscious lucidity in healing; the problem, of course, is that I don't know

anyone but myself who is truly biconscious. I sincerely wish you and everyone in your network and with your experience a long life in the world and the dream.

Ohh You REMbrandt:
Please find attached some very revealing pics of me. I'd love it if you can find me in your dream and figure out what's best for me. PLEASE let me know when you do your dream ravaging to this body (I know you will), I'm hoping I feel a little something...that would be so cool! Have fun with me!

Dear Ooh:
Just did, thanks! I hope you at least hiccupped or something. A tingle, maybe?

Note: Surprisingly, I get a lot of email like this. I certainly go through some dry spells in relationships, and I find porn to be as boring as drugs, so thank you all.

Hey GVE:
Fascinating stuff, especially in regard to current theories on the role of consciousness in the universe (as in, it ain't the universe if we can't consciously perceive it, right?). I'm wondering though about the "phasing" or "shifting" that you say you do regularly between the world and the dream. Since you don't always go back and forth to the same exact places, especially when you phase into the dream, isn't it possible that you are phasing into not just the dream but any number of infinite dimensions? Is the dream not a gateway to all the multiple realities and dimensions so many scientists are starting to think are out there (or in there)? Isn't the dream just more layers of the multiverse?
Coop in Iowa City

Hey Coop:
Yes. And No. And both, then neither. Always, sometimes, and never. The fish.

Eeden:
You are a sexist pig. Your dreams are power trips and are all about conquering and subjugating women. You try to come off as some "mystical rebel." You and Freud are both sexist degenerates, because you reduce the profound experience of dreams to sex and violence. You have nothing original to say and you're a fraud.

Dear Hater:
Sorry, I was only half reading; the other half of me was fucking you in the dream. Though you were much better looking in the dream, I think.

Hey REMbrandt:
Been reading a lot about the theories of the collective unconscious and how that might explain a lot of the phenomena we humans keep claiming to exist, locally (Bigfoot, Loch Ness Monster, Virgin Mary sightings and the like) and globally (UFOs). See anything in that dream of yours that would provide some evidence of the collective unconscious theory?

Hey Theorist:
There's never anything in the dream that I could call "evidence" of anything in any way, shape or form. Evidence denotes something that is "factual." The dream is experiential; it is a fact as I am alive and conscious within it, but it denotes nothing factual outside of itself. We are frequently trying to determine if all that reported phenomena, and even our dreams themselves, are "real." From my perspective, I'm frequently trying to reassure myself that the world is "real." I guess the moral you're looking for would be that, if Bigfoot impregnates your wife, ask for a paternity test.

Hey REMbrandt:
Has it ever occurred to you that, with all the freewheelin'
sex and carnal plundering you've perpetrated within
your dream, that there might be some babies out there
with your dream DNA? Have you ever subsequently encountered a baby as the result of your countless couplings?   I'm guessing not, since moral responsibility
vis-a-vis your spiritual journey, does not seem to be of
any concern. Or have you used your dream powers to
"disappear" any evidence of responsibility?   Have you
ever encountered one of your dream victims, whose life
is broken and shattered as a result of your actions? You,
who play "god" then move on to the next encounter?
Anything like that?
SAD (sad about dreams) in Topeka

Dear SAD:
No. You are confusing the dream with our story culture,
in which there are morality lessons. There are no victims
in the dream, and there is no real procreation. There is
desire, however, and drive. Perhaps it is the spirit that
is procreative. If I may be so bold as to suggest that you
are projecting your own negative life experiences (which,
if true, I'm genuinely sorry you've encountered) onto my
dream journey. Please stop doing this and you will feel
better. Not about me, which is, of course, pointless—but
about yourself.

Dear REMmy:
Isn't it possible that God, our Creator, has created the
dream as a secondary proving ground for moral behavior? If we act morally in the world, and God gives us
another realm that seems too good to be true, in which
we indulge in all our hedonistic fantasies (as you seem to
encourage?), what if we fail His test to proceed into the
true heavenly realm?
Heaven Bound in Provo

Dear Heaven Bound,

If there is a creator--which is entirely possible, and no science can truly deny it--he should just copy the DMV approach to tests and give us written exams and a mind-driving field test once a decade. But OK, let's say God is a moral God bent on judging us, having taken 14 billion years to create the one species important enough to captivate his attention. He creates a physical world in which we must navigate pain, pleasure, destruction, humility, and cruelty on large and small scales; then decides that we need a parallel proving ground in which He can tempt us to indulge in whatever we want, but only for the tiny, tiny portion of the population who can maintain lucidity and are aware of the choices. Fourteen billion years of creation to find a handful of people who maintain some unknowable litmus test of purity? The rules on morality were written by man. You are assuming the mind of a God.

Mr. Eeden:

I am gay, having come out when I was 19 to a less than enthusiastic family. I went through puberty with dreams where I interacted with both men and women. Safe to say the "dream" left me more confused than anything about my true nature. There were no healing visions, no rapturous orgasms, just frustrated encounters where clothes could never be fully unbuttoned and partners turned into monsters. I've been in therapy—thanks so much for asking—and am healing. But what good is the "dream" if it can't be trusted to point us to our true nature?

GAY (Gender's Aimless Youth) in Seattle

Dear GAY:

Believe it or not, yours is not my first letter from a gay person regarding their confusing experience, especially during adolescence, in the dream. They also had a confusing experience in the world; the dream has no authority within the world, or vice versa. It is the same journey, as far as my experience relates. I'd have hoped you felt freer in the dream to explore whatever nature you leaned toward, without ramifications (emotional or physical). Some certainly have used the dream as a safe outlet. The common denominator in cases such as yours is that they have not achieved any level of lucidity, at least in the dream. I know I have been adamant that lucidity cannot be forced, only the groundwork laid for when it aligns, but for many people, creating the atmosphere for lucidity to be achieved does take effort. I and many other writers about dreams have published extensively about methods for attaining lucidity. Therapy is great, congratulations—to me, the dream is not therapy any more than the world is. It is a parallel experience, but just like life, to fully enjoy its benefits, you have to put in some effort, and there is no conspiratorial "they" in the dream that is trying to keep you down, other than your own uncertainty and confusion.

Hey Mr. Gardner Van,
How do you know that, when you're in the dream, you're not plugged into some "Matrix"-like alternate reality that simulates thought and sensation and forms a world around you while your body is being used as a battery?
Red and Blue Pills Please in Vancouver BC

Hey PILLSbury,
I don't. I don't know anything. My body is a battery, in fact. It has a shelf life as to when its charge will be depleted. As to whether we are or aren't in some virtual world in the actual world or in the dream, we don't know. Have fun with it, have purpose with it, while you can.

Dear REMbrandt:
I have never had a "dream." Never will. No little stories in the night for me. Like most "new age" hogwash, I think "dreams" are made up. Maybe I'm the exact oppo-

site of you—someone who doesn't dream, ever. I'd say I have a plenty healthy imagination, I have a high IQ (yes, measured), and I'm perfectly well-adjusted with a good job and social life. Like snake-oil salesmen, faith healers, and vitamin enthusiasts, you're a fraud who takes money from people to feed them an illusion that makes them feel good about themselves or what might come after this life. It's too bad you get away with this, I hope you and the whole dream racket get exposed and sued someday.

Dear NonDreamer,
I'm just going to come right out and call you a liar. If something about the notion of the dream offends you, then you have been creating a fantasy about something you consider a fantasy. You are not the first person unable to look in the mirror and understand your own denial.
Go ahead and sue me. You'll win (in your dreams!)

Dear REMbrandt:
Do you ever make some big mistake in the world, then re-enact the scenario in the dream with a better outcome?
Curious

Dear Curious,
No, because this kind of exercise would give me some false sense that I'd somehow addressed the mistake in the world. Any mistake in the world needs to be rectified in the world. I have attempted to play out scenarios (Cleopatra, will you marry me?) within the dream, to futile, humbling and often hilarious effect.

Dear Mr. Eeden,
I'm a researcher with degrees in biochemistry, pharmacology and neuroscience studies. I have personally been involved in projects for a client of ours in which we are developing a drug that inhibits REM atonia, allowing the dreamer's body to move in accordance with whatever dream activity they experience. This research is not funded by any university or academic interest; it's funded by commercial interests, and I suspect potential military application. Please do not publish my name but keep the information I've sent you. Could be that nothing comes of this research. If we succeed, there's no guarantee of any commercial application; I fear some potential applications in the military or some kind of psychological warfare. Stay tuned.

Dear Researcher:
I am indeed very tuned; please keep me apprised of what comes of this. Consider your note published, just in case.

Dear REMbrandt,
Do you blink in the dream?
Eye-Batting Beauty from Boulder

Dear BBB,
Most involuntary bodily functions (blinking, swallowing, heartbeat, digestion) and actions like itching, cracking knuckles, and taking out the garbage aren't things you need or want to do in the dream. They occur due to biological necessity. I have wasted plenty of time trying to replicate actions in the dream that are necessary in the world. So the answer is, no. Unless I want to.

Dear REMbrandt:
I have fantasies, and the dream feeds them. My fanta-

251

sies would not be considered legal in our society. They wouldn't be ethical in any religion I know of. You are the first person I know of who has written explicitly about performing "taboo" acts in the dream. I come very close to maintaining lucidity in the dream, achieving it for short stretches, then I become distracted by my desires. Don't you think that, if this activity recurs so frequently, that it's an invitation to try the experience in the world?

Dear Fantasist:
No one can fault any one or judge the actions of others in the dream; but what happens in the dream is not a license to re-create that activity in the world. Different playground, different rules. I can't believe I'm saying this, but honestly, get some counseling to help you deal with the fantasies and keep them on the side they belong.

Dear Mr. Eeden,

I work with a collective of artists, photographers, filmmakers, illustrators, and performers, and we have been involved in projects that re-create scenes or images from our dreams. Not that there's anything new in that, artists in all media have been trying to re-create the dream since forever; but we've come up with some interesting shit down here, we all love your writings, and you have a standing invitation to visit and take part. I think you'd find a lot of original stuff happening here.

Dear Collective:
Next time I'm in New Orleans, I'm knocking on your door. Please, please have beignets.

Dear Mr. Eeden,
I work for an insanely wealthy individual who has created quite a compound in the desert, and he spends a fortune having craftsmen, actors, set designers, and even call girls enact his own private dream world here. Seriously, this place is like a movie studio. It's highly secure. I got into this job through a friend and we're not supposed to talk about it, but I am one of the workers who have contact with the boss, and I have seen your book on his shelf. I thought you might want to know. I'm withholding all details because I don't want to lose my job, but there is some seriously wicked stuff going down here—wanted to give you a heads-up in case he started calling you up. I'm not saying he's crazy, just the opposite, actually. I don't even know what happens behind some of these doors.

Dear Job Insecurity:
I consider myself warned, thanks. When the insanely wealthy spend insane amounts of money to recreate their internal insanity, I guess anything can happen. Enjoy those paychecks while they last, friend.

Dear GVE,
Isn't true "lucidity" as you describe it pretty much just the Buddhist notion of nirvana or satori?
Nirvana Bound

Dear Smells Like Teen Spirituality,
If "nirvana" means the ultimate fulfillment, or freedom from the cycle of rebirth and worldly tribulation, then no. Lucidity is a clarity, a phase of hyper-consciousness that enables you to wrest some control from the universe so you may more deeply explore it. It's a beginning, not an ending. Lucidity would be essential to achieving the Buddhist notion of Satori, however; I believe Satori is an "awakening," or discovery of one's true nature. Lucidity

gives one clarity, but not necessarily "truth." That's the big subjective in the universe, pal.

Dear REMMy,
Why don't you just commit suicide? If you believe our consciousness just fades into "the dream," then why not just make it permanent?
Fade to Black

Dear Kevorkian,
Well, that would be one solution...but what's the problem? Whether there is or isn't a reason I'm in this body, I still feel that I haven't asked all the right questions, and that I still have some stuff to do in the world, repressive physics and all. Some suicides may feel they're ending misery here to find a better place (or nothingness)—but your consciousness, your problems and self-worth, don't change between the world and the dream. You will take your problems with you. If I'm going to be permanently in the dream, I'd like to shed some world baggage.

Hey GVE,
Light in the world is composed of photons. Since we can see in our dreams, is the light in the dream comprised of photons?
Lit in Toronto

Dear LIT,
I don't know. It's fairly impossible to conduct true scientific experiments within the dream, as every step of the way, our own subjectivity, observation, and biases are woven into the fabric of the dream, and we will always affect the outcome. I know that I can mimic any quality of light, shade, and dark, from blazing noon to near pitch-black (the mind wants desperately to see, and even

if you close your eyes in the world or dream you visualize something, photons or not). I can close my eyes within the dream and visualize myself closing my eyes and I will keep visualizing something, no matter how many layers deep I go. Poe's "A Dream Within a Dream" begins to resonate quite clearly here. So maybe the question isn't "are photons (or any element of quantum matter) active in the dream," but "does the dream produce elements that interact with the world on a quantum level?"
I would be happy to be shot around the Large Hadron Collider to see what we can find.

Dear Gardner,
How do you know when people are telling you a fake dream? I suspect people make them up all the time. Just sayin'.
Faked in Fairbanks

Dear Faked,
I often listen to people's dream recall and heed my gut instincts to discern what may or may not be a real account of actual dream events. If the dream is telling a particular story, for instance, or if famous people conveniently appear for a punch line. I usually question their motivation for relating the dream in the first place; if it's to prove a point, or if it's overly populated with tropes from dream interpretation books, then it begins to seem suspect. People often want to impress me with their dream adventures, and figure no one knows because most dreams are quirky and weird and filled with disparate stuff, and what's the harm? But the kicker is, they can make up whatever they want, but until they are able to achieve some level of lucidity, they will never have control over their truths or their lies.

Hey Gardner of E,
The most successful species on Earth are hive-minded,

"groupthink" societies where the species welfare is the primary concern, not the individual. Individuals are constantly sacrificed for the good of the species. Even human culture—many Asian cultures come to mind—have historically prized the society over the individual. So, I'm wondering why, then, would humans evolve into a "lucid realm," plane or dimension, whatever, that is completely subjective and driven solely by the individual's consciousness? Don't you think that creation, and life itself, favors the group model?
Felicia in Pittsburgh

Dear Felicia,
Well, that's a lot to chew on, and a fascinating conundrum you present. It's a lot to think about, should I put it out to the group for a collective answer?
That wasn't an (overly) snide retort...there are just too many unknowns to give any satisfying answer that doesn't involve yet more questions. Is consciousness part of biological evolution, or extenuation of a species? Are those species which have benefitted from a "hive mind" capable of the kind of consciousness we have? I suspect sociologists, cultural anthropologists, and even biologists might take issue with your assumption that some Asian cultures have truly used the "groupthink" over the individual, as that could well be the result of more social or political necessity than any natural biological necessity, but I get your point. Why did consciousness give us an individual point of view, individual reasoning, individual experience and desire? Can we truly say that other species do not have this capability—apes, whales and dolphins, the loner octopus? I invite any and all scientific theory on the idea that we'd be better off with a hive mind (it never works so well for the drones and minions in science fiction movies, but hey). All I can dumbly say is that maybe there's a reason we call it the "singularity."

*Darest thou now o soul, walk out with me toward the
unknown region,
Where neither ground is for the feet, nor any path to fol-
low?
No map there, nor guide, nor voice sounding, nor touch
of human hand,
Nor face with blooming flesh, nor lips nor eyes, are in
that land.
I know it not o soul, nor dost thou, all is blank before us,
All waits undream'd of in that region, that inaccessible
land.
Till when the ties loosen, all but the ties eternal, time and
space,
Nor darkness, gravitation, sense, nor any bounds bound-
ing us.
Then we burst forth, we float, in time and space o soul,
prepared for them,
Equal equipt at last (o joy! O fruit of all!) them to fulfill
o soul.*

—Walt Whitman

I think, therefore I think I am
—Gardner Eeden

SUBJECT HAS WRITTEN LUCID: AWAKE IN THE WORLD AND
THE DREAM. SUBJECT LIVES IN SOME MIDWESTERN CITY.
SUBJECT IS AVAILABLE FOR SPEAKING ENGAGEMENTS
AT SCHOOLS, CHURCHES AND OTHER ORGANIZATIONS
INTERESTED IN NEW LEVELS OF CONSCIOUSNESS OR
LURID ENTERTAINMENT. SUBJECT IS AVAILABLE FOR
PRIVATE SESSIONS AND WORKSHOPS WITH GROUPS AND/
OR INDIVIDUALS. SUBJECT IS NOT NOW NOR WILL
EVER BE A PROFESSIONAL PSYCHOLOGIST, COUNSELOR,
OR PSYCHOANALYST. SUBJECT WILL TRAVEL FOR
SESSION FEE AND EXPENSES. DO NOT ASK SUBJECT
WHAT A DREAM MEANS.